Melting her Wolf's heart

Weres & Witches of Silver Lake
Book 9

Vella Day

What must a dark goddess do to win back the heart of the werewolf she betrayed?

Goddess Vinea Summer wants to make amends to hot and sexy Devon McKinnon—the man she knows is her mate, but Devon refuses to accept her apology, damn it. So what's a spurned goddess to do? Giving up is not an option.

As much as he wants to put Vinea out of his mind, Devon's wolf can't live without her. Her enticing scent, long legs, and sensual allure draws him in like a magic spell. But for his own sanity, he has to keep her at arm's length. Yeah, right. Try explaining that to a hungry wolf—or a goddess determined to win back her destined mate.

When trouble finds Vinea, Devon quickly discovers he's willing to risk everything in a life-or-death battle for the woman he loves.

Beneath the calm and shimmering surface lie intrigue, power, magic, and danger.
Welcome to Silver Lake—where appearances can be deceiving, and what you see isn't truly what lies below.

Chapter One

To learn about Vella Day's other new releases, contests, and find new authors, subscribe to her newsletter and get three free books!

An Unexpected Diversion (book 1 of Hidden Hills Shifters)
Bare Instincts (book 2 of Hidden Hills Shifters)
Montana Desire (book 1 of Rock Hard, Montana)

VINEA SUMMER'S BEST friend, EmmaLee Donovan, leaned forward and rested her elbows on her knees. Even with her light brown hair hanging down over her face, it failed to block the circles under her eyes.

"You've got to go back to Silver Lake, Vinea, or the guilt will eat you alive."

Vinea jumped off the bed in her efficiency apartment and paced. "And leave you?"

Not only was EmmaLee her best friend, she might be her only one. Vinea wouldn't feel as guilty about leaving if EmmaLee's boyfriend didn't use her as a punching bag. That kind of violence cut Vinea to the core.

To think six months ago she'd never experienced compassion on any level. Now guilt and the desire to make amends were her constant companions. Ever since Devon McKinnon had held her down under the lake water against the pink quartz, she'd changed, erasing the goddess of the dark realm forever. Now she was a down-and-out waitress, taking orders from demanding people then smiling about it. No wonder her boss, Androf, god of the dark, told her killing her wasn't enough of a punishment for her failures. To him, developing a conscience was worse than death. Well, the laugh was on him. She might be staying in a dump, but at least she'd stopped hurting people.

EmmaLee stood and hugged her. "You have to go back and make things right. It hurts me to see you like this."

"I know I need to set some things straight with those I've hurt, but you need to fix things too."

EmmaLee waved a dismissive hand. "Slater doesn't mean it when he hits me. He just drinks too much, that's all. He's real sorry afterward."

In the past, Vinea wouldn't have thought a thing about such violence, but not anymore. "He's no good for you. Trust me—I know *bad* when I see it."

EmmaLee returned to her chair and crossed her arms. "Slater's a good man at heart." She looked up at Vinea. "He's nothing like the bad gods you were with, right?"

Slater wasn't much better, especially if he continually felt the need to drink to escape his life and then hit the person he supposedly cared about. She'd have said something, but every time Vinea voiced her opinion, it led to an argument. Her sweet friend was so naïve to the ways of the world, and nothing Vinea said seemed to help.

"He can't strike someone dead if that's what you mean. Slater might be a human, but at times, humans can hurt others as much as gods can." Okay, that was a lie. Slater was a shifter, but if Vinea told her friend, EmmaLee would never leave him.

Vinea sighed. She and EmmaLee made an unlikely pair, but it was her friend's love of the supernatural that had bonded them in the first place. Vinea could still remember the look of awe when EmmaLee caught Vinea changing her clothes with a wave of her hand. Instead of freaking out, EmmaLee wanted to know more. Desperate to talk to someone about all the changes she had been experiencing, Vinea told her new friend everything, and to her delight, EmmaLee believed her.

Vinea stabbed a hand through her hair. "I should go to Silver Lake. I hurt Devon badly, and I need to explain why."

"From what you said, you hurt a lot more people than him."

Vinea laughed. "You're not going to let me forget, are you?"

EmmaLee jumped up again and rushed over. "I'm sorry. I didn't mean to bring up that touchy topic."

"It's okay. I was a bad person back then, a really bad person. When I was a goddess in the dark realm, I thought nothing of doing unspeakable acts. It's hard for me to even believe I was that person."

"What can I do to help?" EmmaLee asked.

Vinea didn't deserve her friendship. "Tell Slater to go to hell."

ONCE EMMALEE WENT back home after delivering the promise of leaving the SOB, Vinea changed into some warmer clothes. Billard might not be very far from Silver Lake, but the Tennessee mountains were a lot colder than north Georgia. Now that she was living in the human world, she had to deal with the different temperature changes.

Before Vinea left Billard, she called her boss at the diner and explained that she needed some time off.

"How long will you be gone?" Warren asked. Thankfully, he sounded more concerned than pissed.

"I'm not sure." How long did it take someone to right a lot of wrongs—a week, a month, or would it take a lifetime? "I want to be fair to the girls. Maybe you should get a replacement."

"I'm sorry to hear that, Vinea, but I lost Carol because so many waitresses needed more time off. Poor girl had a breakdown after working double shifts for a month. If you come back sooner than planned, stop in. I might be able to squeeze you into the rotation."

Vinea smiled. "I appreciate it."

What a change Warren was from Androf. One was kind and accommodating and the other pure evil. While it sickened her to leave EmmaLee and the rest of the staff at Billard Eatery, it could take weeks if not months to do what she needed to do.

Because she didn't have a car, she figured no one would be harmed if she teleported to Silver Lake. Thankfully, she still possessed a few of her goddess talents.

Picturing her destination, she disappeared from Billard and reappeared across the street from McKinnon and Associates in Silver Lake, Tennessee. Darn. Her aim was a little off. Even though she'd pictured the front entrance, she landed a hundred feet away. It seemed the longer she resided on earth, the more erratic her talents became. Glancing around, she was pleased she hadn't appeared in a crowd of people. That would have been really hard to explain. The humans weren't even aware of shifters, let alone goddesses.

At least she was here—ready to confront her past. The outcome might not turn out to be what she hoped for, but she had to try. A lot depended on whether Devon would even be in Silver Lake. From what he'd told her, he only came when his brother needed an extra hand. Most of the time, he worked in Pittsburgh. Either she'd have to visit him there once she learned his address, or she'd have to wait in Silver Lake until he returned.

Stop procrastinating!

As she crossed the street, she surveyed the cars in the lot. Tucked behind a larger vehicle was a white truck like the kind Devon drove. Vinea crossed her fingers, hoping this one belonged to him.

Once at the front door, Vinea rang the bell. A lot could happen in six months, but she expected Lexi would be manning the desk. Vinea might have lied to Devon repeatedly, but at least she hadn't tried to steal his powers—like she had from Sam Pompley—Lexi's mate. While she hadn't harmed Lexi, she doubted the woman harbored any positive thoughts toward her. More than anything, she wanted to help Lexi in some way to show her that she was no longer an evil goddess.

"May I help you?" asked a voice that came through the intercom.

Vinea looked up at the camera. Didn't Lexi recognize her? "Hey,

Lexi, it's me, Vinea. Is Devon around?" Good. That sounded a lot calmer than she felt.

"Vinea? What the hell? You have some nerve to come and—"

A muffled voice sounded in the background. It was deeper, lower, and commanding. Sam perhaps? Or was it Devon?

"Never mind, Vinea. Give me a minute, and I'll check." Her tone came out professional, and while Vinea detected a blend of anger and disappointment, she didn't blame Lexi one bit for her distrustful attitude. Actually, Vinea deserved a curt no and a quick disconnect.

Chills raced up her spine at the anticipation of seeing Devon McKinnon once more. Sure it was cold out, but this was more than a reaction to winter. This was more sexual in nature—a feeling she had yet to understand.

Picturing their last encounter, however, doused the pleasant feeling. Okay, only part of it had been bad—the part where he'd almost drowned her—but the part where he was naked had been oh so good.

The intercom crackled, and Lexi's voice came through. "Devon is in an important meeting and can't be disturbed."

"Can't be disturbed or doesn't want to be?" That came out snarky, but it couldn't be helped. She was trying to make amends here and needed to make it past the door.

Sure, she expected some hostility, but she had hoped curiosity about why she was there would have gained her access.

A disgusted huff came over the mic. "Does it really matter? Please leave. You're not wanted here," Lexi said. With that the intercom went silent.

That didn't go well, but she didn't need an open door to get inside. After she made certain no one was watching, she disappeared. Too bad when she reappeared, she was in Connor's office, though she swore she'd pictured where Devon worked. Whoops.

Connor looked up. To his credit, he managed to school his features. "Vinea?" He shoved his chair back and stood. "Get out!

Haven't you done enough damage?" Well, so much for him not showing any emotion.

Her stomach burned hot at the censure. Sure, she deserved it, but being the recipient of such disdain still hurt. "I'll admit I lied a few times." *And stole, and...*

"You did a lot more than that. You tried to ruin Sam, not to mention Devon."

Devon? "I might not have been honest with him, but I never tried to hurt him."

"You hurt him just the same." Connor stepped toward the door and held it open. "Just leave."

"I think I'll go the same way I came."

With a nod, she disappeared. This time, her aim was better, and she appeared in the correct office, not that she expected the reception to be any better.

Devon's head was down, and it was as if he wasn't aware she was there. Her body, however, was going crazy with spikes of sexual need. He looked so fucking hot. His dark hair was cut even shorter, which on him looked good, but she didn't like that he had more lines around his eyes. While he had lost weight, he still was a hot, sexy man.

"Devon." Her throat nearly closed up at saying his name.

He didn't look up. "I told Lexi not to let you in." His words came out harsher than she had hoped.

A sarcastic remark shot to her lips, but she stopped herself. Now wasn't the time for the old Vinea to surface. "She didn't let me in. I just kind of appeared." When he didn't look up, she continued. "I came to apologize."

"Apology accepted. Now go away."

Damn, but this was harder than she thought. "When you dipped me in the water, the pink quartz cleansed me."

He finally looked up, but his eyes were angry swirls of black, laced with that deep rich brown she found so attractive.

"Is that so?" Devon said. "Is that why you held Missy captive in a cave while you lured Zane to his death—after this dunking occurred?"

The words wouldn't form. "Zane died?"

When she'd left him, he was merely unconscious. Surely his bear would have healed him.

"No. He survived, but you thought about killing him. Why?"

Her quick comeback seemed to have disappeared. "It took a while for the cleansing to work. Like I told you that day six months ago, the pink quartz works well on Changelings; maybe I was so evil that it took longer for me, but eventually, all my bad thoughts disappeared. I swear."

Something in her voice must have resonated with him, because his features softened. "I'm happy for you then. I suppose you came here for my help?"

"No! I want to help you."

He leaned back and laughed, though she doubted it held any joy. "You? Help me? That's rich. Unless you can infiltrate the Changeling's headquarters and take them all out, I don't see how you can be of service."

She stood up straighter. "I don't kill anymore."

"Oh, really? Well, that's good to know. What about stealing and lying?"

"No." It was better to keep her answers short. "Listen, can we grab a cup of coffee or something. We really need to talk."

A knock sounded on his door, and Kip Landon stuck his head in. "Oh, sorry. I didn't know you had company." His eyes narrowed slightly before he returned his focus to Devon. "Connor wanted to let you know the meeting's about to begin."

Devon pushed back his chair. "Do everyone a favor and get the hell out, Vinea. You can leave the same way you came."

The hatred rolled off him. Each wave cut her deeply, but it was what she deserved. She'd hurt him more than she'd realized.

She had to find a way for Devon to see how much her heart and soul had changed, and that meant this journey was going to take a lot longer. "I'm not leaving until we talk."

Chapter Two

"KIP, WATCH HER," Devon said.

It took all of his resolve to walk out of his office and not strangle Vinea first. His claws were attempting to break through the skin, and his teeth had already sharpened. Had he not ordered his wolf to stand down, no telling what might have happened. This whole attraction thing was absurd. Why couldn't his wolf understand what an evil, wicked person she was?

She's changed, his wolf shot back.

The cleansing doesn't work on goddesses. Even Vinea said that.

She said it was a delayed reaction. Remember, she's still your mate. Give her a chance.

Devon refused to continue this discussion with his horny animal. Six months ago, he thought he had found the woman of his dreams. Then he learned how she'd lied and deceived him in order to gain more power. Good thing her attempt failed or his good friend Sam wouldn't be the same person he was today.

Turn around and look at her, his wolf said. *Being on earth has changed her.*

He'd seen enough. Devon headed toward the conference room, trying to block the raging emotions swirling through him, as well as the fact his cock was pressing against his zipper. Unfortunately, the light steps following prevented him. Asking Kip to watch her meant his coworker was to keep her in his office, not walk behind her down the hallway.

No one ever listened. But just because she was there didn't mean he had to acknowledge her. If Vinea wanted to come into the room with him, she'd have to walk through the closed door.

"Devon, please?" she begged.

He ignored her. As he entered the conference room, he glanced behind him, but Vinea was gone. Okay, that worried him.

"Where did she go?" he asked Kip.

"She just disappeared."

It was for the best. "See if you can find her."

"I'll try."

Inside the room were his dad and his uncle, along with Connor, Jackson, and Sam. "Where's Rye?" Devon asked.

"Izzy just showed up, and he went to speak with her," Connor said. "I assume you saw our unexpected visitor?"

"Vinea? Yes. She stopped by with some sob story about wanting forgiveness."

Sam stiffened. "Vinea is here?"

Devon held up a hand as Sam started toward the door. "Hold on. I admit she's evil, but I do think she has changed a little—softened since your attack." While her hair was back to what he believed to be her natural auburn color, her eyes held a depth like never before.

Sam Pompley got in his face. "She's fooling you, like she fooled all of us before."

He hoped that wasn't true, but he sure as hell wasn't going to stake his life on it. "Remember, I told you I held her down against the pink quartz."

You're softening toward her, his wolf said with too much glee. *I'm glad.*

I most definitely am not. I just don't need Sam to go off half-cocked after her, that's all. No telling what she might try again.

You're wrong.

"I know," Sam shot back. "But then she kidnapped my cousin. Does that sound like someone who's all goodness and light?"

Devon pulled out a padded chair from the table and sat down. "She's had her say. I think she left, but I asked Kip to check."

Jackson grunted. "Sam's right. You were a fool once, Devon. I don't want to see it happen to you again. That woman does something to your brain every time she comes near you."

Vinea did more than just affect his brain, but he'd keep that fact to himself. "I won't let her get to me this time." What sounded like a deep growl came from the main area of the building, and all he could think of was that Vinea hadn't left and was up to her old tricks. "I need to check that out." She might have done something to Kip.

"I'm coming with you," Connor said.

Devon and Connor shot out of the room then rushed down the hallway to the large room off the lobby. The scene before him took him by surprise. Izzy was holding her baby boy, Logan, while Rye was looking on. The part that didn't fit was Vinea had her hand on Logan's forehead. Her eyes were closed, and her lips were in a grimace. Kip was standing nearby.

"What's going on?" Devon demanded. Surely, Rye remembered who she was.

Connor rushed up next to her, and Vinea stepped back and then staggered. Not thinking, Devon shot around Rye to steady her. Vinea opened her eyes, and when she looked up at him, he swore he could see into her soul. Inside was pain, an expression he didn't think she was capable of experiencing.

"I wanted to help," she said, her voice weaker than before. "That's all."

"Help?" Connor asked. "Since when do you help?"

"Logan has a raging fever," she said. "I really was only trying to take it away from him."

Izzy placed a hand on his arm. "Logan ate something this morning, and I think it might be poisoning him. I called Missy, but even her magic only helped a little. Rye could sense something was wrong and said to meet him here to decide what to do."

The pain crisscrossing Vinea's face almost hurt Devon. Once he made sure Vinea was stable, he let go, his hand burning at the touch. With sweat beading on her forehead, Vinea stepped away, her face pale. As much as he didn't want to care, he did. "Are you okay?"

Her lips seemed to want to smile, but she appeared to be struggling. "I just need to sit for a moment."

Devon led her over to the sofa. "Would you like a glass of water?"

"Yes, thank you."

"Dev, please," Connor chastised.

Right now, he didn't need his brother's scorn, but it would help remind him not to get sucked into her siren ways.

Izzy passed Devon's nephew to Rye. "I think he's improving," she said.

Connor moved closer to his oldest brother and placed the back of his hand on Logan's forehead. "He's still hot to me."

"Connor, why don't you get the meeting started. Rye and I will be right in." Devon didn't need his headstrong brother to cause any more problems. That was Vinea's job.

His brother glanced between Vinea and Devon. "Sure, but watch her." With that, he strutted off.

While Devon wasn't sure what he believed about Vinea, he didn't need Connor stirring the pot. As soon as Connor left, Devon poured Vinea a glass of water and took it over to her. He then sat across from her, partially because he wanted to make sure she didn't try anything else. He also had to ensure she wasn't really sick. While Vinea looked human, she was still a goddess, or so he assumed.

Rye stroked Logan's forehead. "Izzy, his fever is gone!" With the baby in his arms, he walked over to the sofa across from Vinea and sat down. "How were you able to heal him?" His older brother's tone was filled with awe.

Vinea smiled weakly, as if it took her effort. "Once the evil left my body, I was able to heal people. Personally, I think it was meant to be a curse for me, or some kind of punishment, because after I draw out the illness, I'm affected. I've never had any long term effects, but I do feel a lot of pain."

Izzy rushed over and sat down next to Vinea. Devon wanted to tell her it was some kind of goddess trick. Sure, she might have cured Logan, but it had to be a ploy.

"Will you be sick for long?" Izzy asked.

"I hope not. So far, my immune system has been holding up. I'll be back to normal in maybe twenty minutes, but those minutes are not pleasant." She sipped her water.

Devon stood. "I have a meeting to attend." Rye needed to be there too, but perhaps he had doubts about Vinea and would want to stay.

Instead, Rye stood and handed a sleeping Logan over to Izzy. "You should take him home. He needs to rest."

Izzy cradled the baby in her arms and then touched Vinea. "Thank you."

"Sure." She looked up at Devon. "Mind if I sit here for a few minutes?"

He'd look like a real cad if he said no. Besides, even if he tossed her out, she could reappear at will. "Sure. Take all the time you need." He nodded to Kip who motioned he'd keep watch.

With that he rushed toward the hallway with Rye at his heels.

VINEA FELT LIKE crap, but the pain and nausea would pass. While she was thrilled to be able to help Logan, she questioned her own motives. The moment she saw the baby having difficulty breathing, her heart went out to him. Poor little fellow seemed to be in such distress. Without thinking, she had rushed over and placed a hand on his forehead, despite Kip telling her to stop. Izzy's hold had tightened, and Rye actually growled, but once she told them what she was doing, they calmed down. It only took a minute to draw out the fever and his pain.

Vinea wondered if she had cured the child because she felt sorry for the baby, or had she hoped that Rye, the Clan's Alpha, would decide to support her? After all, he was Devon's older brother.

If nothing else, Vinea was practical. Reaching Devon would take a whole lot more than helping his nephew. Devon was skeptical by nature—or at least he'd become more so after Vinea had tricked him one too many times. His job meant the world to him, and she understood that. Curing a sick baby, while nice, wouldn't convince him she'd changed. The only thing that would help would be if she aided in taking down the Changelings.

Vinea had to inwardly chuckle. To those in Silver Lake, the Changelings were these terrible creatures. Compared to those in the dark realm, they were tame. Nonetheless, they harmed people, and that had to stop. Who else but a goddess could get the job done?

Feeling a little better, Vinea wanted to try something new. Sure, she could disappear at will—if that was even the right word—and appear someplace else, but she could be a little directionally challenged sometimes. At least by her second attempt, she would usually be at her desired location. This meeting that Devon was attending seemed very important. If their Clan's Alpha was in attendance, it could only mean one thing: the Changelings were acting up again.

If she had any chance of proving to Devon that she was a legitimately nice person, she'd have to help take these evil werewolves down. How she would do that Vinea had no idea, but sitting here wouldn't get the job done.

"I'm going to head out," she told Kip.

He crossed his arms. "Goodbye. I don't think Devon wants you back."

"I know."

With a nod of her head, she disappeared, but instead of leaving the building, she hovered outside of the conference room door. Kip's footsteps sounded down the hall. Most likely he planned to attend the meeting, which meant she'd have to maintain her shield of invisibility. Holding it for more than a few seconds, however, took a lot of strength and concentration. Rarely had she needed to stay invisible for longer than it took to go from one place to another. This clandestine activity would be quite a challenge.

Kip entered the conference room. Concerned voices sounded inside. Because she wouldn't be welcome if she walked in, she floated through the door, hoping she didn't suddenly take her human form. That could be catastrophic. Hell, then they'd never trust her.

Vinea planned on staying for only a short while, just enough to learn what was going on. Once inside, she looked around, recognizing most of the men in the room. While she'd never seen the two older gentlemen before, it was easy to guess who they were: Mr. McKinnon and Mr. Murdoch. Rye looked strikingly like his father, and Jackson was a spitting image of his dad.

Connor stood at a table on a raised platform that faced a large U-shaped table big enough to seat twelve. Devon and Rye occupied the end positions.

Connor glanced around to each and every member of the team. "While we lost a good man in Will, and he will be sorely missed, the good news is that Roger Devoe is out of surgery, but it's still touch and go. The bullet missed his major organs."

Mr. McKinnon's shoulders sagged. "If the paramedics hadn't been called, I bet he would have been able to shift and heal himself," the elder McKinnon grumbled.

"Dad, some things can't be controlled," Connor said.

"I know. That's why I told Roger time and again that he was too damn old to be a guard on an armored truck."

"He knew the risks," Connor said.

She had to conclude that someone had tried to rob the truck, and gunshots were exchanged.

"Is anything being done for the Rosewood family?" Devon asked.

Connor nodded. "After the funeral for Will, Lexi started working on a fundraiser for his wife and children. I know she's placed a few ads in the paper for help too. Will had two kids, one being a newborn. It's such a shame. He will be missed."

They all bowed their heads for a moment. Vinea had never seen anything like it. The sorrow in the room was almost palpable, and even her own soul had turned heavy. When she too bowed her head, one of her hands appeared. *Dear Androf.* Heart beating hard, she focused on remaining invisible. She couldn't go until she at least learned who they suspected of the robbery. Knowing the McKinnons, and this team, they'd blame it on the Changelings. Though from what she knew of them, they might be guilty.

"Did you learn anything else?" the elder Mr. Murdoch asked Connor.

"Rye? You want to tell us what you know?" Connor asked.

"I've asked around to see if anyone has heard anything, but so far there haven't been any rumors. Personally, I'm voting for the Changelings to be behind this."

Told ya!

Connor held up a hand. "I don't want to accuse anyone without proof, but the craft store is up for sale, and the map Jackson has indicates there is sardonyx under it. Maybe they needed the money to help pay for the purchase."

Mr. Murdoch had a piece of paper in front of him and was taking notes. Seeing how everything was so state of the art around here, she would have thought he'd have a tablet or a phone to record the proceedings. "So they might have motive," the father said.

Rye nodded.

"How much did they take?" Mr. McKinnon asked.

Connor looked over at Jackson who scrolled through his tablet. "It looks like a little less than fifteen thousand. Will was able to press the alert button in the van, and the cops were out the door in seconds. We're guessing the thieves heard the sirens and then high-tailed it out of there, which would explain why so little was taken."

"Did the cops see what happened?" Mr. McKinnon asked.

"No. When they arrived, they found Will dead in the front seat, the back door open, and Roger laying on the sidewalk bleeding. With so much of the money still in the back, the cops clearly had interrupted them."

What a shame to die while trying to do a good deed. She wondered, if she were ever in that kind of situation, would a bullet kill her too? Before the cleansing, only cutting off her head would do the trick. Now? She wasn't sure of her limitations. Maybe she shouldn't take any chances with her life.

"Wasn't the van equipped with cameras?" Mr. Murdoch asked.

"Yes, but the robbers wore masks," Jackson said.

Connor nodded to him. "Tell the group what the bank's doing about tracking the bills."

"The bank knows the serial numbers of the stolen money, but because it's not a lot of cash, it will be harder to trace, especially if the thieves spend a little at a time."

"So what you're saying," his father said, "is that if they buy groceries, the money won't be discovered until after the store deposits the money?"

"Yes and then there'd be no way of knowing who paid with that bill."

"Well, shit."

Vinea smiled. She liked Mr. McKinnon.

Once more, a foot appeared, and she now realized that every time she lost her focus, the ability to stay invisible decreased. Time to go. She had some work to do if she had any hope of helping.

Chapter Three

CONNOR HAD ASKED Devon to come down from Pittsburgh with the express purpose of finding the murdering thieves. While happy to help his brother whenever he could, seeing Vinea again had put a sour taste in his mouth. His wolf, however, refused to stop rejoicing. Sure, she looked hot, especially with those long legs of hers, and goddess only knew, his mouth hadn't stopped watering, but her deceitful behavior from the past spoiled all chance of them ever being together—cleansed or not.

"What do you think, Dev?" Connor asked.

Huh? "About?"

Connor's brows furrowed. "Bro, if you can't keep your head in the game, you might as well go back to Pittsburgh now."

That stung. "No, I'm good."

Connor nodded. "Okay then. One of us needs to speak with Roger, once he's alert enough to talk. He might be able to tell us something, though I suspect he won't add much, which means we'll have to keep our eyes open and our ears to the ground."

"Sounds good." In other words, they had no idea who killed Will. That sucked.

"Jackson, can you send the drone up to periodically check on the Changelings' behavior?"

"I already have it programmed. We know where John Ernst lives and one or two of the other council members, but that's all. We can't track everyone."

Connor nodded. "Do what you can."

Sam leaned back in his seat. "I wish we could be a fly on the wall in that compound. Surely, they'd be discussing what to do with the money."

Jackson sat up straighter. "If you're suggesting Ainsley sneak in, I would prefer not to bring her into this. You all remember what happened the last time when she used her shield of invisibility. I don't want a repeat performance."

Connor nodded. "I agree. We'll try to keep her out of this."

Devon had an idea. "I'd like to speak with the owners of the craft shop to see if there's been any interest in the sale. I went to school with Lydia, the owner. She might be willing to let me know who's put in a bid."

"What reason will you give her for wanting to know?" Connor asked.

Lydia was not a shifter, so he couldn't discuss the Changelings. "I could say a few of the city council members have been worried that outsiders might come in and tear down her place. I could say I'd heard rumors that someone wants to put in an adult sex shop. Lydia would be appalled."

His dad looked over at Uncle Daniel and then at the rest of the group. "How about I ask Lydia? I'm on the city council. It'll make more sense coming from me."

"Sure. That works," Connor said.

That didn't leave him with anything to do. "What's my role?" Devon asked.

This time Sam answered. "How about making sure Vinea keeps out of our hair?"

His muscles tensed, and his stomach soured. That would require him to be close to her, watching her every move—assuming she didn't disappear on him. If he said he'd rather not do that, they'd question his reason. He couldn't say she altered something inside him, though he bet a few suspected it. "Why me?"

Damn. He hadn't meant to jump down their throats or imply he had an issue being around her.

"Seems to me," Connor said, "you're the perfect person. We can't afford to have her messing things up, and she did say she wanted to prove to you that she's changed. I think she'd listen to you."

Well damn.

VINEA'S HEAD WAS spinning with all the ways she could help Devon and his crew capture the thieves. Not only would that bring closure to the poor woman whose husband was killed, it would show Devon that she wasn't the bad person he believed her to be.

It was clear that achieving her goal of winning over Devon would take time. That meant she'd have to find a place to live. Being short on cash, a hotel room was out of the question. While she had the capability of stealing a car, her newfound morals forbade her.

Riding a bike in the cold would suck, but what choice did she have? To minimize frostbite, she wanted a place as close to McKinnon and Associates as possible while being fairly near a grocery store, restaurants, and her place of employment—assuming she could find a job. She didn't have many qualifications other than waitressing. It wasn't like she could program a computer or do someone's taxes.

Okay, now she was even more depressed about her current state. The only thing she'd been good at was harming people.

As much as Vinea wanted to simply disappear and reappear at her destination, she had to stop using her abilities. If this had been last year, she wouldn't have cared if anyone saw her and learned about goddesses and shifters. Now, she understood how detrimental that could be to some people—like Devon.

Basically, she had to live like her goddess status was a thing of the past. That meant she'd have to walk or ride a bike if she wanted to go anywhere. Ugh. In order to find a place to live, she had to do some research, and that meant a trip to the Silver Lake Café where they offered free Wi-Fi.

The walk turned out to be more pleasant than she thought. The last time Vinea had been in Silver Lake she still had a lot of hatred on her mind and couldn't enjoy anything nice. Today was different. Seeing two people hold hands made her a little jealous, but then she squashed that emotion. That was what caused her expulsion from the light realm in the first place.

The Valentine's decorations in the Silver Lake bookstore looked festive, but she didn't think she'd ever understand that holiday. Why only pick one day of the year to express love? From what she'd been told, it should be done daily.

As Vinea entered the café, she noticed a *Help Wanted* sign. Well, wasn't that convenient? For a brief moment, she wondered if anyone from above was watching her. If so, she'd have to thank them if she ever saw her family again.

While she couldn't be certain how long she needed to stay in Silver Lake, her money would run out long before she could convince Devon she'd changed. Vinea definitely needed a job. If she hadn't just stepped inside the restaurant, she would have swiped a hand over her body and put on a more appropriate interview outfit. She sighed at having to make do with the sweater and jeans she'd put on this morning.

Wanting to see if she could find an apartment before asking about a job, she followed the waitress over to a table in a relatively quiet corner. After she ordered a cup of coffee and a Danish pastry, Vinea began her search on her smart phone. Had her friend EmmaLee not helped her find a place to stay when she first arrived in Georgia, Vinea wouldn't have any idea how to locate rentals. By the time she worked her way through her second cup of coffee, she had three potentials.

After she ate her Danish, she made her calls. The first place was available, but between the deposit and first and last month's rent, it was too expensive for her—especially since she didn't have a job yet. The second apartment had already been rented, and the man apologized for not removing the listing. The last one—her least favorite—was an old trailer. The good news was that it was available, close to McKinnon and Associates, and affordable, so she made an appointment to meet with the landlord in an hour. Even better was that she could rent it month to month, and that served her needs perfectly.

After she finished eating and paying, she mentally readied herself to ask about the job. Fingers crossed, she hoped she would succeed.

VINEA THOUGHT THE interview went rather well. The manager said he'd have to check her references, but she was confident Warren would give her a good recommendation. With a bit of pep in her step, she hurried to reach the rental place on time, hoping the space was livable.

When the landlord showed her the trailer though, she tried not to express her disappointment. Compared to her place in Georgia, this trailer was a big step down, and the Billard efficiency was nothing to cheer about. However, the trailer was warm and it provided enough amenities for her to survive. Best of all, it came furnished, and even though the sofa cushions were sagging, and the place needed a good scrubbing, the bed looked decent.

While someone from above seemed determined to make her pay for the bad things she had previously done in her life, she was fine with it. Vinea had been an evil person. If that were the case though, why help her find a job—assuming she was offered it? Ugh. She'd never understand the universe.

The dingy trailer was unoccupied, and once she gave the landlord her first month's rent, he handed her the keys, wished her well, and left. With nothing to do, she checked out her new abode, making a list of what she needed to purchase. Food was the first thing on the agenda. Thankfully, the supermarket was within walking distance. At least by living here, she'd stay in shape.

On the way to Save-a-Lot, her mind spun, trying to think of ways to help Devon and his team. Even though they had no concrete evidence the Changelings were involved in the robbery and murder, everyone in the room seemed to think they were the most likely suspects. Not liking when people drew unfounded conclusions—especially when it was directed at her—it was her duty to find some evidence one way or the other.

When she'd come to Silver Lake the first time, her goal had been to steal Sam Pompley's magic. Because she hadn't been imbued with the ability to fight, she'd had to elicit help. Planning had been the key. In the process of figuring things out, she'd researched Silver Lake, thinking she might need to join forces with their evil residents—the Changelings. Vinea had learned that Jacob Richards, aka Brother Jacob was their current leader. At the time, they had something like twelve councilmen, but somewhere along the way, a few had been put to rest. Their second in command, John Ernst, seemed to be the most visible of the Changelings and perhaps the meanest.

Because Vinea had found someone else to help her, she hadn't needed to contact the mutated werewolves. When her sister thwarted her goal of stealing Sam's powers, Vinea had been livid. Now, she could look back and thank her. That cleansing sure had changed her perspective on life for the better.

Once at the grocery store, Vinea piled the needed food items into her cart, but because she was on foot, she could only carry two bags, so she didn't buy a lot.

However, by the time she returned home, a plan began to formulate in her head as to what she could do to help Devon. It was one that carried little risk, but had the possibility of a great reward.

After she put the groceries away, she decided on what to do next. She would float on up to Brother Jacob's home. Because the workday hadn't ended, she might even get lucky and learn something. If nothing else, she could search his office. Staying invisible for any length of time would be tricky, but as long as she didn't lose focus, she should be successful.

With a nod of her head, she was inside his house a second later.

Not knowing the location of his office, she'd imagined landing in his living room. In reality, she ended up closer to the kitchen. Invisibility sure had its benefits.

A voice wafted toward her, and she followed the sound. Even though the door between her and the voice was closed, she went right through it. A man sat at his desk. Head bowed, the top of his head was bald with gray at the temples. This must be Brother Jacob. He was thinner than she'd expected. His hawk nose and sunken cheeks made for an unattractive appearance. Then there were those thin lips that were pressed into a line. He had a similar appearance to Androf, and the coincidence wasn't lost on her. Perhaps this was what evil looked like.

"How much?" he asked, leaning back in his seat and tapping a chewed pencil on the desk.

For a second, Vinea debated wrenching the annoying thing from his fingers, but he'd hang up for sure if she did that. Staying as still as possible, she mentally urged him to continue.

Brother Jacob shook his head. "Fifteen thousand is as high as I'm able to go." A moment later a small smile lifted his lips. "Very well, I look forward to meeting you tomorrow."

That conversation sounded like it had potential, especially since the price quoted matched the amount of money stolen, but she wished she knew what he was buying. This might be a wild goose chase, but if she didn't follow through, she'd never know for sure.

Brother Jacob pressed an intercom button. "Marcy, can you purchase a round trip ticket to Los Angeles—direct flight only—for tonight or early tomorrow morning. Yes, LAX airport. And get me a rental car and a room at the Windsor Hotel in Laguna Beach for one night." He then disconnected.

Well, that was interesting. Vinea always did like to travel, and California in February had to be warmer than here.

With the when and where figured out, Vinea only waited another minute before teleporting out of there. This time her internal GPS worked, and she returned to her kitchen. Compared to Brother

Jacob's elegant office, her place was dingy, but at least she had a roof over her head, for which she was thankful.

When she had originally transported herself to Silver Lake, she'd carried two suitcases and a backpack since it was all she could manage. She might be a goddess, but her current powers didn't extend to moving objects from one location to another.

From her knapsack, she dragged out her computer and booted it up. There couldn't be that many direct flights from Tennessee to Los Angeles. Identifying the exact flight would make it easier on her.

A quick search revealed he wouldn't be able to fly out tonight, which meant he'd take an early morning flight out of Nashville and arrive in Los Angeles by noon. From what she'd heard Brother Jacob say, he'd make his deal, spend the night, and return the next day. This was going to be so easy. Poor sucker, wouldn't know what happened.

Happy to have a plan, Vinea debated passing it by Devon, but then she decided she wanted to surprise him. If whatever Brother Jacob was buying wasn't anything important, she'd only disappoint Devon by getting his hopes up. The last thing she needed was for him to look down at her for being incompetent. No, it was best to have something tangible to show him.

Though she wouldn't need much while in California, she would need money and her computer, in case she needed to email something to Devon. Just as she'd finished packing her toiletries and computer, her cell rang, jacking up her heart rate. Believing it was Devon calling to ask for her help, she rushed to answer it.

"Hello?"

"Ms. Summer, this is Charles DuPree calling about the waitressing job."

Vinea grabbed hold of the kitchen counter. "Yes?"

"I'm calling to offer you the job at the café, if you're still interested."

She pumped her fist. "I am."

"Can you start tomorrow morning?"

Crap, she'd be in California tomorrow. "I'm afraid I have to make a quick trip across the country. It just came up before you called, but I can come in on Sunday if that works for you?" She held her breath, awaiting his answer. She had to guess that one or two additional days without help wouldn't be too big a burden on the other waitresses.

"That would be fine. Your shift is from ten am to six pm."

"Great. I'll be there." They spoke a bit more about how he'd provide her with three slightly used uniforms, and that she would have to purchase any other ones. Vinea had learned her lesson the hard way about not being grateful. "That's perfect. Thank you."

Pleased things were falling into place, Vinea finished gathering her gear. *California here I come.* From what the men at McKinnon and Associates seemed to think, the Changelings' main focus in life was obtaining sardonyx. Maybe because it was so rare that the price seemed to be quite high.

Had she still been a goddess of the dark realm, she would have created the stone herself and then made oh so much money. Being honest sure did come at a cost, but she was happier now because of it.

Chapter Four

T HE NEXT DAY Connor waltzed into Devon's temporary office and pulled up a chair. "I wonder what Ms. Vinea is up to today," his brother said with a smug look.

Did Connor really care, or was he here to bust his chops? "I don't know, and frankly I don't care. Just as long as she stays out of my hair, I'm happy."

"I thought you were going to keep an eye on her."

"If I hear she's making trouble, I will. As long as she behaves, I'm not giving her a thought."

His cheerful demeanor evaporated. "You are so full of shit. You still like her, I can tell." Connor leaned forward and rested his elbows on his knees. "What I don't get is why do you like her? Sure, she has a smoking hot body, but she's overly self-confident and arrogant, not to mention a liar, a thief, and an attempted murderer."

Devon bristled. He didn't like that Connor had even noticed Vinea's body. It didn't matter that physically she was gorgeous. Her auburn hair, coupled with her long legs and stupendous tits, made his own mouth water, but to hear his brother say it didn't sit well. He would ignore the other slanderous remarks.

"At the time I met her, I thought she was a caring person. I bought into her sad sack story about how some guy had stolen all of her possessions. I realize now that it was a lie to get me to help her. Now that I know what kind of person she is, I'm totally over her."

You know I still want her, his wolf whined.

"Yeah, you did fall for her line," Connor said. "I trust you've learned your lesson?"

Was that supposed to be a warning? Devon was doing a good job here and had only occasionally let his mind wander. "I have. I already told you, I'll be happy if I never see her again—unless, as I said, she does something to interfere with our job."

His wolf whimpered. Vinea might cause his animal to make these outrageous accusations about them being mates, but logic said it was impossible. Vinea was a goddess, and goddesses couldn't mate with humans, albeit a human who could shift—or so he'd always believed.

"Good." His brother slapped his thighs and stood. "I just needed to find out if you're fully on board here. I don't need you pining over what could have been. I know you said you cleansed her, but you can never be sure."

"I'm pretty sure I failed. She even told me right after I dunked her that cleansings only worked on Changelings. I guess I was being overly optimistic at the time."

Sure, she had attempted to kill Zane shortly thereafter, but then she tossed down her weapon and ran away, saying she couldn't do it. Would a purely evil goddess do that? Or did she have an ulterior motive for not following through? Maybe she didn't really need to kill Zane, and she was after a bigger fish to fry—namely him. He inwardly growled. The woman would be the death of him if he let her.

"I'm glad you've seen the light. We have to find out who killed the guard and robbed the armored car sooner rather than later. I want to bring some closure to Lori, Will's wife. If the Changelings are responsible, we need to let them know they can't terrorize our town and get away with it."

"I couldn't agree more." Devon shut out Vinea's image. "What would you like me to do?"

"Help Jackson go over the security tapes. Kalan sent over a copy of the camera footage from the back of the van. The sheriff's department couldn't see anything, but maybe a second set of eyes will help."

Devon pushed back his chair, happy to have a specific job. Once Connor returned to his office, Devon found Jackson in their control room where all of the video equipment was located.

Jackson looked up. "Hey, you here to help?"

"I'm going to try." Devon pulled up a chair. "What do you have?"

Jackson made a few mouse clicks. "I've combined the footage from the security cameras on the armored truck with the street cams to give us some added angles." He pointed to the screen. "This is where the black SUV pulls in front of the armored car, forcing Will to slam on the brakes."

Thankfully, Jackson had turned off the sound. Hearing the squeal of tires and glass shattering would only make it that much more real. "How convenient that they picked a spot where there wasn't any traffic."

"Exactly. The SUV driver knew when and where to pull the heist. Plus, he managed to only damage the rear panel of his vehicle. It's not easy to disable the armored car while maintaining the function in your vehicle."

"I don't think I could pull that off," Devon said.

"Me neither." Jackson pointed to something on the screen. "It's hard to see, but this looks like Will is leaning forward right after the crash and pressing a button to alert the cops that there was an attack."

That was smart thinking. "At any point did you get a read on the license plate?" Devon asked.

"Yes, but it turns out it had been stolen that morning."

"Figures." The footage continued to roll, showing Roger jumping out of the front seat of the armored car as three armed men approached. The guard got off one shot before he was hit in the stomach. "That man closest to Roger flinched. Do you think Roger hit him?" Devon asked.

"If he had been hit, he has to be a shifter because he was able to take the bullet without collapsing."

"That's one reason to think the Changelings are behind this."

"I agree," Jackson said.

"This robber opens the door, shoots Will point blank, and then grabs the vehicle's keys. He then rushes to the back and unlocks the door."

"So?" Jackson asked.

"Take a look at this other robber," Devon said.

Jackson replayed the last scene. "They all are dressed in black, and they all are wearing masks."

"That third man has really long legs." His mind shot to Vinea.

"What are you saying? Do you recognize him? With their bulky jackets and masks, I don't see how you could."

Devon waved a hand. For a moment, he wondered if the third robber could be Vinea. She was tall enough to be a man, and that person had a distinctive gait, but he couldn't be sure if that was how Vinea walked. Too often she wore heels. "It's nothing. Did you learn anything about the men we can use to find them?"

"I measured their bodies and compared them to the height of the armored van. I was able to calculate their heights, but that's all."

"It might be enough once we have suspects."

Jackson turned up the sound. "Here comes the sheriff's department. The thieves must have practiced what would happen if the cops showed up. They each grab two bags and then run back to the vehicle and leave. No hesitation or squabbling about wanting to take more."

"So basically we have squat," Devon said.

Jackson nodded. "If you didn't see anything, then I'll have to admit we're at a dead end."

"There doesn't seem to be any witnesses either. It was almost as if the thieves had someone clear the sidewalks right before the crash. While the accident happened just outside of downtown, I would have thought someone would be around."

Jackson held up a hand. "No one might have been on the sidewalk, but possibly someone inside that office building saw something. Maybe you can question the building occupants while I ask some of our Clansmen to discreetly ask around. Hopefully, someone heard some scuttlebutt about a heist."

"We can only hope."

VINEA WAS PLEASED that she'd timed her arrival to when Brother Jacob's plane touched down on the tarmac. She couldn't chance that he'd go to his meeting first and then head to his hotel. If she missed the exchange, she'd be screwed. Regardless of what he was purchasing, she wanted to get a hold of some of that stolen money. If she could prove it came from the armored car robbery, then Devon and his team could go after Brother Jacob.

Never having been in the Los Angeles airport before, she was overwhelmed by the chaos. People were swarming the gateways then jamming into buses to take them here and there. Not wanting to lose sight of Brother Jacob, she hovered above him but refused to ride in one of those trams. She'd meet him on the other end.

He was only carrying a large briefcase, so maybe he needed to stop at the baggage claim area. When he rushed outside without stopping, she declared him the lightest packer she'd ever known. Brother Jacob hailed a cab, and then Vinea snuck into the front seat just as his ride took off. She'd never ridden in a car in her invisible state before, and she rather liked it. The only issue would be if part of her appeared and the driver saw her; he'd crash for sure.

After fifteen minutes in heavy traffic, Vinea began to worry she might become visible sooner than she'd like. When she felt her body trying to regain its form, she quickly flew out of the cab. A moment later, she found herself behind a building in her fully human form. Damn.

She looked around and sighed a breath of relief that no one was around to see her. The problem with this invisibility stuff was that she had no idea how long she had to wait before turning invisible again. Losing so many of her powers sure sucked.

Not wanting to have come all this way and not witness the exchange, she nodded and prayed. Thankfully, she was once more on her way. This time, she flew above the line of cars and taxis, believing she was safer in the sky. However, a new problem arose. Which of the hundreds of cars was Brother Jacob in?

Eventually, she had to fly low in order to search each car for him. Finally, she spotted the right one. When that taxi exited the highway she was happy, because Brother Jacob would be easier to track.

Twenty minutes later, the cab pulled in front of some loading docks, and Brother Jacob exited. He spoke with the driver and then headed into a warehouse. Given that the driver remained, Jacob must not have believed the exchange would take long. With his briefcase in hand, he strode inside. Let the fun begin! It was time to see what this man was buying.

Vinea entered the large, dark warehouse before Brother Jacob did. The air was stale, and the vast room was filled with shipping containers. Whatever Brother Jacob was buying probably wasn't legal, or he would have insisted meeting in an office building or at his hotel room. Then again, in case of a double-cross, Brother Jacob might need to shift. A warehouse would then be perfect.

"Hello?" called Brother Jacob, his voice echoing in the vast space.

A short, thick man stepped out from behind a container. "Did you bring the money?"

While Vinea didn't watch much television, she had sat through a few detective shows with EmmaLee, and this sounded like a script from one of them.

Brother Jacob held up his suitcase. "Yes, may I see the sardonyx?"

Aha! So she'd guessed right. The man also had a briefcase. He opened it up, and inside was a large red stone, about six inches in length and two inches in diameter. It was huge. No wonder it cost so much. Brother Jacob extracted a bag from his case and then handed it to the man.

If this had happened in the dark realm, about ten armed men would have rushed out and killed Brother Jacob as well as the man selling the stone, taking both the money and the sardonyx. Humans seemed to be a lot more trusting. Just in case the man had a small army nearby, she surveyed the warehouse. Sure enough, two men with guns were hidden near the rear.

Once the items were exchanged, Brother Jacob left, slipped into his cab, and took off. Because she knew where Brother Jacob would be spending the night, she decided to follow this buyer and his newly acquired stash of cash. She wanted to get her hands on some of the money to see if it came from the robbery. Wouldn't Devon be pleased if she showed up with the sardonyx as well as the incriminating cash!

DEVON WAS QUICKLY becoming discouraged. He'd spoken to a half dozen employees of the accounting firm whose office faced the street where the robbery had occurred. One woman heard the crash as she was returning to her office, but by the time she glanced outside, the cops had already arrived. Yes, Will's death was a tragedy she said, but she had nothing else to add.

Throughout the discussion, he half expected Vinea to show up either at the office building or back at McKinnon and Associates. When she didn't, he refused to name the emotion he was experiencing.

You miss her, his wolf chimed in.

I do not. I'm becoming increasingly worried because I don't know what she's up to.

Well, I miss her. Her scent. Her body. Her smile.

Devon had it with his animal trying to lead him down a very dangerous path.

THE NEXT DAY Devon helped Jackson look through the database that Lexi had been creating ever since her arrival. She'd done an amazing job documenting each of their cases. Anytime someone was arrested, she attached a photo and a description. Kalan or Dalton often provided her with additional information. Now, when anyone wanted to look through a list of those suspected to be a Changeling, they just needed to ask Lexi. Unfortunately, there were only a handful of men identified as belonging to that Clan. Most were the correct height, but five foot ten was average for a man. He was slowly losing faith that they would find the men who'd killed Will and injured Roger.

Devon retreated to his office, wondering if he truly could be of use in Silver Lake any longer. Connor, Kip, and Jackson seemed to be at a dead end too, so why should he stay around when his team in Pittsburgh could use an extra hand?

Rye had known Will and his family quite well, and he kept calling the office, asking for an update. Devon hoped something broke soon.

He was just about to find something to eat and then discuss his return to Pittsburgh with his brother when Vinea appeared in front of his desk, scaring the crap out of him. He swung his legs off the desk and jumped up. "What are you doing here? And please stop just appearing."

She had the nerve to laugh. "You look cute when you're taken by surprise."

"Surprised? I'm pissed." He slipped his hands behind his back, hoping she didn't spot how his nails had grown just from being close to her. And her scent that smelled of lilacs? It was driving him crazy. He could almost feel the hair on his face sprouting.

Down boy, he chastised.

I've missed her. Haven't you? his wolf shot back.

He didn't respond, not needing to enter into a discussion with his horny animal.

She waved a hand and then pulled up a chair. "Devon, sit down.

I have something to show you, and I think you will be pleased."

Please do as she asks, his wolf begged. *Remember, she is your mate,* his wolf reminded him for the umpteenth time.

That doesn't mean she isn't up to something. "What do you have?" Devon attempted to soften his tone, not wanting to antagonize her further.

Vinea looped her large bag off her shoulder and dug her hand inside. When she withdrew a huge red crystal, his heart sputtered.

She handed it to him. "I believe this is sardonyx."

Devon had never seen such a large specimen before. "Where did you get this?"

"I kind of lifted it off Brother Jacob."

Brother Jacob? How did she know about him? Was she working with the Changelings? "I don't understand."

Vinea looked away for a moment, almost as if she were embarrassed. It was an expression he'd never seen her use before. "I know you didn't believe me when I said I've changed." She held up a hand, as if she recognized he was about to interrupt. "But I have. I am nothing like the lying and deceitful potential murderer I once was. Words are only words; that's why I wanted to show you I'm here to help. What better way to do that than to steal something precious from your archenemies?"

Devon sat up straighter. He wasn't normally this slow, but he didn't want to jump to any conclusions, especially when it involved Vinea. "How did you know they had this?"

"I knew you wouldn't tell me what you're working on, so I kind of listened in the other day."

His pulse spiked at the implication. "Listened in to what?"

She didn't answer for a moment. "You know how I can appear and disappear, right?"

"Yes." He could fill in the blank. "Don't tell me you came into the conference room and eavesdropped?" His gut churned. If she were working for the Changelings, their entire operation would be compromised. The ramification of the evil stunned him. Devon stood. "Get out."

She didn't move. "Don't you want to know how I got the sardonyx?" she asked.

"I thought you said one of the Changeling council members gave it to you."

Her mouth opened. "I said no such thing. I overheard Brother Jacob on the phone making a deal about spending fifteen thousand dollars to buy something. That number sounded familiar."

"Yes, it was close to what was stolen." He dropped back down onto his seat. She had his full attention now. "Go on."

"I thought perhaps he wanted to buy some sardonyx. It's all you people ever talk about."

"That's because when they get a hold of some, they use it to steal powers—powers that don't belong to them."

Vinea huffed out a laugh. "I know what stealing means."

"This isn't funny, Vinea."

"It's not meant to be. Since I thought you wouldn't want those people to get a hold of the stone, I followed Brother Jacob to California."

That wasn't what he expected her to say. "California?"

"Yes. Brother Jacob took a plane. I kind of…well, flew there on my own, so to speak."

As much as he wanted to ask for more details, he needed to hear what she had to say first. "Then what?"

"Long story short, I followed him to a warehouse where the exchange took place." She stuck her hand in her purse and drew out a handful of bills. "I overheard where Brother Jacob was staying for the night, so I followed the seller instead. When he wasn't paying attention to the wad of cash Brother Jacob gave him in exchange for the sardonyx, I helped myself to some."

"And you're just giving this to me?"

She blew out a breath. "Yes, so that Jackson can ask the bank to check the serial numbers."

Holy shit, she had been listening to their plan. "Thank you." *I think.*

"So do you believe me now that I'm on your side?" she asked with such innocence he wanted to say yes, but he just couldn't.

Chapter Five

I F VINEA HAD an ulterior motive, Devon needed to find out what it was. "I guess I have to believe you," Devon said, hoping she'd not see the lump in his throat at the lie. "You know I deal in facts. Having the sardonyx and the money proves you've changed."

In truth, it proved the opposite. Had she not given the stolen goods to him, he'd have condemned her immediately. His mind raced, trying to think of all the ways she could have come into possession of the precious gem and the money and yet not be culpable.

Believe her! She's your mate. And she's a good person now, his wolf begged.

I'm not listening to you or my body when it comes to her. I am listening to my mind, and it is screaming for me to be cautious.

You're making us both suffer. You want her, and you know it. We need to be with her.

Devon worked to shut him up, but when she grinned, his body went haywire. His teeth sharpened, and his bones cracked. Until he was positive she had abandoned her dark goddess ways, Devon couldn't take what she seemed to be offering—a mate with exceptional talents.

"Great," she said. "What else can I do to help?"

"Nothing. You've done more than enough. Except it would really help if you didn't *float* around without my knowledge." No telling what mess she could get into. He stood. "I'll give this money to Jackson and then put this crystal someplace safe. We can't let the Changelings get a hold of it."

Vinea stood. When she licked her lips, he almost lost it. From the gleam in her eye, her plans weren't finished, and he needed to rein her in. The best way to accomplish that was to keep her close.

Yes! His wolf rejoiced.

"What do you say we celebrate your find? Dinner tonight?" he asked. His pulse sped up as his conscience rebelled. Half of him wanted to believe her, but the other half didn't want to be duped again.

I'm proud of you, his wolf said.

"That would be great." Vinea's enthusiasm seemed so genuine that he had to fight his urge to reach out and touch her. He needed to protect his heart and caution had to be his game.

"How about I pick you up at seven?" he asked.

She hesitated for a moment but then nodded. "Sure."

When she told him where she lived, never would he have guessed a goddess would live in a trailer. He'd been to that trailer park, and it wasn't upscale.

"Shall I walk you out?" he asked. He'd feel better once she was gone. While he'd asked her not to float about, he wasn't convinced she'd obey.

She shook her head. "When I'm sure no unsuspecting soul can see me, I'd rather teleport. I don't own a car, and it's quite blustery out for walking."

Once more she surprised him. She had no problem stealing a few vehicles in the past. Maybe she had changed.

Told ya, his wolf taunted.

As soon as Vinea left, he and his wolf needed to have a stern talk and get on the same damn page.

"Then I'll see you at seven," he said.

She smiled, and his insides stirred, as did another body part. Damn. He hated how fickle he was. His wolf desperately wanted to taste her, touch her, and be intimate with her, yet his human part was smart enough to know she wasn't good for him.

"Tonight then," she said. With a slight nod, Vinea was gone.

Devon leaned against his desk and ran his hand down his face, feeling like he had just been through a twilight zone.

For the next few minutes, he went over everything she'd said, looking for inconsistencies and hidden motives. He then studied the sardonyx, wondering if it was real or a cheap imitation. The only way to be sure the money Vinea gave him came from the heist was to have Jackson run the serial numbers against the ones the bank gave him, so Devon gathered the crystal and the money and headed to Jackson's office. When he entered, his friend was totally focused on his computer screen.

"I had a visitor," Devon announced as he placed the money and the gem on his friend's cluttered desk.

Jackson looked up, and when he spotted the stone, his eyes went wide. "Where did that come from?"

Devon filled him in on everything Vinea had told him. "I can't be sure if it's real."

"We'll have to check it out."

"Good. Then can you see if the serial numbers of the bills match the bank's list?"

"Absolutely." He picked up the first bill and typed the information into his computer. His brows rose. "Well, I'll be damned. It is a match. And you said she lifted these from the seller?"

"Yes. Vinea only took a few so as not to tip the guy off."

"That was actually rather smart, especially if the money hadn't been stolen from the bank here."

"True," Devon said. He had to give her kudos for not being greedy.

"Do we know who this seller is?" Jackson asked.

"She didn't say, but I don't think she knows."

"If this guy was able to find a gem this size, there's no telling how much more he could locate. It could be critical to our survival to make sure he understands the type of person he's dealing with."

Jackson nodded. "Let's nail Brother Jacob first before finding out who this dealer is." Jackson picked up the crystal, leaned back in his chair, and looked off to the side for a moment. "Maybe Anna would be willing to touch the stone and tell us."

"Anna?" She was mated to Dalton, but he hadn't been told she had any special talents.

"When Anna touches sardonyx, it makes her ill."

While unpleasant for her, Anna's talent could be useful to them. "If Brother Jacob spent fifteen thousand dollars for it—assuming what Vinea said was true—I'll bet this is no fake."

"That's assuming she really did follow Brother Jacob to California. She could have created the sardonyx. She is a goddess, you know." Jackson handed him back the stone. "As for the money, she might have been in on the heist."

His gut clenched. "I thought that too."

She's telling the truth, his wolf whimpered. *Did she sound like she was lying?*

No.

Jackson waved a hand. "See what Connor says. We need to make sure we can trust her."

He could hear his brother now. The man would be skeptical of anything Vinea said or did. On the other hand, it might do Devon some good to talk with him. Connor might be able to knock some sense into his thick skull.

"You're right. I'll let you know what he says."

Devon left Jackson and headed straight to Connor's office. When he walked in, Devon waved the huge stone. "Special delivery."

Connor jumped up and stepped around his desk. "Where the hell did you get that?"

"Sit down. It's a long story." He went through the entire conversation with Vinea once more, including how he'd invited her to dinner to see if he could catch her in a lie. "If she is telling the truth, then maybe she can remember a few more details about who this dealer is. I can't recall if she said she followed him to his home or not. If she did, we might be able to locate him."

"That's smart thinking. See what information she has. And you said the serial numbers matched?"

"At least one did."

"Son of a bitch. The problem is that we have no proof that the money came from Brother Jacob. The fact that Vinea basically stole the money from this seller means it won't hold up in court."

"True. Jackson suggested that since she was a goddess, she might have made it."

"I wouldn't put it past her. Shit. I wish we could ring up her sister and ask if goddesses are capable of manufacturing stones."

"Wouldn't that be nice? I'm having a hard time with trusting her too. I do know that with a swipe of her hand, she can change her hair color and its length. Hell, she can be wearing a dress one minute and shorts the next. Why not be able to recreate a stone?"

"Damn," Connor said. "So even if we prove the stone is real, we won't know for sure if Jacob purchased it from someone in California. I don't suppose she showed you her airline ticket."

Devon's heart was sinking fast. "She flew, but not in an airplane."

"You do realize that she could basically destroy us if she created sardonyx for the Changelings."

"Yes, but let's not jump to conclusions. If she is working for them, then there is nothing we can do to stop her. If she did learn about the purchase and went out to Los Angeles, we'll know soon enough."

"How? She deceived all of us before!" Connor's anger rose.

"Just calm down and listen to me for a minute. If the Changelings robbed an armored car and then spent the entire sum on the stone, only to have it stolen, they will be furious. They'll have to try another heist soon. If they do, we'll know Vinea was telling the truth." Relief poured through him at that thought.

"Hmm, you might have a point. Did you know Vinea was going to follow Brother Jacob?"

"No! The last time I saw her was right before our meeting, which apparently she was listening to—from inside the room!"

"I knew she could teleport, but she has invisibility power too?" Connor asked.

"Yes."

His brother slammed his hand on the desk. "Unless we can invoke a soundproof spell as well as one that prevents invisibility, we all need to be careful around her. You are right to want to ask her more questions. You know the old saying about keeping your enemy close?"

"I hear ya. When I meet with her this evening, if she's guilty, I'm hoping I can catch her in a lie."

Devon was torn. He didn't trust her, but he didn't want to believe he'd been duped again. Having the sardonyx implied she was trying to help him—unless she'd made it. The stolen money was another matter. She could be in possession of the money because she was in on the heist. How he was going to find out the truth was anyone's guess.

"Good luck," Connor said. He tapped the stone. "I'll hand the sardonyx over to Rye. He'll check the authenticity. If it's legit, he'll stash it in a special place."

"Let me know."

"I will."

VINEA WAS NERVOUS. She was going out on a real date with Devon McKinnon. Yes, it would be wonderful to sit across from him and just talk, but she wasn't hundreds of years old for nothing. The man would not be flirting with her. Even after she had handed over the sardonyx and the stolen money, she could see his wheels spinning, clearly questioning whether to believe her or not.

Sure, she could have returned to his office to see what he told the others, but that wouldn't have been right. As of six months ago, Vinea Summer didn't break the law or lie or cheat anyone—and she especially didn't want to upset the man who haunted her dreams.

Did she believe in fated mates? Hell yeah, she did. She believed in them so strongly that she became obsessed with wanting to be the one to pick and choose who was paired with whom. But alas, it wasn't meant to be. When Naliana, her younger sister, was chosen instead of her, Vinea saw red. Somehow the jealousy had turned her so evil that she'd been kicked out of the light realm to repent. And now she had, only she doubted anyone noticed or cared.

Truthfully, she hadn't expected them to. It had taken her too long to change. If Devon hadn't dunked her in Silver Lake, she might never have seen the light. Even after he tried to cleanse her, she'd rebelled and lied to him, saying that only Changelings could be cleansed. In truth, she'd had no idea what the pink quartz would do to her. It wasn't until the next day that the truth revealed itself. She'd held that knife over Zane Hunter's head and realized that she couldn't go through with killing him. It was why she'd run.

Bottom line, Vinea needed to move on and stop blaming others for her problems. She needed to face what she'd done, and if Devon refused to be convinced that she was a different person, then she'd have to deal. Of course, it would kill her to lose him. After all, he was all she thought about. Hell, his image was the one that helped her cope with all the adversity. While she deserved the pain, at some point, she'd like to find happiness—with Devon McKinnon.

But happiness would never come if she didn't get ready for this date. This was another chance to convince him she was no longer the evil goddess. If she dressed too provocatively, he'd think she was only interested in seducing him for her own gain.

If she tossed on a pair of baggy jeans and a loose T-shirt, she'd be throwing away her one advantage of appealing to his wolf side. Even though Devon acted as if he couldn't stand her, she hadn't missed the signs that he wanted her—or at least his wolf half did. In her heart, she wanted to believe they were fated mates.

The only problem with her theory that they belonged together was that never in a million years would Naliana allow it. Would her sister ever pair a goddess with a shifter? Ugh. Vinea hated not knowing.

Even when she was part of the dark realm, the moment Vinea had spotted Devon in Vermont, her body had gone crazy with need. At first, she hadn't understood what that meant, but the more time she spent on earth, the more she recognized that emotion as lust mixed with love. Admittedly, she didn't know Devon that well, so love seemed ridiculous, but she certainly loved his noble ways. Plus, him being an incredibly hot and sexy man certainly didn't hurt either.

A knock sounded on her trailer door. Damn. She wasn't ready. Seductive or unattractive? *Quick, decide.* To hell with it. With a swipe of her hand, she opted for straight-legged jeans, knee-high leather boots, and a soft peach sweater that outlined her breasts quite well—the perfect blend of sexy and sweet.

"Coming!" she called.

Now that Devon was here, she wished she'd told him that she'd meet him at the restaurant. Men like Devon probably had never stepped foot in a run-down trailer, and he might judge her poorly.

She pulled open the door and drank him in. Wow! He looked so hot in his white button-down shirt, dark blue jeans, and highly polished boots that she wanted to jump his bones right then. Her body sent so many sparks of need throughout her that she thought she might combust.

In the dark realm, sex was a means to an end, not something that one enjoyed. But here on earth, the right man could change her life.

"Hey," he said. His hands were stuffed in the front pockets of his jeans, and he was looking past her as if he was curious about her place. He finally returned his gaze to her face. "You look nice."

Those kind words melted her and gave her hope. "Thanks. Come on in, but enter at your own risk. I've tried to scrub every surface, but some grime even I can't get rid of. My goddess powers only go so far." Devon actually chuckled, and the tension in her shoulders relaxed.

He glanced around. "It seems livable."

That was a nice way of putting it. "Let me put on my jacket." Vinea swiped a hand over her body, and suddenly, she was covered in a long wool coat.

"I hope you're careful who you're with when you do that. I bet a lot of people would freak out if they saw that display."

She smiled. "I'm careful. Trust me."

"Ready?"

Not at all. "Sure."

She crossed her fingers, hoping that EmmaLee's superstition worked.

Chapter Six

N OT ONLY DID Devon smell divine, his truck had that new
leather scent she found pleasant.

Devon glanced over at her before starting the truck. "During
dinner we need to remember that the walls have ears."

Vinea thought she detected a hint of humor coupled with the
warning, which to her implied kindness. "I promise not to say the
words Changeling, sardonyx, or armored car heist."

He smiled then fired up the engine. "Good. You warm enough?"
he asked as his fingers hovered over the heater knob.

"I could use a bit more warmth."

"Don't tell me the dark realm really is as hot as hell?"

She laughed. "No. For centuries humans have fabricated what
they imagine their version of hell is—heat, brimstone, and men with
horns running around. I can assure you, none of that is true. It's far
worse, but I don't think discussing the various realms at dinner
would be wise either."

He flashed a grin, and butterflies tumbled in her body. She had
to stop reacting so viscerally to him. She'd end up saying something
like she wanted to spend the rest of her life with him, and then he'd
run for sure. Until Devon trusted her, she couldn't chance even
bestowing a kiss on him. It would kill her to wait when she wanted
him so badly, but she had to be patient.

A few minutes later they arrived at the Lake Steakhouse. At
night, the restaurant appeared almost glamorous with its rope lights

bordering the door and windows. "It looks so festive."

He stopped in front of the entrance. "It's the best Silver Lake has to offer. While I park, how about waiting in the lobby where it's warm?" To punctuate his comment, a few snow flurries kissed the windshield.

That was considerate of him, but she didn't want him to think she was delicate. If she had any chance of a new start with Devon, he needed to see her as someone worthy of being with him—an equal more or less. Regardless of what life had dealt her these last six months, she was a survivor, and Devon McKinnon deserved someone who wouldn't crack under pressure or adversity. "I'm good."

"Suit yourself."

They parked in back and by the time they rushed down the back alley to the front of the restaurant, her nose was nearly frozen. It would take a few winters for her to get used to the chilly air.

Lit candles sat on each table, making the restaurant romantic, and the paneled walls and shelves lined with glassware and artwork created an upscale vibe. The hostess gushed over Devon and then sat them close to the bar. Apparently, the name McKinnon held a lot of weight in this town. Vinea could only hope that if they did mate, the town accepted her as well. It was what Devon deserved.

While she'd been on a few dates in the last six months, in the back of her mind, Vinea always believed she'd end up here—with Devon. It was why she never even considered a serious relationship with anyone else.

He helped her off with her coat and then slipped off his. Once seated, he unfolded his white napkin, removed the steak knife, and then placed it next to his plate. The waiter rushed over to take their drink orders. While alcohol didn't affect her much, she opted for coffee. Most likely she'd be up all night anyway going through the conversation they were about to have, so she might as well enjoy the caffeine.

"So tell me," Devon said. "How did you end up in Silver Lake? I would have thought this would be the last place you'd want to return to."

"I told you. I needed to apologize to you. I hurt you and your friends, and I wanted to make amends for the pain I caused." Vinea waited to see if he believed her.

"Why else?"

While she'd expected the doubt, she was hoping for a different outcome. "That's it. My life has changed dramatically since we last met."

"How so?" His hand curled around the knife handle. That wasn't good.

Even though she'd practiced what she'd wanted to say to him for so long, her brain was moving too fast to remember much of it. "After I set up Zane Hunter, I was about to kill him when my life passed in front of my eyes. It's clichéd, but it's the truth. Trust me, I didn't like what I saw one bit. I was so upset that I ran. I know now that I should have stayed and tried to help him, but I think Missy was just as happy that I left."

"I imagine she was. Where did you go?"

"With no destination in mind, I jumped into my stolen car and headed south." He flinched at the word *stolen*.

"Why not *fly* somewhere?"

Now came for the embarrassing part. "I would have, but my powers had taken a nosedive. After the cleansing, nothing seemed to be working. Even the force field I had erected in front of the cave couldn't remain active. It was how Missy was able to escape and toss that powder-like substance on the demon. How it killed him I have no idea."

"I heard something like that had happened. Were you scared?"

"Scared of seeing a demon melt or of losing my powers?"

He chuckled. "I was referring to the loss of powers, but I imagine seeing someone turn to dust would be disturbing too."

"The dust thing was actually cool—or at least I thought so at the time. The demon deserved to die." Devon acted as if he cared about her state of mind. "As for losing my powers, I was petrified. Our life down there is defined by our abilities. Take that away, and I became nothing. Fortunately, some of my powers have returned."

"That's good, I guess."

She glanced off to the side and inhaled. "You want to know what really scared the crap out of me?" He nodded. "It was my sudden concern for others."

"Like when you tried to kill Zane?" he said, his lips thinning and his brows pinching.

Shit. This wasn't going as well as she'd hoped. "No. As I said, growing a conscience didn't come on suddenly, but rather in bits and pieces. I felt it building, but I wasn't sure how to handle it. Hell, I didn't even know if I could deal with the ramifications. Remember, I spent almost my entire life being cruel. Realizing what I had done all those years was wrong, really tore at my very soul. When I had that knife in my hand, the truth of my actions hit me squarely in the face. I couldn't kill him." Devon said nothing. "You don't believe me, do you?"

"On Earth, we judge people by their actions and not by how much power they have or by what they say they'll do."

He didn't answer her question, but hopefully he'd judge her by the fact she dropped the knife instead of using it. "I get it. Words mean nothing if my actions don't back it up. It's why I want to help you—to show you I'm serious."

"I'm glad." From the way his jaw tightened, he was trying to placate her.

She leaned forward. "I know it's hard to understand, but remember I *was* a goddess of the dark. Without my evil thoughts, who was I? It's scary having your entire world turn upside down."

"I imagine that's true. Have you figured things out now?" Each word came out controlled and rather forced.

Wasn't that what she'd been trying to explain to him? "Yes."

"And you want nothing to do with your old life?"

"No." What more could she do to convince him?

¦

"Let me ask you this. Could you return to your former home now if you'd wanted to?" This time, his words held more curiosity than anger.

"Perhaps, but I have no desire to return."

Devon adjusted his placemat and silverware, and she let him think. He finally looked up at her, his eyes nearly black. "As long as you're *baring your soul*, why did you target Sam Pompley? I've always been curious how you found out about his abilities."

His bitterness ate at her, but it was what she deserved. "The second question is easy. His powers are legendary. Just because I'd never been to Silver Lake before then—at least not in my human form—doesn't mean other gods or goddesses of the dark haven't been here. One goddess in particular, Darinda, was the one who discovered his abilities. She was playing around with some of the Changelings and actually watched the guards walk away from their bunker—a bunker they were supposed to protect. I believe the Changelings had stolen some Wendayan magic and Sam was helping to get it back, right?"

"Yes. Kip's brother had his magic taken from him."

"I'm sorry. Because Darinda was impressed by his prowess, when she returned to the dark realm, she told everyone what he could do."

Devon fiddled with his fork. "And that was when you decided you'd like to have power like his?"

She didn't like the scorn in his voice, but she couldn't blame him for having a negative attitude. "Yes."

"Was it in order to make Naliana do what you want?"

Vinea stilled, not expecting him to be so smart. "In small part yes, but mostly I needed something that would allow me to curry favor with my boss—Androf."

"Sounds like you were ambitious."

"I guess that is as good a way as any to explain it."

"If you were this high and mighty goddess, why involve Justin Kapok to help you with Sam?" he asked.

Talking about her past wasn't one of her favorite topics, but

Devon deserved answers. "I needed Sam incapacitated first so that I could carve out his magic with my special crystal knife. It's not like I can fight. My powers aren't strong enough." She shivered at that gruesome thought of actually removing someone's powers. How had she even considered doing something so terrible?

"Carving out someone's magic is horrific," he said, his eyes narrowing.

"I know, but it is how the dark gods do it. It was as if I was on autopilot all those years, obeying my boss, not thinking about why I did things. Feelings only got in the way."

He sipped his drink. "And yet you claim to have feelings now?"

"I do. I was cleansed, remember?"

Devon held up a hand. "Fair enough. Where did you meet Justin? Did he know you were a goddess?" Bitterness tinged his tone. Dare she hope he was jealous?

"No! I happened to run into him when I was on another assignment. When I learned he liked to gamble, I figured he could be of use to me." She held up a hand. "Trust me—my days of using others are over."

He clenched the napkin on the table and curled his lips. "Yet you got a job at a casino just to set him up?"

"I don't see why that's important now. I hate myself, okay?" Talking about her horrible deeds burned a hole in her stomach.

"I just want to understand you, to learn what you had to go through to get where you are today." His tone softened, and hope surged. It was almost as if her outburst had punctured a hole in his balloon.

"How can learning about what a terrible person I was help you understand me now?" she shot back.

"I think it's obvious." His voice came out tight again. Damn her and her big mouth. She hadn't meant to attack.

Only because Devon wanted to know about her dark side did she continue—with great reluctance. "All right, I'll tell you, but it doesn't paint me in a good light." His brows rose, but she didn't defend herself. Nothing she'd done so far made her look good. How much worse could it get? "I mentioned when we were in Vermont that I worked at an Indian casino. My goal was to worm my way into Justin's good graces. I wanted to have him willing to help me when and if I needed him." Her voice trailed off at the memory of what she'd been like.

"You were something else." His harsh tone cut her.

"I know. I was pure evil. I can't change the past."

"How did Lexi fit into the scheme of things?"

While she could feel Devon rethinking this date, she wanted to finish the history lesson and move on. "I overheard Justin talking about winning her in a poker game, but apparently, she managed to skip town before he collected his winnings. I figured I could help with retrieving her." Just saying those words made her realize that no one would forgive her—certainly not Devon.

"Go on," he said through gritted teeth.

"After a few well placed questions and a couple of fly overs I found her."

He narrowed his eyes. "Were you responsible for the men who robbed her?"

She glanced down at her lap. "I'm afraid so. Sam was in Silver Lake, and I needed Lexi to become stranded there. At the time I thought I was being quite *clever*." She hoped he could tell her sarcasm was really self-loathing in disguise.

"You are devious."

"I *was* devious."

Devon leaned back and lifted a palm. "I stand corrected. And thank you for the explanation."

That was it? While his tone had softened, she wasn't convinced she'd made any headway. "You're welcome, I think."

"Now that you've answered my questions about your past, I have another one."

"Anything." She didn't want there to be any secrets between them.

"This may sound strange, but I need to ask. If you're Naliana's sister, how did you end up with the last name Summer? I thought Naliana said they don't have last names where she comes from."

"I needed one to get a job, so I made it up."

"I never thought about that. Why Summer?"

"My life began the day I met the pink quartz at the bottom of the lake. It was summer time, and I figured it was as good a name as any."

His brows rose, and she swore one side of his mouth quirked upward. "I like it."

Some of the tension in her chest that had built up released. "Thanks. Before you ask what I've been doing since that dip in the lake six months ago, I've been in survival mode and have had to be creative."

"Creative?"

"Yes, when answering people's questions, like where have I lived for the last thirty years, or how old I am?"

Devon stared at her. "I can't imagine how hard it must have been to reinvent yourself."

He understood? "Yes. Even telling a lie bothers me now, if you can believe that."

He finally smiled. "As a matter of fact I can."

Relief, and a rush of giddiness, sped through her, and she couldn't help but smile back.

Their drinks magically appeared in front of them, and Devon held up his beer. "To new beginnings?"

Hope surfaced, but his hesitant reaction told her he wasn't ready to forgive her completely—yet.

"To new beginnings."

She sipped her hot coffee, enjoying the rich brew while Devon downed most of his beer. His nerves were probably as taut as hers.

"So where exactly did you go after you left Silver Lake the last time?" Devon asked.

She set down her coffee and twirled the cup. "Once I left Silver

Lake, I headed south with no clear destination. I'd just crossed the Georgia border when I had to stop for gas. When I went inside to pay, I heard two men making a fuss near my car, and I got a real bad feeling about it. As I ran out, both men jumped in my vehicle and took off."

"They stole your stolen car?" Devon raised an eyebrow, and she felt her cheeks heat at the hidden reprimand.

"Yes."

"I do like the irony of it all. What did you do then?"

"What could I do? The car was stolen; I couldn't exactly go to the cops."

"I guess justice was doled out."

"It was. I figured Androf was pissed that I hadn't returned and sent these men to do me harm."

His brows rose. "Androf? Oh yes, your down under boss."

"Yes."

"Then what?"

"I was tempted to disappear and pick a new location, but there were too many people around. In fact, the cashier saw the whole thing and offered to call the police for me. I laughed it off saying one of the men was my boyfriend trying to teach me a lesson. In truth, I was so upset that I didn't know what to do."

"You must have done something." His voice came out a whisper as if he was reliving her nightmare along with her.

"I walked into town and stopped at the Billard Eatery for a cup of coffee to think and plan. That's where I met the woman who would become my best friend. Her name is EmmaLee Donovan. She's a waitress who looked more down and out than I was. I figured if she was surviving, so could I."

"I would have thought you'd be so frustrated that you'd break down and cry."

"A normal woman might have, but remember, feelings were new to me. I was confused more than anything. I understood that something major was happening to me—namely the evil was being sucked out of my body. That meant my emotions were all over the place. I'll admit that when I was at the bottom of the lake, I felt something amazing transpire. It was a feeling I hadn't had since being kicked out of the light realm, and it scared the hell out of me."

He flashed a grin, and she quickly caught on to the double entendre. She shot him back a small smile.

"I can only imagine that you needed time to think. Nothing was as it should be." He stunned her with his compassion.

"Totally. When I saw EmmaLee running around like crazy waiting on impatient people and smiling at them, it gave me hope for some reason."

"People like her inspire me too."

"We started talking, and I told her I needed a place to stay until I could figure out my life. She actually offered me her sofa. Her trailer was a step above where I'm currently staying, but I wanted to be on my own. I appreciated the gesture immensely." She leaned back and smiled. "EmmaLee was so open and trusting that I told her my whole story."

Devon polished off his beer. "The whole story? As in what you tried to do to Sam and Zane?"

"Not at first. I started off by telling her I was a goddess."

"And she believed you?"

"Yes. There were things I could do to prove that."

"And she didn't think you were performing some kind of parlor trick?" Devon asked.

"Believe it or not she didn't."

"How did she react when you told her more?"

"That didn't go over so well at first, possibly because I might have glossed over my failure with Sam, but I did tell her about you and my role in trying to send Zane back home."

"I'm not sure I'd have been so open. Admitting how horrible you were couldn't have been easy."

Her heart melted at his words. "It wasn't, but if I wanted a fresh start, I needed to tell her everything. I trusted EmmaLee to keep her mouth shut, despite the fact she was doing research on the existence of shifters at the time."

"Really?" His brows furrowed. "What makes you think she won't tell the world about goddesses?"

"She won't. She knows how dangerous it can be. She said meeting me was the best thing to happen to her in her life."

"I guess you can never know when you meet someone how important that person will become to you." He looked deep into her eyes, and Vinea was tempted to suggest they leave and find a more intimate place so they could learn more about each other. But she wouldn't. Not yet.

Reality then crept in. He wasn't talking about her and how important she was to him. He couldn't be. Evil goddesses didn't change a person for the good. Sure, he was a werewolf, and as such would know if they were mates, but since he wasn't anxious to be with her, they probably weren't mates after all. Damn. She had been so sure of it.

Vinea had to stop dwelling on the future and worry about not widening the trust gap between them. "You're right. EmmaLee changed my life."

He nodded. "What have you been doing for the last six months then?" he asked.

"Since I needed money, I got a job. Unfortunately, my skills were limited."

"Seriously?"

She appreciated that he thought she had skills. "I'd picked up a few things along the way about computers, how to drive, and how to deal cards, but not much else. About all I could do well was to wipe down tables and wash dishes. You see, we were given missions, and we did them. That's all. There weren't universities where I'm from."

"I would imagine not, but you're good with people. Why not try a sales job?"

"I wasn't given an opportunity to advance myself in the traditional way, and I didn't know if I'd be good enough."

"I'm sorry."

She didn't need his sympathy. "Don't forget I was imbued with hate and evil, and I didn't believe those people skills you think I have would translate well here." She kept her voice low. No need for the rest of the customers to hear how bad she had been. "For most of my time living below, I did what I was told since the consequences for failure were dire. As a matter of fact, my boss came to visit me right after I was hired at the diner and informed me of that fact."

"You mean your former, dark realm boss?"

"Shh." Once more she looked around. "Yes. Someday I'll tell you about that unpleasant conversation. Let's say I was relieved when he left without killing me."

"I thought you were..." He leaned forward and whispered, "immortal."

"I'm not sure what I am anymore. I do know that I'm aging just like every other human, so I have a feeling I might be even less immortal than you."

"Me?"

"Well, you do heal quickly."

"That hardly makes me immortal, though it might keep me alive a bit longer than the average human."

The waiter stopped by for their order. Vinea wasn't really hungry because her stomach was still in knots, fearing she'd mess something up with Devon. So far, he hadn't called her a liar or a thief, so she considered that a positive. "I'll have a six ounce prime rib, medium."

"Very good. And for you, sir?"

"The Lake Steakhouse special, also medium and another beer."

"Thank you." The waiter jotted down their order and left.

Devon studied her for a moment. "Being a goddess, I know you can alter your appearance with a swipe of your hand, disappear, and teleport. Is there anything else can you do?"

"Heal people, but that talent is new. Ever since Naliana shot that light through me, it's been getting stronger and stronger by the day."

"You sound as if that's not a good thing."

"No, it is good, but it takes a toll on me. Every time I help someone, I wonder if I'll be able to survive it. So far, I've only helped those who weren't in serious need."

His brows pinched. "What if someone were dying?"

She liked the protective tone to his voice. "Then I might die."

Chapter Seven

A FTER LISTENING TO Vinea's struggles, Devon's attitude slowly
began to change. At first, he thought she was merely spinning a
tale, but the pain in her eyes convinced him she wasn't making it up.

After dinner, he took her home to her trailer. While he wasn't
quite ready to say goodnight, he needed time to reflect on everything
she'd told him. The rational side of his brain said not to rush things.
His wolf however was clamoring for satisfaction. Hell, he'd had to
readjust himself during the drive the second he imagined kissing her
goodnight.

Devon jumped out of the truck and rushed over to her side to
open the door. When he held out his hand to help her down, her
touch nearly scorched him. That wasn't good. While he couldn't
deny a definite connection existed between them, he wasn't ready to
act on it.

"Thanks for dinner," Vinea said as she stepped to her trailer
door.

"I enjoyed it." That was the truth. At least the last half, after he
adjusted his attitude.

Her lips pressed together, and the next second, she spun to face
him and wrapped her arms around his neck. Before he could even
think, her warm, delicious lips were pressed against his.

Take her! his wolf urged.

His human brain was telling him to stop, but his body wouldn't
obey—not before he enjoyed the sweetness of her lips and her heady

scent a bit more.

It was Vinea who broke the kiss and then stepped away. "Good-night."

Before he could say anything, she'd unlocked her door and rushed inside. After she closed it, Devon just stood there a bit stunned. He hadn't been ready to stop.

It was the whistling wind carrying a fresh wave of snow that jolted him back to reality. Time to go. Devon spun on his heels and dashed to his truck. He couldn't believe he'd actually let her kiss him. For the first time in six months, he didn't regret just letting life happen.

When he walked into his house, Devon grabbed a beer and then began pacing his living room, doubt suddenly springing up. Had he been a fool to fall for her story? Right now, his mind couldn't be more scrambled if he spun in endless circles.

Devon probably should call Rye, his wiser older brother, to hear his opinion, but not only would he be busy with Izzy and the baby, he would just tell him to go with his gut. And Devon's gut told him she had changed. Or was that his wolf talking?

Connor, on the other hand, would tell him to stay as far away from her as possible, that goddesses couldn't be cleansed. If it were possible, Naliana would have done it long ago. The fact that the gods of the light hadn't cleansed those from the dark realm proved it.

Damn. Devon was so confused. Yes, he wanted a mate, but was Vinea the one? All the signs were there. His body went crazy every time he was near her, and her scent made him lose focus too many times to remember. She did something to him, but was that enough to prove they belonged together forever?

She'd admitted that her abilities were such that she really couldn't hurt him physically, but emotionally he'd been out of sorts from the moment he'd laid eyes on her.

The most open-minded person around was Jackson, but Devon didn't want to disturb what little time his best friend had with his mate, Ainsley.

Devon strode over to the sofa and dropped down. Vinea had said she'd been a waitress at a diner in Billard, Georgia. He assumed she was telling the truth as it was something that would be easy to check.

After tipping back half of his beer, Devon went into his office and retrieved his laptop. A quick search brought up the email and phone number of her place of employment. At least the town and diner existed—so far so good. He shot off a quick email to the owner saying he was considering hiring Vinea and wondered if he could give her a recommendation.

With that taken care of, Devon stripped out of his clothes. All night his wolf had been pacing and panting over Vinea and creating chaos on his libido. He needed to rein in some control, and a cold shower would hopefully cool down his overly active wolf.

"YOU WON'T BELIEVE what I did tonight," Vinea said with the phone pressed against her ear. She unzipped then kicked off her boots before curling her legs under her on the sofa.

EmmaLee squealed. "Do tell."

"I had a date with Devon."

Her friend sucked in an audible breath. "You didn't. Tell me everything."

"The best part was that he never once called me a liar. In fact, he seemed to believe my story, though I have to admit something was holding him back. I could see in his eyes that he was waiting to catch me in a lie."

"For starters, what you went through was not a story," EmmaLee said. "It was what really happened."

"I know."

"You should be happy. When you left here, you didn't even think he'd talk to you."

"You're absolutely right. And you know the best part?" Vinea asked.

"What?"

"When he walked me to the door, I kissed him."

EmmaLee squealed again. "And?"

"It was everything I'd dreamed about and more. I broke off the kiss and rushed inside before he had the chance to voice any regrets. Hopefully that kiss will open his heart a little bit more toward me."

"That was a smart move," EmmaLee said. "So what happens now?"

That was the big question. "His team is having some issues with a bunch of bad guys, and I tried to help out, but I don't think Devon believed me when I told him what I had done. It doesn't matter. Eventually, my contribution will convince him that I am on the up and up."

"You are a good person, Vi. Devon and the others will see that as well."

Vinea felt the tear run down her cheek. "You're the only person who believes in me. I don't know what I would ever do without you. I love you, EmmaLee."

"I love you too, but you don't need to sound so sad. I'm not going anywhere. I will always be here for you. Just remember to believe in yourself, girlfriend." Someone knocked on EmmaLee's door. "Oh, that must be Slater. I gotta go. Call me whenever you want. I miss you." Then she hung up.

Slater? Hadn't EmmaLee promised to kick his ass to the curb? Ugh. That girl would never learn.

Vinea leaned back against the sofa and swiped away the tears that fell. She missed having someone to confide in. Sure it had done wonders to tell her tale to Devon, but while he seemed to really understand what a struggle it had been for her these past six months, at times lines would form around his eyes, giving her the impression that he was waiting for her to slip up. While that saddened her, it also made her more resolved to earn his trust and forgiveness. EmmaLee was right, Vinea needed to believe in herself, and hopefully, Devon would start to believe in her as well.

First, however, Vinea needed to work on their friendship, and then in time, she'd earn his love.

THE LEADER OF the Changelings, Brother Jacob, brought the gavel down on the hard wood table that was atop the platform facing all nine of his council members. They were seated and silent—just as they should be. He inhaled to control the roiling anger that was nearly ripping him apart. His men didn't need to see their leader become unfocused or show any weakness. Losing the sardonyx was a huge blow to them. Jacob's new goal was to find the thief and personally kill him.

"Normally, I am the one demanding answers when something goes wrong, but this time, I am to blame." Despite the injustice perpetrated against him and his Clan, he almost smiled at the look of shock on their faces. It was the first time in a long time he'd taken blame for anything. "I have no idea how the sardonyx was stolen since I had stored the gem in the hotel safe in my room, and I even slept with the room key card under my pillow. But the next morning, the sardonyx was gone. It took all of my control not to punch a hole in the wall or put a curse on the manager. The man assured me that the lock couldn't have been breached, yet it must have been. How else could anyone have gotten in?"

"What happened?" one of his disciples called out.

As much as he wanted to discipline Charles for not raising his hand, he didn't. "I may never learn how the theft occurred, but I will be more careful in the future." In retelling the story, his blood pressure rose a few notches, but he didn't want the others to see him lose his cool. Brother John raised his hand. "Yes?"

"I assume you asked the management to check the security footage. Whoever entered your room had to have entered from the hallway, right?"

His room had been on the fourth floor. "Yes, and I did ask for the security tapes. In fact, I missed my plane the next day because I spent hours poring over the footage. Unfortunately, I saw no one enter my room. Anyone have any suggestions on how it was stolen?" The men glanced at each other, but no one offered any solutions. "Bottom line, the sardonyx is gone, and that means we have to buy more."

"We'll have to pull another heist," John Ernst said.

That was what he'd been thinking. "I agree. The armored car company is sure to take extra precautions. We'll need someplace new—any thoughts?"

DEVON HAD SPENT the last few days trying to handle the problems in the Pittsburgh branch remotely. Apparently, one of the women whose husband had been banned from being anywhere near her had violated the restraining order. Now, a few of his men had to give her round the clock protection. Handling the details over the phone had been hard, but at least it kept his constant focus off Vinea. To his dismay, he'd hear a female voice in the hallway and think Vinea had arrived. He'd then remember she'd probably just show up in his office instead of coming in the front door like everyone else.

A knock sounded on his office door, and he jumped, immediately picturing her. Connor barreled in and pulled up a chair. "Things are too quiet in town. The Changelings are surely mounting some revenge, and I was wondering if you'd heard any rumors?"

Devon glared at his brother. "I've barely been out of the office. Their whole crew could burn down the town, and I'd be the last to know!"

Devon had no right to take out his frustration on his brother. He should direct his irritability at the cause—Vinea. He'd been avoiding visiting some of the more popular spots—like the diner and McKinnon Pub and Pool in order to put some distance between them. If he was too near her, his wolf would go crazy with want. It was already getting harder than hell to rein him in. Even worse, he didn't trust the human part of him around her either.

"You need to get out and ask around," Connor said, looking at him rather strangely. While Devon should explain why he was out of sorts, he didn't need to hear Connor tell him that he'd told him so.

Devon refocused. "I know I should. And I will. Have you heard anything?"

"No, and that worries me. Assuming the sardonyx that Vinea gave us came from Brother Jacob, he should be on the warpath."

"He can't tie the theft to us. It happened in California."

"He doesn't need proof," Connor shot back. "We'll be the first ones he'll point his finger at."

"You might be right. We're the only ones who realize how important that stone is to them."

Connor nodded. "I have this sixth sense something is going down soon. Have you spoken with Vinea?"

"Not since the other night when we went to dinner."

Connor scrubbed a hand down his jaw then looked off to the side for a moment. "I still think she's screwing with us. She's always had an ulterior motive and looks at everything for her own gain. The bitch is bad news, and I don't trust her."

His need to shield her flared, and that protective streak scared him. "I think she's changed."

Connor lowered his chin, clearly not changing his mind. "I bet she knows the Changelings' next move."

Devon couldn't prove otherwise. "It's possible."

"If we assume she isn't working for them, why not use her to help us?"

Use her? Now Connor sounded like Vinea when she'd admitted that she'd used Justin to get what she wanted. He tried to tell himself that this situation was different, that the Changelings were pure evil, but he wasn't sure if he was merely fooling himself.

"She said she was willing to do anything," Devon said.

"As much as I hate to admit, it's because of her that we got a break in the case in the first place."

"Agreed. We were at a dead end," Devon said.

Connor leaned forward. "As much as I don't like asking her,

maybe you can find out what she knows, and what she's willing to do. Just be alert if she gives you any bullshit."

His brother's hostile and negative attitude about Vinea pissed him off, but he wasn't going to argue with him, especially since most of what Connor said had crossed Devon's mind at some point. "While she promised she wouldn't eavesdrop in our office, she said nothing about not visiting Brother Jacob again."

"That's great."

"I don't think that's a good idea," Devon said, trying to keep a neutral tone.

"Why not? She did it once. If she can investigate while remaining invisible, we could learn a lot. She will either prove to us that she is a changed person, or her true colors will show."

Devon inhaled slowly. "Which way are you leaning?"

"I'd put my money on her remaining true to her dark side."

Damn. The image of Vinea in danger crumbled another brick of his heart. Because he refused to mention that fact to Connor, he went on the offensive. "If she does snoop, how do we know what she'll tell us is the truth? Vinea could lead us into a trap."

It seemed better if he, rather than Connor, brought up the argument that it could backfire. Maybe then his brother would back away from using her. Devon wasn't happy about these new stirrings of emotion he was experiencing.

Connor laughed. "You sound like me. Maybe it's best if we leave her out of it."

"I agree. Besides, Vinea told me her abilities weren't extensive anymore. If she did become visible by mistake, we could be in big trouble. She's not like Izzy who can shoot fire at someone or strangle a person with a vine."

"Then we are better off without her."

What really worried Devon was what if she were restrained? Could she become invisible and transport away? Ainsley, Jackson's mate couldn't. Devon probably should question Vinea further in order to understand her limitations.

Stop fighting your true feelings, his wolf growled. *Admit it. You want to protect her from all harm.*

Devon shoved back his wolf. If he accepted any of these unwanted feelings he was having for Vinea, his wolf would take advantage of Devon's weakness and come out full force to get what he needed.

Connor stood. "If nothing happens in the next few days, you might as well head back to Pittsburgh. I know your office is short-handed with that restraining order case. The farther away you are from that evil woman, the better off you will be."

His gut clenched, as his wolf rammed against him, growling and snapping. Devon had to admit his brother was right, and a wave of disappointment swept over him. "I will."

Here he thought he was ready to walk away from Vinea forever, but maybe he wasn't.

Chapter Eight

T HE NEXT MORNING, Connor walked into Devon's office bright
and early, a scowl marring his face. "The hardware store was
robbed last night," his brother announced.

There went his quick return to Pittsburgh. Devon's wolf rejoiced, but he didn't. The image of the armored car robbery surfaced.
"Was anyone hurt?"

"No. Best the owner could tell was that they were robbed during
the day without anyone being aware. The owner was about to put
the day's receipts in the vault when he found his stash of money from
yesterday's deposits stolen."

"How was that possible?"

Connor pulled up a chair. "It had to be an inside job."

He could buy that. "Were there any security cameras in the
office?"

"No, and that's the problem. The person must have known
that." He glanced around as if he wasn't sure how to approach the
next topic. "When I was in the hardware store around six last night
buying some wall anchors, I saw Vinea there."

He bristled. "So?" His brows creased. Devon could see where
this was heading. "You were at the store. Does that make you a
suspect?"

"Devon. Think about it. How hard would it be for her to become invisible, hover over the owner's shoulder as he opens the safe,
and memorize the combination?"

"She would have had to case the store for days in advance to learn the owner's routine and how the money was handled. I'm not saying she isn't capable, but do you have any other proof? Did you see her go into the office?"

"Of course not. How could I if she was invisible?"

Devon didn't want to get into it. If Connor could provide him with proof, he might believe Vinea hadn't changed. Right now, she was an innocent bystander. But damn, she was making it hard for him to trust her.

The kiss convinced you, didn't it? his wolf asked with way too much glee.

No, maybe… I don't know.

Devon cleared his throat. "What do you want me to do?"

"Talk to her again. Pretend that you believe her. Find out if she saw anything suspicious. She might give us something to go on."

"I don't have to pretend. I do believe she's innocent unless I'm convinced otherwise."

Connor stood. "You need to think with the head on your shoulders and not the one between your legs."

Devon refrained from giving his brother the finger. He loved Connor, and he believed he meant well. Vinea had hurt Devon emotionally, and that pissed his brother off, but if Connor had gone to dinner with them the other night, he'd know Vinea wasn't the spiteful and deceptive woman she had once been.

Devon closed his door, returned to his desk, and then called her. His heart thumped, and he tapped his fingers on the desk waiting for her to pick up.

When she didn't answer, he couldn't help wondering if she was angry because he hadn't called her in the last couple days or if she was where she shouldn't be. In truth, it was probably best that he not speak to her right now. Devon needed time to sort through some issues. His stupid wolf kept insisting Vinea had changed and that she was his mate, but Devon didn't know how his wolf could know so much when he didn't.

Her voice message came on and then the beep sounded for him to leave a message. "Vinea, it's Devon. Can you call me when you get a chance? I need your help." That should appeal to her good senses.

Once he disconnected, he went over what Connor had said about the theft. It might be time to find out what Kalan could tell him. While Kalan and Rye were best friends when the three of them were growing up, they'd played alongside each other for years. Kalan would be straight with him.

Grabbing his gear, Devon left the office. As he drove to the sheriff's department, Devon checked the sidewalk, hoping to spot Vinea. If she didn't have a car, she most likely would be walking, since Vinea didn't seem the type to hole up in a dingy trailer.

Unfortunately, he arrived at the department before he saw any sign of her. He would give her some time to return his call, and then if he hadn't heard from her, he'd head on over to her place to speak with her. If she had been at the hardware store even close to the time of the robbery, she might have seen something suspicious. He didn't want to believe that she would have robbed the store or that she was in league with the Changelings.

Once inside the station, Devon spotted his friend at his desk. "Hey, Kalan, how's it going?"

His friend looked beat. Being a werebear, his beard grew faster than most, but it didn't look like he'd even shaved this morning—or slept.

"To be honest, I'm dead tired. I was in the middle of working on the armored car heist when Dalton and I were asked to head up the theft at the hardware store. It's like we're the only ones on staff."

Devon wasn't sure if he should mention Vinea and her connection, but it might help him with his case. Knowing where to focus his attentions could save him time. "Can we go someplace private?"

Kalan pushed back his chair. "Absolutely. Follow me."

He escorted Devon to an interrogation room then pressed two buttons. "No one can see or hear us," Kalan said. "What is it?"

They sat opposite each other across a worn brown table. "I'm not sure how much you know about Vinea's recent arrival or how she came into possession of a big chunk of sardonyx."

"Rye told me Vinea removed it from Brother Jacob's hotel room in California."

"Yes, but a few have questioned if that was where she got it."

Kalan leaned back in his chair. "Is that so?"

"Let me back up. I need to start with how she became involved in the first place." Devon detailed everything from about how she came to his office the first time to how she listened into their discussion of the armored car heist. He finished with how she'd retrieved the sardonyx and the money.

"I take it you aren't sure whether to believe her?"

"At first I wasn't. Connor still doesn't believe her, but because I was eager to hear her side of the story, I asked Vinea out a few days ago. I have to admit she was convincing in that she had no involvement in any way with the Changelings. She said she just wanted to help us—to make up for all the wrong she'd caused."

"I hope that's true. Besides Vinea's testimony, do you have any other evidence that the Changelings are involved?"

"No."

"I see. What can I help you with then?"

Devon told him about Connor seeing Vinea in the hardware store yesterday.

"And you think she might have had something to do with that theft?" His words came out rushed.

Devon blew out a breath. "I don't want to believe it, but she is capable of disappearing, which means she could have done it. I'm here to see what you can tell me."

"So far, all we know is that the safe was wiped clean of fingerprints."

His heart spiked. "That implies Vinea is innocent. She wouldn't need to wipe the safe clean. If she even has fingerprints, she'd know they wouldn't be on file." Devon tried to hide his relief, but from the brief smile on Kalan's lips, he hadn't succeeded.

"We should ask her for them," Kalan said. "How about talking to Vinea? If she is guilty, you might be able to sense it. If she had nothing to do with the crime, she might have an idea who's guilty. I don't know how much she knows about what's going on, but she is a goddess. They know things we humans don't."

He really appreciated Kalan not automatically assuming Vinea was guilty. "I plan to do just that. Thanks."

Kalan stood. "Keep me in the loop, okay? The red moon is tonight so there's no telling what crap will hit the fan. A few of the shifter officers know to keep an extra eye out for the Changeling shenanigans."

They always caused trouble around the red moon. "Whatever I find out, I'll let you know."

"Appreciate it."

Once Devon left the station, he drove straight to Vinea's trailer. The inside was dark, but he knocked anyway. She didn't answer. Given how small the place was, he was certain he would have sensed if she'd been there. Not that he would blame her for ignoring him, but he believed he could sweet-talk her into speaking with him even if she had been angry.

Just as he jumped into his truck, his cell rang. "Hello?"

"Devon, it's Vinea. I just got your message."

A lot of banging and talking sounded in the background. "Where are you?"

"At work."

How did he not know she had a job? *Because you haven't called her*, his wolf was quick to mention.

"Where is that?"

"Just a sec." She must have covered the phone because all he could hear was muffled voices. "I'm sorry. This is a bad time. I gotta go."

"No, wait. I have to talk with you."

She hesitated, and his gut churned. "I get off work at six," she said. "So how about stopping by at six thirty?"

"I'll be there."

As soon as he disconnected, he let out a breath. He'd been about to say he'd bring over dinner, but if he did that, he wasn't sure what might happen. The more he was around Vinea, the less control he seemed to have.

Devon had a sinking feeling that if she had asked him in the other night, he might have agreed. Once close to her, no telling what his wolf would have made him do, Until he was sure of her, Devon couldn't let his animal have his way.

AS SOON AS Vinea hung up, she rushed to pick up an order and then delivered it. "Here you go, Mr. Sanford. I'll be back to check on you."

"Can you stay and chat? I won't bite." The seventy-five year old human smiled, his perfectly white dentures lighting up his face.

She'd only been on the job for a week, but already she'd become attached to some of the regulars. Mr. Sanford's wife had died about two years ago, and he said he liked to have either lunch or an early dinner at the Silver Lake Café several times a week. He was fast becoming one of her favorites.

"I have to take care of a few people first, but I'll come right back."

"You do that." He winked, and she wondered what Devon would be like when he was that age. Handsome, sexy, and quite virile, she was sure.

Vinea rushed to the kitchen, picked up another two orders, and then took the food to the waiting customers. The whole time she was hustling about, she replayed her strange conversation with Devon. She understood that he was a busy man, but did he have to wait four days before contacting her? From his tone, something urgent had come up.

All day, she'd heard the gossip about the hardware store robbery, and she hoped he didn't want to ask if she had anything to do with it. The Changelings were bad, and she'd been bad in the past, so it made sense he'd think she was working with them—only she wasn't.

Just today, she'd wondered if her presence in Silver Lake was causing Devon more anxiety. Part of him seemed to want to believe she'd changed, but the other half was still skeptical.

Once she finished with her customers, she returned to Mr. Sanford. Knowing how lonely he was, she slipped in across from him. "So how are you doing?"

"Not so good. Marie died two years ago today. There's not a day that goes by that I don't think of her, but today is extra hard."

Vinea reached out and placed her hand on his gnarled fingers and squeezed. The irony of her sympathy didn't escape her. Seven months ago, she might have laughed at the old man, relishing that he was in pain, but not any longer. His hurt resonated with her—like the ache in Devon's eyes whenever he looked at her.

"What was Marie's favorite dessert?" Vinea asked.

"A brownie sundae."

She smiled. "How about I fix you one in honor of Marie? My treat."

"I think that is a wonderful idea, as long as you can spare some time to sit with me while I enjoy it?"

"I would be honored, Mr. Sanford."

Vinea slipped out of the booth, paid for the dessert, and then went to work on making the best brownie sundae ever. When she returned with it, they sat in silence as he enjoyed the treat. Once he finished, he leaned back, looking full and content.

Mr. Sanford smiled. "That was the best dessert ever. Thank you, my dear."

For the rest of the afternoon, Vinea rode high. Being nice was addicting.

When her shift finally ended, Vinea was actually nervous about seeing Devon again. If he accused her of some wrongdoing, her mood would plummet. The hardware store robbery was sad, but several of the customers claimed the owner had insurance. She imagined the violation was just as devastating whether he was covered or not.

It was possible the Changelings had been responsible. After all, she'd stolen their precious stone, which meant they'd have to buy more. If they had to steal money the first time, they'd need additional funds.

Maybe taking the stone hadn't been the smartest of moves. No telling what they'd do next. In the future, she should pass her plans by Devon before interfering.

Once she clocked out, she headed out the back door.

"Goodnight, Vinea," Charles DuPree called.

"Night."

It was snowing out, but the cold didn't bother her as much as it had in the past. From all the running around during her shift, Vinea was quite heated. In fact, the cool air was actually welcome. She liked her job at the café, but she missed EmmaLee something fierce. Most of the other waitresses were nice, but she doubted she'd find anyone as understanding as her best friend.

The walk home took fifteen-minutes. During that time she let her mind wander to that wonderful moment when she'd kissed Devon, and how his lips had been warm yet firm. While the contact had been brief, it was something she'd remember for quite some time. Devon McKinnon was an outstanding kisser.

Once home, she hurried inside and slipped off her coat. After the afternoon she'd had, she needed to shower. Vinea was so wiped out that she didn't even have the energy to swipe her hand across her body to change. Instead, she peeled off her clothes then ducked into the bathroom.

As soon as the water warmed, she stepped under the hot flow and sighed with relief as the heat pummeled her body. With little time to spare, she quickly washed, dried off, and then tried on a few outfits. Satisfied with the jeans and Kelly green sweater, she drew on wool socks and boots, and then padded out to the living room to wait for Devon. Taking the time to dress, instead of swiping her hand, made her feel as if she was growing accustomed to life here on Earth.

Six thirty turned into six forty-five, and she began to wonder if Devon was coming. When the knock finally sounded on her door, Vinea jumped. Nerves were never part of her character before, but now she was almost skittish. She wanted to believe it was because she cared.

When she opened the door, the cold air rushed in. Devon was bundled up in a navy blue parka, and his cheeks were a little red. Holy hell, he looked good enough to kiss. "Come on in."

Once he stepped inside, she closed the door. Devon glanced around, but his expression didn't change. For the past four nights, she thought Devon might stop by, so every evening she'd cleaned, but no matter her effort, the trailer would never be considered spotless.

"I haven't eaten, and I thought perhaps we could go out to dinner again," Devon said.

Did that mean he'd had such a good time before that he wanted a repeat performance? Here she thought he wanted to merely question her. "Sure. Do you want to go now, or would you like a drink first?"

The last time she went shopping, she'd picked up a six-pack of beer in case he did stop over.

"I'd just as soon go now."

Two things rushed to her mind. Either he couldn't wait to get started on their dinner date, or he was going to tell her something she wouldn't like and believed that being in a public place would lessen the chance of her storming off or disappearing.

Not wanting to jump to conclusions, she pretended it was the first case. Without thinking, she swept her hand and dressed in a matching blue parka. His eyes widened at her selection, but he said nothing about her choice. Damn. If she wanted to blend into this world, she needed to dress the way a normal human would—by putting one arm at a time into the jacket.

"Let's go," she said.

Vinea crossed her fingers, hoping this date would lead to something wonderful.

Chapter Nine

"W HERE ARE WE going?" Vinea asked as she slipped into Devon's truck.

"How about McKinnon's Pool and Pub?"

It made sense that he'd want to be surrounded by his family when he asked her any unpleasant questions. "Works for me. Maybe you can show me how to play pool while we're there." Not only would it allow her to spend more time with him, she could accidentally on purpose brush up against him.

Devon chuckled. "And be embarrassed when you clear the table in one turn? No thank you."

She laughed. "I've never played in my life."

"That doesn't mean you won't use your skills to win."

He was being silly, but she enjoyed that he was worried about losing. She liked a man with ambition. "I'd never do that. Well, I might, but only if I had to."

"Had to?"

"A girl can't let a man have the upper hand all the time."

He smiled. "Ah, the real Vinea Summer appears."

She held up her palms. "What you see is what you get."

Devon glanced over at her then returned his focus to the road. "I'll store that comment for further study."

A few minutes later, they arrived at the pub. "Does your father own it?" she asked.

"No. My uncle Garrett does. His daughter, Molly McKinnon

waits tables. She's finishing up school, but she likes the extra cash waitressing brings in. My youngest brother Finn is the bartender and recently became the manager."

She remembered Finn; she'd tried to extract information from him about the demon from Cargonia. Man did that seem like a lifetime ago. "You must be proud of him. That's quite an accomplishment."

"I am proud. I'm very lucky that everyone in my family has done well." He parked and then cut the engine.

Devon came over to her side and opened the door. Vinea wasn't sure if she'd ever be used to such chivalry. She'd certainly missed out on a lot of things living in the dark realm.

Once she stepped inside the dimly lit pub, it took her a moment to become accustomed to the smells that seemed to be some combination of beer, old wood, and what she thought might be peanuts. It wasn't unpleasant so much as unique.

A two-piece band consisting of a guitar and a set of drums was setting up on the small stage to the left as they walked in. A poolroom sat straight ahead with a large bar to the right. The dining area consisted of eight tables surrounded by a lot of booths ringing the walls. How had she not remembered any of this the last time she'd been in here?

A cute girl rushed up to them, and when she hugged Devon, Vinea had to tamp down her jealousy. It was her big weakness.

"Molly, I'd like you to meet Vinea. Vinea, this is my cousin Molly McKinnon."

Ah, yes, the owner's daughter. The relief was so great she almost hugged the girl. "Nice to meet you."

Devon placed a hand on Vinea's back and heat seared up her body. She was fast falling for this man, even though he might never accept her. Damn.

"Can we sit anywhere?" he asked his cousin.

"Sure, but my station is along the back wall."

"Great." Devon led Vinea to the back.

He was being so nice that Vinea was waiting for the other shoe to drop. Molly took their order and then rushed to fill it.

"Did you hear about the theft at the hardware store?" she asked, wanting to get the ball rolling if this was the real reason for him asking her out.

"I did. Do you know something about it?"

Vinea couldn't detect any anger or censure in his tone, but Devon was good as hiding his emotions. "I only know what I heard at the café."

"Café?"

"I work at the Silver Lake Café now."

"Ah. So that's what the noise was in the background when we spoke earlier."

She studied him for a moment. "And you call yourself a detective?"

His chin lifted, acting as if she'd offended him. "I could have found out if I'd tried."

Vinea didn't even want to ask why he hadn't. "I'm sure you could have."

"Why didn't you mention it?"

She was embarrassed. She also wasn't ready for the censure of taking a menial job. It didn't matter he seemed okay with her working tables in Billard. "I didn't think it was important."

Devon studied her for a moment, probably deciding whether or not to say if it was. "You know I like to know what you're up to."

She couldn't decide if that was because he wanted to keep tabs or her, or if he was interested. Right now, her emotions were so erratic, she couldn't be sure of anything. "Good to know."

"So, back to the robbery. Did you hear any gossip?"

Talking about facts would be easier than discussing what they felt about each other. "All I know is that the hardware store was robbed around six, but that the owner might have insurance." She held up a hand. "Not that it makes it right."

"I heard that too, and I agree. Did anyone speculate who might be responsible?"

She chuckled. "Even if anyone knew, it's not like they're going to point a finger. It would be unhealthy for them, if you know what I mean?"

"True. Connor said he saw you in the hardware store yesterday. Are you sure no one looked suspicious?"

The blood drained from her face, until anger scratched back. So that was what this was about. "I didn't see Brother Jacob if that's what you're asking." She hadn't meant her comment to be curt. While he hadn't come out and asked if she had been responsible, he'd implied it.

"I'm sorry. I'm not asking if you did it."

Wasn't he? "But you were thinking it."

He slipped his napkin onto his lap. "Connor wanted me to ask, that's all."

"Connor? I suppose he suggested that I probably disappeared, waltzed into wherever they keep the cash, and stole the money."

He glanced off to the side. "More or less."

She swallowed her anger. "I know I tried to harm both Sam and Zane. I also understand that I hurt you by leading you on, lying to you, and then stealing from you. I broke any trust I had with Lexi and a lot of other people, but that is all in the past now. I'm not sure what more I can do to prove to you and your family that I'm not out to harm anyone."

Molly chose that moment to deliver their drinks, and Vinea appreciated the chance to cool off.

Devon tossed back half his beer. It was as if he needed the fortification. "I want to believe you, but as you so nicely stated, your track record isn't the best."

"You're right, but I'm determined to prove to you that I can be trusted. I should do a little more snooping up on the hill."

"No way." Devon clasped his hands on his drink.

Was he kidding? "What do you mean? You accuse me of wrongdoing or possible wrongdoing, and then say I can't prove my innocence?"

Devon leaned forward. "It's not safe. You don't understand what kind of animals live in the hills."

The Changelings. "It won't be dangerous for me. Remember who I am and what I can do. Besides, I want to do this."

He waved a hand. "You said yourself that your abilities aren't what they used to be."

Me and my big mouth. "I'll be in and out in a minute. The last time went fine. Nothing is going to happen. One head bob and I'm gone, poof."

He leaned back and shook his head. "No."

Vinea huffed. "No? Since when did you become my keeper?"

Please say it was right after I kissed you.

"I'm not, but I would be lying if I said it wouldn't affect me if you were caught."

When backed into a corner, the Vinea of old seemed to come out. "Why? Do you think those people would assume I was working for you and then come after you?" Here she thought he cared for her.

Devon blew out a breath and glanced at the ceiling. "I have no idea how you came up with that conclusion, but you have it all wrong."

"Then explain it to me," she said between gritted teeth, trying to keep from shouting.

"Despite my better judgment, I like you."

Her pulse shot up. "Does that mean you believe me?"

Once more, he glanced to the side before returning his gaze to her. "I think so."

She'd been about to say that she wanted him to believe her un-conditionally, but then decided that was unrealistic. She needed to be content with baby steps. "Okay, if I have to stay away from *those people*, what are *you* going to do to find the person responsible for the hardware store theft?"

Devon finished off his drink. "I don't know."

"You see? You need me." There had to be a way to convince

him. Sure, she could go there without telling him, but that would only add another lie to her pile of offenses.

"What if something goes wrong?" he asked. The anguish in his eyes told her a lot.

"I'll make sure it doesn't." *Please say you're okay with this.*

He blew out a breath. "Fine, but I want to hear your plan first."

Excitement raced through her. If she could learn something, it might bring Connor over to her side too. Hopefully, this job would convince Devon once and for all that she'd really changed. "I'll do the same thing I did before. I'll enter quietly, listen for a while, and leave. Simple."

Devon knotted his fingers together. "Fine, but on one condition."

She had him. "What's that?"

"Call me as soon as you get out of there and let me know what you've learned. No heroics, hear?"

Vinea smiled. "Absolutely none."

Devon cleared his throat. "Okay then. So tell me about your new job."

Vinea was thrilled that the inquisition was over, and they could finally get on with their date. "As I mentioned, my skills are rather limited, so when I spotted the help wanted sign at the Silver Lake Café, I applied."

"I'm impressed you looked for work so quickly."

She hadn't expected him to say that. "Why? I do need money to live on."

"I know you worked as a waitress in Georgia, but it has to be harder for you to do manual labor than the average person."

She laughed. "Because you think my life was so cushy before?"

He shrugged. "I'm not sure what to think, but if you were still up to your old ways, I guess you wouldn't be working a regular job."

Vinea sipped her beer, liking the taste. "I'm glad you're finally willing to see the real me."

"So am I."

Molly returned with their meals. Vinea had ordered the breaded chicken breast with a mushroom sauce and Devon a hamburger. Now that he wasn't shooting daggers at her, she could enjoy her food.

"So, how long will you be staying in Silver Lake?" she asked Devon.

"It depends on what you find. Just today, Connor suggested I return to the branch office in Pennsylvania because we'd reached a dead end, but then the hardware store was robbed."

"Isn't finding the perpetrator a job for the police?"

He chuckled and nodded. "They are handling it, but the owner is a good friend of my father's, and he asked if we could lend a hand."

So when this mess was cleaned up would he head on home and not give her a second thought? That idea upset her so much that her chicken no longer looked so appetizing. "What would you like me to listen for, or to find, when I visit your *friends* in the hills?"

"Anything you can find that relates to them having newfound money, whether it's in relation to the hardware store theft or the armored car heist. Hell, if they discuss anything about a new attack, we'd love to know."

"That's a tall order. I can float around for a bit, but my ability to stay invisible for long has always been an issue."

He leaned forward. "I take it back. I don't want you to go."

Shit. Devon really did care about her safety. A warm and embracing liquid shot through her, filling her with joy. However, if she had any hope of being with him long term, she had to do this job. "I want to help you. If I feel myself appearing, I'll leave. I promise."

He chewed the inside of his mouth. "Fine, but be careful."

She smiled at Devon. "I will."

Maybe he was starting to care for her again. She could only hope.

THIS TIME WHEN Devon dropped her off at her trailer, he said he had some business to take care of and couldn't stay. She didn't believe that was the reason for him bugging out so fast. True, he had received a phone call on the way home, but a few minutes extra to say goodnight wouldn't have hurt him. Men. She wanted to believe it meant he didn't trust himself, fearing a kiss would turn into something more, but getting her hopes up meant it would hurt more when he left.

If he had to leave, she'd let him go. Even a goddess couldn't make someone care if he didn't.

"Okay, while you're working," she said, "I might head on up to Brother Jacob's house sometime tonight."

"Shouldn't you wait until tomorrow?"

"Why?"

"It's late. Brother Jacob might not be conducting business at this hour."

Vinea leaned closer. "Are you worried about me?"

"Yes." His voice came out strangled.

So he was afraid what might happen if he stayed—or so she told herself. "You are a sweet man, Devon McKinnon."

He cleared his throat. The man definitely had issues with expressing his emotions. "Remember to call me. Okay? And don't stay too long."

She ran a hand down his arm. "Don't worry. What can go wrong?"

"Plenty."

Quite happy with the way things had turned out this evening, Vinea slipped out of his truck and rushed to her trailer. Anxious to learn something, she decided to head up right away.

But when she stepped inside her trailer, she instantly knew something was wrong. The heat had gone off. After investigating the heater, she realized it was beyond her scope of expertise to fix, and no amount of hand waving would help. Damn. Fortunately, she had the landlord's number and called him.

"I can send someone over in a half hour."

That would give her enough time to head on up to Brother Jacob's, listen for a few minutes, and return before the repairman showed up. "That would be great. Thank you."

Not bothering to take off her jacket, she nodded once, and to her delight, she found her prey in his study again. He was on the phone talking to someone about buying more sardonyx. Perfect timing!

His conversation certainly sounded promising, however that alone didn't mean he'd stolen the hardware money. She should have asked Devon how much was taken so if Brother Jacob haggled over the price, and the two prices matched, it might indicate he'd been the thief.

From the casual way they were talking, he was calling the same man who'd sold him the stone in California the last time. Before she would traipse out to the west coast again, she'd ask Devon first if his crew wanted her to get a hold of some of the money and the stone like she had the last time. If the Changelings lost their precious sardonyx a second time, no telling what kind of retribution they'd engage in.

"If you do," Brother Jacob said, "call me." He tossed his cell phone on his desk and leaned back.

Guess that didn't go as planned. The man looked tired, as if he had the weight of the world on his shoulders. She couldn't imagine being responsible for a large group of people, especially since he believed he needed something as rare as sardonyx to ensure their existence. That would put a toll on anyone.

Vinea waited a few more minutes, but he just seemed to be surfing the Internet. As she was about to call it a night, a knock sounded on the door.

"Come in," Brother Jacob said. The scowl on his face implied he wasn't in the mood to be disturbed.

John Ernst walked in with his chest puffed out. "I have some news."

Well, she couldn't leave now!

Brother Jacob stood and came around to the front of the desk and peered down at the newcomer. He was a good four inches taller than Ernst, so perhaps this was his way of intimidating him. "What is it?"

"Were you able to secure any more sardonyx?" Ernst asked.

"No, but Archer says he'll explore other avenues."

Archer? Having a name might help Devon.

"I might have a lead. I spoke with the realtor about buying the craft store."

Brother Jacob waved a hand. "The hardware store safe didn't yield even enough to buy a hunk of stone, let alone a down payment on the craft store."

Bingo! Too bad she hadn't thought to record the conversation. She was slipping.

"We'll have to find more money," Ernst said.

Now things were heating up. In her excitement to find out more, she lost focus and appeared. Oh shit. Vinea tried to become invisible once more, but it seemed she needed a moment to regroup. This was bad. Really bad.

"What the hell?" Brother Jacob said as he grabbed her arm.

The shock of being exposed enabled her to activate her flight mechanism, and a second later she was back in her trailer, her heart pounding so hard, she thought she might go into cardiac arrest.

Shit, shit, shit. While he hadn't captured her, he'd seen her face. Jacob would be more careful now than ever. She hadn't prayed in years—make that hundreds of years—but she believed now might be time to start. If she caused these men to go underground or go on a witch hunt for her, Devon would never forgive her.

Vinea paced her living room, knowing Devon was waiting for the call. If she told him she'd found out nothing while in Brother Jacob's house, he would think she was in cahoots with those evil Changelings. Telling the truth was the only option, and the sooner the better. Calling wasn't an option. She would need to tell him in person, and then calm him down when he began shouting.

With a nod, she disappeared and reappeared in the McKinnon and Associates office. Devon wasn't there, even though he said he was heading to the office to do work. Using her cloak of invisibility, she searched the other offices and spotted Sam and Connor at their desks. While she wanted to tell someone about her fiasco, she believed neither of them would be likely to hear her out.

Next stop was Devon's house. She'd never been inside, but she knew where he lived. In fact, she might know more about Devon McKinnon than he did—other than where he was at the moment.

Her arrival was a little misplaced however, and she landed in his unlit bathroom. Whoops! That would have been embarrassing if he'd been in the shower or worse on the john.

The rest of the house was dark, implying he wasn't home. While she doubted he was on a date, given her frazzled state of mind, it might be better if she headed home and waited. After all, the repairman would be there momentarily.

Because she didn't have time to search, she should just call him, but she was a chicken. Not talking to him in person would be disastrous. Maybe after the heater man came and went, she'd call, assuming she'd figured out what to say to him.

Chapter Ten

WHEN DEVON ARRIVED home after his meeting, he debated calling Vinea to see what she'd found out at Brother Jacob's house. She'd promised to call, so why hadn't she?

Because it was close to ten, he decided not to disturb her. Most likely, Brother Jacob either wasn't home or he wasn't divulging any Clan secrets. Devon was sure that if she learned something earth shattering, she would have contacted him.

Tomorrow would be soon enough to speak with her and find out. And while he never doubted her sincerity in trying to convince him she had changed, whether she really had was up for debate.

I believe her, his wolf said. *And so do you. Stop being so fucking stubborn and tell her you do. That way she won't have to put herself in danger.*

For once, his wolf might be right.

No sooner had he removed his coat than his cell rang. Thinking it was Vinea, he didn't bother to check the ID. "Yes?"

"Dev, its Finn. You need to get down to the pub right away."

Finn was never this serious. Something bad must have happened. "What is it?"

"Vinea is here with John Ernst."

His heart nearly turned to steel. "Are you sure?"

"Sure, I'm sure. She's the same woman you came in with a few hours ago."

Fuck. "I'll be right there. Call Rye."

"I already did."

Devon dragged on his coat but didn't bother with the buttons. He dashed out to his truck, hopped in, and took off. He might have taken a few of the turns too fast, but that couldn't be helped. As much as he wanted to rant and rave at Vinea the moment he saw her, approaching her when she was with John Ernst would put her life in danger—and possibly his. Was she there because she believed she could get Ernst to divulge some secret? Shit. She better not be trying to convince the Changeling that she could help them.

He slammed his hand against the wheel. He didn't know whether he was angrier with himself for believing what she'd told him or royally pissed at her. Mostly likely it was a little of both.

Screeching to a halt in front of the pub, Devon yanked his keys from the ignition and stormed inside. Just before he entered, he forced himself to calm down. He wanted Vinea to think he just happened to stop by for a drink—nothing more. With his vision straight ahead, he strode toward the bar.

She's not here, his wolf said. *I would have sensed her.*

Nonsense. How can you say that? She isn't my mate.

Seriously? You're in denial, his animal responded.

Finn rushed over to the end of the bar. "She's gone."

"What? When?" Finn would have never pranked him.

"She and John Ernst left right after I called. I figured you were on the road already, so I didn't contact you." He nodded toward the door. "Here's Rye now."

His brother slid onto the seat next to him. "Where is she?"

"Conveniently gone," Devon answered. "I wonder if she knew Finn had called us."

Finn shook his head. "I purposely ducked into the storage room before contacting you. She couldn't have seen or heard me."

Rye placed a hand on Devon's arm, probably hoping to calm him down. "Finn, tell us exactly what happened," Rye said.

"There's not much more to tell. Vinea came in here with John Ernst, and they sat in one of the back booths."

"Who waited on them?" Rye asked.

"I did."

Finn never left the bar. He must have known something was up. "Did you hear anything?" Devon asked.

"Just bits and pieces. When I neared the table, I heard the words *thanks for your help*. That was all."

Acid burned in his gut. "How could I have been so stupid?" Devon asked to no one in particular.

Rye faced him. "You need to find her and ask her what she was up to. Maybe she was trying to learn something, and she believed coming here would give her some safety."

He hadn't thought of that. "I will ask her, but I don't expect anything more than a claim of innocence."

"You won't know until you try," Rye said.

His brother seemed to be on her side. "If she fucking conned me yet again, I just might kill her." Not wanting to listen to either of his brothers tell him not to overreact, he pushed off from the stool and strode out. He just hoped he didn't implode before he reached her. If Vinea wasn't home, which he suspected she might not be, he might drive up to the hill and confront John Ernst himself.

By the time he arrived at her place, Devon was having a hard time thinking straight. Nothing made sense. He couldn't imagine why she would have a meeting with one of the Changeling council members in the family pub. Why not stay on Changeling ground? The only explanation was that she feared for her life, as Rye said. Her plan had been to remain invisible, so what had made her change her mind?

Devon shut off the truck's engine in front of her trailer and then sat there, trying to come to grips with what he'd found out. He always prided himself in keeping his cool, but this time he wasn't so sure he could do that.

The lights were on in the trailer, implying she was home. Needing an explanation, he shot out of his truck, strode up to her door, and pounded instead of lightly knocking. "Vinea, I need to talk to you."

A second later, she pulled open the door dressed in full winter gear—jacket, wool cap, scarf, and gloves. Most likely she'd just beaten him home.

Her eyes widened. "I didn't expect you."

"I'm sure you didn't." He stepped inside, readying for the confrontation. Before he could even form the scathing words, the lack of warmth startled him. "Why is it freezing in here?"

"The heater broke."

"When?"

She rubbed her arms. "Maybe two hours ago? After you dropped me off, I walked into a freezing trailer. When I couldn't get the heat to turn on, I called the landlord. He came over a half hour later, checked out the heater, and said it was caput. He promised to have a new one installed by tomorrow—assuming he can get a hold of someone at this late hour."

His head swam. "Are you saying you've been here since I dropped you off? In this cold?"

She glanced to the side. "Not exactly."

"What does that mean?" He failed to keep the anger from his tone since he knew where she'd been.

"After you left, I made a brief stop at Brother Jacob's house."

"And?" It was all he could manage to say.

As she rubbed her hands up and down her arms, she winced. "Things didn't go quite as I planned."

"You don't say." He wondered if she'd mention that she ended up at McKinnon's Pub.

Devon needed to discuss a lot of things with her, but he didn't want to have this conversation here. It was too damn cold. While he was insanely angry, he wasn't so much of a heel to let her sleep here tonight. She'd freeze.

"We have a lot to talk about, but it's too cold in here. How about staying at my place tonight? It'll be warm." He also could keep an eye on her that way.

"Really?"

She smiled, and his wolf rejoiced. He did not. "Yes."

"Okay. Let me grab a few things." Her demeanor quickly changed from sober and a bit frightened to almost happy. "I need to tell you what happened at Brother Jacob's."

"What happened?" he called after her, as she high-tailed it down the hallway.

Vinea turned back around. "I'll tell you when we get to your house."

That was for the best. "I'll be in the truck warming it up."

Vinea practically bounced toward her bedroom. If she had been at the pub, would she have been this cheerful? It was as if she had no clue why he was on the warpath.

It didn't take her long to grab a small bag. Vinea locked up and dashed to his truck moments later. Once she hopped in, it appeared her good mood had evaporated. As much as Devon wanted to wait until they were at his house, he had to ask. "You mentioned something happened with the Changelings?"

Vinea leaned over and turned up the heat. "Yes. I found out a ton, and then the unthinkable happened."

She must want to torture him, but Devon wouldn't cave. "What was that?" He was pleased he was able to keep his voice non-threatening.

"When I arrived—cloaked in my invisibility, of course—Brother Jacob was on the phone to a seller of sardonyx."

Devon's fingers tightened on the wheel. Damn fucking Change-lings. They sure didn't waste any time. "Will you be heading out to California again?"

"No. I couldn't tell if it was the same man, but he didn't have any stone for sale. I did learn this new man's name was Archer. I'm guessing it's his last name."

That was good intel, but Devon hoped like hell she was telling the truth. As much as he wanted to believe her, things kept cropping up that pointed to her not always being truthful. "Did you learn anything else?" he asked as he put the truck in gear and headed back to his place.

"Yes. I was about to leave when John Ernst came into the office."

If she saw John Ernst up on the hill, why go to the pub? Devon had to work at holding his tongue. "What did he want?"

"He said he spoke to the owner of the craft store about selling it. But get this, Brother Jacob said the money from the hardware store theft wasn't even enough for a down payment." Excitement laced her tone.

Devon whistled. "I wish you'd worn a wire."

"Me too. I actually thought of it, but only after the fact. Just so you know anything that touches me also disappears, so they wouldn't have been able to tell."

A few minutes later, he pulled down his parents' drive to the guesthouse, cut the engine, slipped out, and came over to her side. "Let's get inside where it's warm." Devon carried her case as he led her up the steps.

Once inside, he escorted her to the bedroom. "You can stay in here."

"Perfect. Thanks."

He hoped she didn't get any ideas. He'd be sleeping on the sofa.

Share the bed, his wolf urged. *I can only last so long with my mate this close.*

You'll do as I say, Devon warned.

"Settle in. I'll make us some coffee to warm you up."

She smiled, and his libido shot into overdrive. "I'd love that. Then I'll tell you the rest of what happened." She slipped off her coat and followed him back to the living room. "I like your place. It fits you."

That was an odd thing to say, or was she trying to distract him? "It's my parents' guesthouse. I'm here too infrequently to have a place of my own."

"I thought you said you stayed with them in the main house the last time you were here."

Damn, she had a good memory. "Yes, but my parents are on vacation and their house is too big without them. They'll be getting home soon, but by then I'll probably be on my way back to Pittsburgh."

"Oh." Devon headed into the kitchen to prepare the coffee and Vinea trailed after him.

"So finish your story about Ernst and Brother Jacob," he said.

She leaned against the counter, tension creasing her brow. "I was so excited to learn that the Changelings had robbed the hardware store that I...um... kind of materialized." She winced then looked off to the side.

His body tensed. "You what?" Devon hadn't meant to yell, but he couldn't help it.

"The bad part was that they both saw me. I have to say the look of shock on their faces would have been comical had it not been for the fact that they can now identify me. Before I could disappear again, Brother Jacob grabbed me. I thought I was a goner, but the shock enabled me to disappear again."

"That's terrible."

She straightened. "Look, I'm really sorry, but you're safe. They can't tie me to you. There's no way they could know I'm helping you."

A million thoughts flashed through his head, the most important of which was that it was a red moon. It was possible that when Brother Jacob touched her, he was able to transform into a likeness of her. He could only hope that was the explanation for her—or rather her lookalike—visiting the pub. "Can I see your phone?" he asked.

She handed it to him. "You want to make certain that I spoke with the landlord, don't you?"

There was no use mincing words. "Yes, but I'll tell you why in a moment."

He checked her phone log and noticed two calls to the same number: one after he'd dropped her off and the other forty-five minutes later. While it was possible she could have made it to the pub in time, he had a better explanation.

Devon finished brewing and pouring the coffee. "Let's sit in the living room, and I'll tell you what I learned tonight."

They carried their drinks into the small space and sat. "You looked rather relieved when you saw the calls. Why?"

This was going to be difficult to explain while not coming off as being a total ass. "I am relieved. A short while ago, my brother Finn called me from McKinnon's Pub and Pool."

She stilled. "Did I leave something there?"

"No, he called because—" His cell rang. "Hold on for a second." Devon checked the caller ID. "It's Rye. I think I know what he's going to say." He swiped the phone. "Yeah?"

"Did you speak with Vinea?"

"She's with me now. Vinea did spy on Brother Jacob, and when she returned home, she had to deal with a dead furnace. At the time of the incident, she was with the repairman."

"You sure?"

"Yes. Turns out when she visited Brother Jacob she materialized by mistake. He touched her."

"Oh, shit. That explains it. I was calling to remind you that there's a red moon tonight and that I wouldn't put it past them to pull a dirty trick like that. Maybe they wanted to see who responded to John Ernst being with her in order to find out who she was working with."

"Thankfully, Finn was circumspect."

"No kidding. How's it going otherwise?" Rye asked.

Devon didn't want to discuss this now. "Can we talk tomorrow?"

"Got it. Later."

Devon pocketed his phone. "Rye came to the same conclusion I did."

Her brows furrowed. "I'm confused."

"Right before I came over, Finn called to say you were at the pub with John Ernst."

He shouldn't have made that announcement when she had coffee in her mouth, because she almost spit it out, though some did dribble down her chin. She wiped her face with the back of her hand.

"I wasn't. I swear."

"I know that now. You were dealing with a broken heater."

"Why would he lie?"

"He didn't."

She held up a hand, set down her mug, and then stood. "Even after all I've done for you, your family still thinks I'm working with the Changelings?"

"I'll admit that I did too at first, until you told me that Brother Jacob had touched you."

She slowly returned to her seat. "And it's the red moon. Of course. When Brother Jacob grabbed me, he was able to become me." Her jaw lowered. "Holy crap. Finn did see me, or rather, a likeness of me."

Devon was happy that she understood why he'd jump to the wrong conclusion. "Can you see why I overreacted?"

"Yes, but I never, ever would be in cahoots with those scumbags. And if I were—which I'm not—why would I go to the enemy's camp, so to speak?"

That had bothered him. "They obviously wanted to be seen. What worries me is why they assumed you're working with us?"

"Small towns talk, though the last few times I've interacted with McKinnon and Associates, it wasn't to help you."

"That I know."

"So now what?" she asked then raised a finger. "We need to catch them in an illegal act."

Devon's protective nature flared. "You, Miss Goddess, will do nothing of the sort! While your snooping ended more or less without dire consequences, any future actions could ruin everything. They'll know for sure we're on to them if you're caught again."

She set down her cup with a clank. "And if I had never returned to Silver Lake, would you have been any further ahead?" she shot back.

He liked her spunk. "Probably not."

And that was the root of the problem. He needed her. Unfortunately, it was in more ways than just her helping him with the case.

Chapter Eleven

VINEA DIDN'T KNOW whether to be happy that Devon seemed to believe she wasn't the person with John Ernst or upset that he'd assumed she had been. She wished like hell she knew what it would take to melt his heart.

"It's getting late," Devon said right after he drained his coffee. "Why don't you head on in to bed?"

From the rather contemplative way he spoke, Devon needed time to deal with his feelings. Over these past few days, Vinea was more convinced than ever that she and Devon were fated mates. On the other hand, it might be a cruel twist of fate foisted on her by Naliana, but if they were destined to be together, Vinea was going to do everything in her power to make it come true.

So as not to cause the man more grief, she said her goodnight. As if she were still at work, she picked up both cups and took them into the kitchen.

"Just leave them in the sink. I'll take care of them later," he said.

"It'll only take a sec to wash them." She turned on the water and dropped some soap on a sponge.

Devon stepped into the kitchen and touched her shoulders. "I want to apologize again for acting like an ass."

She turned off the water and faced him. "It was an honest mistake. My past was bad, and you didn't want to look like a fool again. I never thought it would be easy to prove to you that I've changed. Just so you know, I'm not giving up."

His smile came out weak. "I hope you don't."

As Devon disappeared down the hallway, she finished washing the cups. When she returned to the living room, Devon was walking in with a blanket and a pillow in hand.

"What are you doing?" she asked.

His eyes widened. "Sleeping on the sofa."

That made no sense, nor was it necessary. "Why?"

"For starters, you're in the only bedroom. You can fill in the blank why I'm out here. Secondly, if the Changelings have connected you with the McKinnons, I don't trust them not to show up here. Hell, I wouldn't be surprised if Brother Jacob pretended to be you again with the intention of convincing me to tell all."

Maybe she had misjudged these crazy bastards. "They have style, I'll give them that."

He dipped his chin. "I hope you aren't serious."

"No, but they are creative if nothing else." She shot him a quick grin and was thrilled when his eyes flashed amber for a moment. *Yes!* His wolf knew they belonged together. "I guess I'll see you in the morning. If you need help with the Changelings, give a yell."

His eyes widened. "Besides listening in on a conversation, what can you do?"

Was he serious? Not that she blamed him for not wanting her to help. Hell, she'd almost ruined things the last time. "Well, if I picked up, say—" Vinea looked around for something that might harm a person and then pointed to a rather heavy looking potted plant. "That. If I were invisible, as soon as I touched it, it would disappear. I could smash it over one of their heads. Or I could rush to the kitchen, grab a knife, and stab one of them without anyone being aware I was there."

He studied her for a long minute. "Here I thought you weren't capable of killing."

"To save your life, I'd hurt anyone." Her pulse pumped hard, and anger welled in her stomach at the thought he'd ever be in danger.

She hadn't meant to sound so vehement, but she wasn't sorry she had. It was about time Devon understood the depths of her commitment to him—and to them.

"I hope it doesn't come to that." He winked, and her whole body seemed to melt with erotic lust.

"Me, too. Sleep well." She spun on her heels and rushed down the hallway to *his* bedroom. Being in a room where Devon slept would cause every nerve ending to fire all night long. She might as well kiss sleeping goodbye.

VINEA YAWNED FROM having tossed and turned all night. Devon's scent permeated the sheets and the room, waking her up time and again with lustful thoughts. She'd been tempted many times to wander into the living room, if only to watch him sleep. True, she could have become invisible and hovered above him, but if they were to be mates, he probably would have sensed her presence, and the last thing she needed was to explain that she wanted nothing more than to have mind-blowing sex with him.

As she lay in bed with sunlight peaking through the crack in the curtains, she listened for sounds of movement. Even with her good hearing, Devon didn't seem to be awake.

Wanting to do something nice for him, she eased out of bed. After she washed up, she quickly dressed in a pair of blue jeans, a yellow sweater, and comfy boots then headed into the main room.

Tiptoeing, she peered over at the sofa. Devon was on his back with the blanket halfway up his chest. His mouth was slightly open, and he was snoring softly. Smiling, she went into the kitchen. While she wasn't a cook at the diner in Billard, she had watched them work, wanting to learn as much as she could about life on earth. She'd practiced her skills on EmmaLee, and her friend claimed Vinea was a born chef.

Because the kitchen was open to the living room, Vinea had to move about quietly. First came the coffee. While it was brewing, she scoured the refrigerator for something to eat, a little disappointed that other than eggs, he had very little in the way of breakfast food. What did the man eat? Not planning to stay for long, he probably decided not to stock up on food. When he was on surveillance, he probably lived on take out. His fine physique had to be due to his shifter metabolism.

Once she found a bowl, she cracked open some eggs, added milk, and then beat the mixture, surprised he didn't wake up from the scraping noise. Just as the coffee finished, she poured the eggs into a hot pan. The kitchen itself was rather rustic, but she appreciated the cast iron pan and metal bowl.

Devon sat up with a start. "What are you doing?" His voice cracked from sleep.

She smiled. "Three guesses."

"You're making breakfast?"

He didn't have to sound so surprised. "I hope you don't mind."

He tossed off the blanket. "I didn't hear you get up."

"I was goddess quiet."

That finally got the reaction she wanted—a smile. "Do I have time for a shower?"

Oh, how she wanted to say she'd join him, but during the night he might have changed his mind about whether to trust her. Devon seemed to be so conflicted. "Sure. I'll turn the heat down."

"I'll be fast."

He grabbed the blanket and pillow and rushed down the hallway. As much as she wanted to become invisible and watch him strip naked, she almost certainly would have become so distracted that she would have appeared. Even if he had been flattered by her need to see him, she doubted he'd be pleased. Vinea had to show him that he could trust her to use her powers appropriately.

While she waited for him to do his thing, she stirred the cooking eggs and then searched for some plates. When the shower turned off, she dished up the food and poured the coffee.

A few minutes later, Devon came out wearing tight jeans, a

white T-shirt, and no shoes, drying his hair with a towel. "It smells wonderful. Thank you."

You smell wonderful too.

This was harder than she thought. When Devon had asked Vinea to stay at his house, she'd been elated. Having the chance to be near him, to show him she'd changed, had thrilled her. Now she realized it was pure torture not to touch him in the intimate way she desired, especially since patience had never been her strong suit. In fact, her rash behavior had gotten her into trouble numerous times.

"Come sit down before it gets cold," she said.

He pulled up a chair and dug in. "This definitely hits the spot," he said.

She detected some darkness under his eyes. "Did you sleep well last night?"

"I got enough. The Changelings' ability to become you for another two days has me worried though."

What did that mean? "You aren't questioning that this is me, are you?"

Before he had the chance to answer, she disappeared, and the shocked look on his face delighted her. Vinea quickly returned to her corporeal form.

Devon held up a palm. "I'm pretty sure no Changeling can do that!"

"You're right. If you're ever in doubt whether it's me or not, just ask me to repeat that trick."

He smiled. "Will do."

As much as she wanted to ask him if he was dating anyone back in Pittsburgh, she didn't want to spoil the tentative thread of trust they were finally building. Instead, she gobbled down her meal and then pushed back her chair after she was finished. "I'll wash these."

He reached out and grabbed her wrist. "Sit down and relax. Or do you need to be someplace?"

"I promised Brother Jacob that I would tell him how my date with you went." Of course, she was joking, but Devon's jaw hardened, and his eyes turned nearly black. "Kidding," she said. Okay, maybe it had been to soon for that kind of dark humor. She had a lot to learn!

He released his death grip on her wrist. "Don't tease me like that."

"I didn't take you for the delicate type."

"I'm not delicate, as you so nicely put it, but I'm confused about some things."

Vinea sat back down and sobered. "Tell me about it. Maybe I can clear them up."

Devon swiped a hand down his chin. He hadn't shaved yet, and she liked the rough look. "A lot has happened in the last few days. Mind you, I want to trust you."

"But shit keeps happening that stops you. I get it. It's almost as if someone is trying to sabotage me."

"Who do you think is responsible? One of your dark gods?" he asked.

"It's possible, but it could be the Changelings, though I don't see why they would have anything against me."

"Before you appeared in Brother Jacob's office, I bet they thought highly of you. After all, you were trying to destroy us."

"True."

"McKinnon and Associates is their main enemy. Perhaps they want to keep us off kilter. When you stole the sardonyx from Brother Jacob, I'm sure we were the first group they considered."

"If they are guilty, I'm worried that some Changeling will now see me with you, putting a bigger target on your back." Damn, and here she was hoping they could have more dates.

He dragged a palm down his sexy chin, acting as if it had put a dent into what he wanted to do too. Didn't she wish?

"If we need to meet for some reason, you'll need to just appear in my office, sight unseen."

"I can do that. Seeing how we shouldn't flaunt our connection, I guess I'll just have to *appear at home* and walk to work from there."

"Are you sure you want to walk? I can drive you."

She shook her head. "I wouldn't be surprised if the Changelings have people watching your house as we speak."

"They aren't close. I would have sensed them."

To be sure no one was watching, she could become invisible and take a look, but she trusted Devon to be able to tell. "Good to know."

Together, they took the plates over to the kitchen, and in no time, she had them washed. Devon dried them and then put them away.

She dragged her wet hands down her pants. "If you need me for anything today, just text. I might not be able to get away from work right then, but I'll find you when I'm free."

"It's a deal."

Good. They had a truce of sorts, and before he could change his mind about her, Vinea nodded and disappeared. Moments later, she was inside her freezing trailer. Flapping her arms to warm up, she walked around the tiny space, trying to sense if anyone had been here. She wouldn't put it past the Changelings to leave something of theirs—like a business card—and place it in a conspicuous place for Devon to find. Damn rabid wolves.

While she didn't have to be at work for an hour, she didn't want to stay in her cold trailer longer than necessary. She quickly dressed in her uniform then put on her coat. If all went well, her landlord would come through with the heater today.

If he didn't, maybe Devon would take pity on her again and ask her to spend another night. Wouldn't that be a dream come true? It would move them one step closer to becoming mates.

With that delicious thought, she headed out to work. The walk chilled her, but to keep from bemoaning the cold, she focused on what she'd do if she ever lured Devon into bed. Heat warmed her lower regions, and she was more convinced than ever that the two of them would combust if they ever made love.

Vinea smiled. She could still remember seeing him naked a little more than six months ago when he stood at the edge of Silver Lake. If he hadn't shoved her into the water, she probably would have tried to take him right then.

But that was in the past.

Before she could dream any more about what could be, she arrived at work. She entered through the back where the cooks were already shouting orders.

"Hey, Ralph," she said to one of the short order cooks.

Elise and Marissa were there picking up their orders. They both waved and smiled. Vinea walked over to the wall to check where her station would be located.

"You're early," her boss said as he pushed open the kitchen door.

"Thought the girls could use an extra hand," she said. There was no reason to tell him her heater had busted. He might then ask where she'd spent the night, and she wanted to keep that information to herself.

He smiled. "Great."

Once she checked the location of her station section, she went to work. While she'd asked Devon to text her, if he needed her, she doubted he would. It would have to be some kind of emergency before he'd contact her.

For a moment she considered returning to Brother Jacob's house without Devon's permission, but that would go against his wishes. Right now, she needed to do things his way. Not only that, she didn't trust herself not to mess up again.

Given she'd already breached Brother Jacob's sanctuary once before, it wouldn't surprise her if he hadn't arranged to meet his Clan elsewhere. He couldn't chance having all of the Changeling secrets exposed. Jackson's mate, Ainsley, could become invisible, so Brother Jacob probably figured Vinea was a relative of hers. Maybe that was how he connected her to the McKinnons. It didn't matter now. What was done was done.

At two, she was on her fifteen-minute break and needed to hear a friendly voice. After pulling on her coat, Vinea stepped into the back alley and called EmmaLee. Today was her day off, and she prayed her good friend wasn't with Slater.

"Hello?" her friend said.

Her pulse jumped at hearing her voice. "EmmaLee, it's me, Vinea!"

She squealed. "Hey, how are you? How are things going with Devon?"

So many things had happened since they'd talked that Vinea didn't know where to begin. Discussing any of the thefts, especially while standing in the alley within earshot of someone inside, wouldn't be smart. "My heater broke in my trailer, and when Devon found out, he insisted I stay at his place."

"Seriously? Did he warm you up?"

"I wish. Nothing happened between us—unfortunately. My primary goal right now is for him to realize I'm not evil."

"How's that going?" EmmaLee asked, a sudden seriousness tingeing her tone.

"It's hard to assess, but I think I'm making progress." She told her about breakfast and while he hadn't been affectionate, he hadn't pushed her away.

Someone called to EmmaLee. It was Slater. Crap. "Can I call you back?" she asked. "Slater and I are about to do something."

"I thought you promised—never mind. Sure. Any time. I miss you," Vinea said.

"Miss you more. I hope you come back soon."

For the first time since her transformation, she wasn't anxious to return. Silver Lake was growing on her. "We'll see."

Once she hung up, Vinea was a bit depressed. She missed her talks with her best friend. For the foreseeable future though, she had to put her social life on hold. Vinea had a job to do, not only at the café but also helping Devon.

Once back inside, she focused on making sure all of her customers were happy. While the next three hours were rather uneventful, there had been one bright spot. Mr. Sanford had come in. He was such a nice man, always smiling and telling her how much she brightened his day. Something about him reminded her of her dad—her dad when she was little that is; not when he suggested Naliana become matchmaker instead of her.

Vinea halted at that thought. Looking back on it, he might have been right. Whoa! Where had that thought come from? Only now did she understand why the gods had expelled her. Her jealousy of her younger sister had caused a mental cancer so great that only a cleansing could expel it. But why had she been jealous in the first place? Had she subconsciously known Naliana was better suited for the job? Of the two, her sister had been the more compassionate. Well, damn.

"Miss?" one of her customers called as he waved.

"Coming."

Once she gave the man his check, she began wiping down her tables and refilling the condiments. Her shift was almost over when a group of six men sat in her section. As she turned to greet them, her blood ran cold.

Oh, shit, oh, shit. It was Brother Jacob and his men.

Chapter Twelve

V INEA DUCKED OUT of sight from the Changeling Clan, and plastered her back against the wall. Marissa exited the kitchen with a tray of drinks in hand, and Vinea reached out to stop her.

"Can you do me a favor?" Vinea whispered.

"Sure. What's wrong? You look pale."

"I'm not feeling all that well. Can you take the drink orders for table nine? I have to use the ladies' room really bad." It was a lame excuse, but it was all she could think of right then.

"No problem. Let me give these drinks to table two, and I'll swing by your table."

"I owe you."

Thankful her coworker didn't ask any more questions, Vinea rushed to the bathroom. Once she checked she was alone, she swiped a hand over her head, hoping the short blonde haircut and overdone makeup would throw off Brother Jacob and John Ernst.

I can do this. Pretending to be out of breath, she rushed up to the table as soon as Marissa stepped into the kitchen.

"Sorry to keep you waiting, y'all." She fanned herself and smiled, acting as if she had no idea Marissa had taken their drink orders. "What can I get you men?" Vinea patted her apron, supposedly looking for her pad. The accent was in honor of EmmaLee. Whenever her friend was tired, her southern phrases came out.

"Someone else took our drink orders."

"Oh? Okay. Do you know what you want to order?" Vinea

focused on the man next to Brother Jacob, not wanting to let on she knew that Jacob was the kingpin of the group.

"Can you give us a minute?"

"Take your time, y'all."

Making sure not to run into her boss, Vinea returned to the restroom once more and then became invisible. Fingers crossed, she returned to hover over their table, hoping to hear something important. She couldn't stay away for too long, as she didn't need them asking her boss where their waitress had gone. Making certain to focus on each man—memorizing their features, their mannerisms, and how they reacted to Brother Jacob—she listened and once more wished she had worn a wire.

"Have we decided who's next then?" Brother Jacob asked, glancing at each of the men at the table.

John Ernst nodded. "The Lake Steakhouse is packed every Saturday. I say we hit them up right after closing."

"I agree. Let's decide who should go in and who should stand watch."

Thank you Brother Jacob for getting right to the point. With a nod, she landed in the bathroom, but someone was already there. Whoops. Trying once more to find a safe place, she pictured the outside alley. When she saw no one was there, she felt safe returning to her human self. The hard part was not looking suspicious when she returned through the back door.

Their cook, Ralph, didn't even seem to notice when she snuck in, but perhaps her short blonde hair threw him off. Avoiding her boss and the other servers, she rushed to the table to take their order. The men seemed so engrossed in their conversation that they barely noticed her.

Vinea smiled. "I'll place this order, but since my shift is ending, Marissa will finish up."

Not waiting for them to complain, Vinea took off for the kitchen. Right before she entered, she ducked into the bathroom once more, and returned her hair to auburn and made sure not a speck of makeup was on her face. Heart still not back to normal, she painted on a smile and located Marissa before slipping out.

"So you believe her?" Connor asked.

Devon had given the events of the last few days a lot of thought. "Yes. There is strong proof that Vinea was at her trailer after she returned from the fiasco with Brother Jacob." He explained about the message from the landlord. "She told me that Brother Jacob had grabbed her arm when she materialized."

"It was a red moon, which means he transformed into her. Bastards."

"Yes." Devon was thrilled Connor believed that.

His brother leaned back in his seat. "So do you have a plan?"

"A plan?"

"About how to nail these bastards? I'm guessing Vinea is still willing to help?"

"Yes, but I don't want her to go back to Brother Jacob's again. It's too dangerous."

Conner's eyes widened. "Okay, I didn't expect that reaction. I'm guessing you're falling for her again." He shook his head. "You didn't learn your lesson, did you?"

Devon's hands clenched. "She's changed. Until there is irrefutable proof she hasn't, I will treat her with respect." He'd do more than that, but he wasn't about to mention it to Connor. His wolf was at the end of his rope, but it wasn't just the sexual release he yearned for. He wanted Vinea in his life.

Thank goddess you've come to your senses, his wolf cheerfully exclaimed.

In reality, it was a relief finally to mentally say those words. His cock hadn't deflated in weeks, and his nails were constantly in a sharpened state. If he didn't get some reprieve soon, he'd go crazy.

"It's your life," Connor warned.

This negativity wasn't doing them any good. *Tell him.* Devon leaned forward. "I know this will sound crazy, especially since Vinea is a goddess and all, but the reason I keep defending her is because I believe she's my mate."

Connor dropped back his head and laughed. "You're joking, right?"

"No. I'm not. I can't deny it any longer. It was why she was able to fool me in the first place. She does something to me. I swear she put a spell on me the last time."

Connor waved a hand in front of Devon's face. "It's because she is a goddess. She can do those things. What makes you so sure she isn't doing it to you now?"

"Give me one thing she's done since she's returned that proves she's in cahoots with the Changelings or out for some personal gain? She has given good intel."

Connor glanced to the side and leaned back in his chair. "I can't, but that doesn't prove that she's good now either."

Devon shrugged. "She risked exposure by going out to California. Can you imagine what would have happened if the Changelings had gotten a hold of that much sardonyx?"

"I don't want to even think about something like that."

"Trust me, she wants to help. I can see it in her eyes. She's a good person now."

Connor held up his hands. "I hope you're right, but please don't do anything rash."

"I don't intend to bite her if that's what you mean." At least not for a while. The problem was that her scent never left him. At night, he could barely sleep, picturing her perfect tits, her delicious scent, and her curvaceous body. He needed her desperately.

Even though she'd kissed him, Devon wasn't certain she wanted to be saddled with him. His lifestyle wasn't conducive to having a great relationship—or so many women had told him.

"Good," Connor said, sounding rather smug.

A knock sounded on Connor's door. His brother glanced over at him and shrugged. "Come in."

Vinea walked in, and Devon's cock shot to attention. His wolf howled and clawed for release. Even though she was still wearing her Silver Lake Café waitress outfit, she looked beautiful. Devon shot to his feet. "Did something happen?"

She glanced at Connor first and then back at Devon. "I need to speak with you—in private."

"If you found out anything, just tell me. It will save an explanation to my brother afterwards." Devon hoped that Connor would be willing to put aside his prejudices and listen to her.

"Fine." She clasped her hands in front of her and worked them into a knot. "I was at work at the café when Brother Jacob, John Ernst, and four other men came into the restaurant."

His pulse spiked. "Oh, shit. Did they recognize you?"

"No." She explained how another waitress took their orders while Vinea ducked into the bathroom and redid her hair and makeup. "I'll show you."

One second, her hair was long, auburn, and sexy as hell, and the next she wore a short blonde bob and a ton of eye makeup.

"Holy shit," Connor said. "You don't look the same at all."

Vinea nodded. "That was my plan. I was worried the most about John Ernst. He sat across from the *other me* at McKinnon's Pub, or so you said. That would have given him a chance to memorize what I looked like."

Connor nodded. "Did you overhear anything?"

She shot a quick glance at Devon. "Yes. Devon said not to visit Jacob's house, but he said nothing about keeping a low profile when I was at work."

Wasn't she the clever girl? "So you hovered about their table?" *Please say yes.*

She smiled. "As a matter of fact I did. And I worked really hard not to become distracted. I couldn't be gone too long, but I learned that on Saturday night, the Changelings plan to rob the Lake Steakhouse after they close."

"What?" Connor said. "Are you sure?"

Devon was pleased Connor didn't scoff at her and call her a liar. "Positive. That's all I know since I had to wait on their table, and I couldn't be two places at once."

Connor grabbed his phone. "I need to let Kalan know. If we can catch them in the act, it might make them think twice about pulling another heist."

Vinea held up a finger, worry crisscrossing her features. "Unless they wanted me to think that was their plan."

"You said they didn't recognize you," Devon said, worry sinking into his gut.

"I don't think they did, but perhaps they believed their invisible mystery woman might be around." She held up a finger. "The Vinea of old would have tried that misdirect."

He had to hand it to her; she was trying to help them. "They didn't mention any other place?"

"No, but I'd make sure the police beef up surveillance all around town. There have to be other places that have a sizeable amount of cash."

Devon addressed Connor. "Can Jackson use his drone to do some surveillance, not only on Saturday but each day this week? We might be able to see them checking out different places."

"That's a good idea." Connor nodded at Vinea. "Thank you."

She smiled warily. "Any time."

Devon pushed back his chair. "How about coming to my office with me? I'm sure Connor has work to do."

"Sure."

There was something about her rushing over to see him that had his juices flowing, along with a few other body parts standing at attention.

Told you, his wolf shouted with way too much cheer, but this time Devon was willing to admit he'd been wrong.

"Have you eaten?" he asked as he escorted her inside his inner sanctum.

"No. I came straight from work. I figured we couldn't afford to waste time."

He liked the *we*. "Would you like to have dinner at my place?"

"Is Androf evil?"

He laughed. "How about I order something to go, pick it up, and take it back to the guesthouse? You can meet me there in say an hour, unless you'd like to come with me?"

"Not if there's a chance someone could see us together."

"You're right." Being this close to her was really messing with his ability to think.

"Besides, I need to check if I have heat," she said.

"If you don't, pack a bag."

Vinea clasped his arm, and the heat from her touch seared him. "Only if you let me sleep on the couch. I don't want to take your bed away from you for two nights in a row."

"Ain't going to happen, Goddess Lady." He tapped her nose. She must have no idea that his protective sensors were now in high gear.

"We can discuss it later. I'll see you in an hour." She winked.

With a quick nod, she was gone. Her ability to disappear like that was so awesome. Too bad it was such a dangerous talent. Even Vinea didn't know the extent of her capabilities or whether she was still immortal. Now that he'd found his mate, he wasn't going to let her go.

He stopped back at Connor's office and knocked. "I'm heading out."

"Hot date with Vinea?" Connor sounded snarky.

"Actually yes, asshole. I invited her to my place. I'm picking up something to eat. She was the one who suggested we not be seen together since she doesn't want to draw attention to McKinnon and Associates." He studied his brother. "You could work on not being such a stubborn dick. I realize you want to protect me, but I got this. Just try to give her a chance, please. For me?"

His brother's eyes closed for a second as he exhaled loudly. "I'm glad she's being careful."

"Me too."

"By the way, I talked with Kalan. He said the sheriff's department wouldn't be able to spare any more men to stake out other potential targets, but they will be ready Saturday night at the Lake Steakhouse."

"Which means it's up to us to help."

"Looks that way."

Devon left and headed straight to the restaurant. Before he went inside and ordered food, he walked around the perimeter to see where the Changelings would most likely enter. If they intended to rob the place after closing, the only viable entry point would be the back entrance. Instead of breaking down the door, all they had to do was wait for the owner to leave with the cash and attack.

Devon would have to ask if Jackson could string up some extra surveillance cameras around the restaurant. Tomorrow, his team would discuss other possible targets. If the Lake Steakhouse was a diversion, they needed to be ready.

Once Devon understood the logistics of the place, he went inside and ordered two take out dinners. If Vinea didn't like the steak, he'd give her his lasagna.

Once his order was ready, he drove home, careful to check his rear view mirror. He wouldn't be surprised if the Changelings decided to create some chaos by attacking a McKinnon. Devon had to make sure that if they came after him, he could keep Vinea safe.

Chapter Thirteen

WHEN VINEA ARRIVED at her place, the heat still wasn't on. Dang. After checking the front door, she found a note from the landlord stating the new furnace would be delivered in a few days. He apologized for the inconvenience but said nothing about discounting her rent. For a moment, the image of a demon appeared, but she quickly dismissed that unpleasant thought.

There was a silver lining. It gave her an excuse to be with Devon once more. For that, she should probably thank the man. If her heater hadn't died, her landlord wouldn't have been able to provide an alibi for her the night Brother Jacob took her form. Whether Devon would have believed she hadn't had a drink with John Ernst without her proof was anyone's guess.

Trying to adapt to the human lifestyle, Vinea packed some clothes instead of swiping her hand over the suitcase to create them. She then headed over to Devon's. If she happened to arrive before him, she didn't think he'd mind if she made herself comfortable. Staying in the chilly trailer just wasn't fun.

One second later, she was in Devon's wonderful house—or rather his parents' guesthouse. He wasn't there yet, but that suited her fine. While the fireplace didn't look as if it had been used in a while, there was a pile of wood stacked next to it. She might never have lit a fire with matches before, but there was a first time for everything. It wasn't as if she hadn't watched Slater build a fire or two when EmmaLee had invited her to a few parties at his place.

Vinea stacked the wood on the grate, stuffed paper underneath it, and lit it. The flames flared, heating the area within a few feet of the fireplace. Sadly, within minutes the fire died without igniting the logs. Determined to conquer fire making, she tried again, only this time, she added a bit of magic. Her ability to shoot fire from her fingertips was almost useless, but it would light the paper and maybe even the logs. To her delight, she had a roaring fire going in less than five minutes. Success! It gave her a warm and happy feeling each time she used her talents for the good now.

The roar of an engine came to a halt outside the house, and Vinea jumped up. Devon was here. As much as she wanted to rush out and greet him, she didn't need any Changelings seeing her pop out of his house. If they were spying on them, they'd have to wonder where the inside light was coming from now that Devon was just arriving home.

However, since the Changelings didn't like coming anywhere near Silver Lake because the pink quartz weakened them, most likely they were safe from their prying eyes.

The door burst open and Devon rushed in. "Looks like it's going to snow," he said as he wiped his feet on the doormat and then set a large bag on the dining room table. Unzipping his coat, he looked over at the fireplace. "I trust the heater didn't arrive?"

"No."

"I'm sorry." He nodded at her handiwork. "Nice fire."

"Thanks. It's my first." His brows rose and then a small smile lit his face. He was so handsome.

"Impressive. You're adapting to regular life quite well, I see."

She smiled. "I'm trying, but sometimes even simple things are a challenge."

"Like what?"

Like lighting a fire without magic. "The first time I came to your realm, I had to learn how to drive a car. I couldn't just appear and disappear all the time. That would have caused a stir."

Devon chuckled. He stepped over to the delicious smelling food and unpacked it. "You had no one to teach you?"

She shook her head. "No. The gods from the dark realm aren't exactly nurturing. We do have powers to help us, but sometimes they aren't enough."

"Come on over and eat, and you can tell me more. Care for some wine?"

"I'd love some."

The wine might help Devon relax, and maybe she could snatch another kiss. The remembrance of the last one they shared still made her body tingle.

Devon located two glasses and poured the wine. "I've been thinking," he said. "For the next few days, I want you to stay here—at least until after whatever the Changelings are planning has passed, and we know there isn't a threat to you anymore."

Her pulse soared. She'd love nothing better. Vinea studied him, trying to detect his motive. Did he want her to stay because he didn't trust her to do something or because he wanted to keep her safe? "I'd like that, but if I'm here, I want to help."

"No."

She smiled. "Afraid I might be harmed?"

"As a matter of fact yes. If they kidnapped you, who do you think would have to save you?"

Her smile faltered as an ache stabbed her gut. "What, you don't want to be inconvenienced?" She tried to keep her tone light, but she suspected she failed.

"It wouldn't be an inconvenience as you so politely put it. Being kidnapped would be frightening for you, not to mention potentially harmful." He opened the two meals. "Steak or lasagna?"

"You're not very good at changing the subject. Since you asked, how about we split both?"

"That works."

She remained quiet while he divided the food, wanting to give him the chance to understand his own motivations.

Once seated, Devon handed her the plate. "Do you want to

know why I have this need to protect you?"

He had a need? This had potential. "I do."

"I've been going crazy from the first moment you walked into that bar in Vermont. This time, since you've returned here, my wolf has been out of sorts, demanding that I believe you."

"Smart wolf." Dare she hope he recognized they were mates? Her pulse soared. "I'll admit that when I first saw you, I was instantly attracted to you too, but being my evil self, I didn't understand what those urges meant."

His eyes widened. "Do you know why now?" He stabbed a forkful of lasagna and ate it in one gulp.

She sipped her wine to give herself a moment to think. "Yes. For lack of a better word, it's called lust. Before I was cleansed, I only used sex as a means to an end. I never really felt anything. I was filled with too much bitterness and hate. Just so you know I've faked every climax I've ever had."

His whole face fell. "Really?"

"I'm pathetic, I know. I'm guessing that in order to have a real climax, I'd have to care about the person I'm with. Until six months ago, I wasn't in the right frame of mind to emotionally give myself to anyone." After she was cleansed, she realized Devon was her mate and that prompted her to keep from committing to anyone. She tasted the lasagna and inwardly groaned at the divine taste.

He whistled. "That must have been tough."

"It was."

"After you were cleansed, did you feel the same about me?"

Vinea pointed a fork at him. "I want to hear your side of the story before I tell you mine. After all, you started it."

He stuffed a large chunk of steak in his mouth and chewed slowly. "Fair enough." He blew out a breath. "Before I was aware that you were this evil goddess, I was highly intrigued by you. But you knew that."

"I suspected it."

"Even after I saw you floating over Sam, I refused to believe that the feelings I had for you were based on nothing."

Vinea reached across the table and placed her hand on his. "It was based on something." Clearly, Devon was having a hard time telling her what she was sure he wanted to say. So she decided to make it easy on him. "You believed I was your mate, right?"

His eyes widened, and his jaw tightened. "You're a witch too, aren't you?"

She laughed. "No, but I can see the signs. Your eyes often turn amber when I'm near. I also didn't miss how your nails sharpened, and your hair sprouted the day I returned to your office."

"Your back was to me. How could you tell?"

She shrugged then smiled. "I'm not giving away all of my secrets."

He leaned back, acting as if a huge weight had been removed from his shoulders. "What are you saying? That I was right in thinking we're mates, or that the whole concept is ridiculous because you're a goddess?"

"That you were right in thinking we are mates. Mentally, you're having a hard time believing it though—and rightfully so. After all I *was* a dark realm goddess."

"That's true."

"So what are we going to do about it?" she asked. Vinea was pleased by her calm delivery despite her heart pounding away faster than a hummingbird's wings.

"How about I show you?"

He pulled her to her feet, wrapped his arms around her waist, and sealed his lips over hers. Between the pressure and his strong, woodsy scent, it was as if he'd poured liquid joy into her, and at that moment, Vinea was convinced that she'd been returned to the light realm.

Goddess, but she wanted him so fucking bad, but she needed him to make the first move. The last thing she wanted was for him to say she'd seduced him and put some kind of spell on him—as if she could.

Devon groaned, and his hands lowered to her rear, pressing her against his hard erection. *Take me. And hurry.* What she wouldn't give to have a telepathic link with him right now.

When Devon deepened the kiss, Vinea could no longer hold back, and she ran her tongue along the seam, begging for entrance. Devon opened up, and it was as if she was once more at the bottom of the lake, drinking in the love and acceptance. Her muscles sagged, and her head swam with endorphins. Their tongues twisted, and as fire swept through her body, she couldn't tell where hers left off and his began.

He broke the kiss and jumped back. "Where did you go?" he asked.

She hadn't gone anywhere, but when Vinea looked down, she wasn't there. Oh, shit. She dragged her hands down his back, and he jerked. A second later she reappeared again. "I'm sorry. I didn't mean to do that."

"Are you sure?"

Why was he angry? "Yes, I'm sure. I was so excited that I just disappeared."

His faced softened. "You were excited?"

"Of course I was. Being with you felt so right that I completely relaxed; my mind floated and my power just did its own thing. For the first time in my life, I totally lost control. That's what you do to me."

Devon grinned. "I see." He then sobered. "Can you warn me next time?"

"If I could, I would."

Devon moved closer and stroked her face. "I guess I need to be a little less passionate. I like being able to see you."

"Don't you dare give me anything less than your full attention. I want all of you—heart, body, and soul." With a sweep of her hand, she disrobed him.

His eyes widened as he looked down at his naked form. "Whoa. I knew you could do that with your clothes, but I didn't know I was fair game."

Vinea giggled. "I didn't know either." But she was very glad that she could do it.

While she had seen him naked once before by the lake—before the cleansing—he was far more magnificent than she remembered. Slim hipped, his waist flared outward to form a broad chest and muscled shoulders. What was happening below the waist wasn't something she could describe—other than he was other-realm worthy.

Devon stepped closer. "If you're going to play dirty then so will I."

She was hoping he'd say that. "What are you going to do, wolf man?"

He laughed. "From the first moment I met you, I thought you'd be a challenge for any man. And I was right."

Vinea kicked off her boots. "Will you do the honors of taking off the rest of my clothes?"

"I can't think of anything better." Instead of unbuttoning her shirt, he rubbed his chin. "Hmm. I need to decide what will torment you the most. Should I make slow love to each piece of clothing, or strip you naked and eat you until you scream my name?"

Vinea's knees lost strength at those fabulous sounding promises. His words were balms to all the hurt hurled at her for centuries, and she ran a finger down his chest. "Why would you want to torment me? I thought you liked me."

"Oh, I like you all right, but you are a wild woman who needs to be tamed."

"Is that so? And you're going to be the one to tame me?" She lifted her chin and then nipped his bottom lip.

"Absolutely." Devon stepped back, grabbed a hold of her button-down shirt with both hands, and ripped it open, the buttons pinging on the floor. "Just to set the record straight, taking off a man's clothes without his permission has consequences." He dragged his gaze up and down her body.

"Like ripping mine off?" She wasn't upset at all. Seeing Devon cut loose like this was such a high.

"Yes."

Excitement sizzled inside her, and she grabbed his cock. "This calls for my big guns. I wonder if I can make you shift?"

"If I let my wolf have his way, he'd be baying at the moon right now."

She laughed. "I'd like to see that."

"Keep looking so fucking sexy and you just might." Devon slipped the torn shirt from her shoulders and let it drop to the ground. Keeping his gaze on her face, he unhooked her bra.

In return, she squeezed his cock to let him know how much she enjoyed what he was doing. Devon's teeth sharpened, and the growth on his face thickened. Yes! When he growled from deep within his chest, she let go. "I thought you could control your wolf?"

She loved challenging him, but she hadn't meant it when she said she'd like to see him in his animal form—at least not now.

"I thought so too, but you've put your spell on *us* once more."

"Have I?" Let him think that. In actuality, she had no magical abilities when it came to that kind of witchcraft.

Devon moved closer until his lips were inches from her mouth. With his gaze transfixed on her eyes, he lowered the straps and let the bra join her torn shirt. He sucked in a breath. "You are more beautiful than I imagined."

Joy shot through her at his words. Over the ages, men had always told her how sexy she was, but none of their words had any effect on her. Only Devon's did. Her nipples hardened under his scrutiny, and heat swamped her core.

"Want to lick them?" she asked with as much innocence as she could muster.

He groaned. "I want to do more than that, but it's a good start. He moved the dining room chair out of the way and backed her up until her butt hit the table. Grabbing her shoulders, he leaned over and kissed her again. This time, he took control, and when he demanded entrance into her mouth, she gladly granted it to him. Vinea wrapped her arms around his waist then ran her palms up his corded back. He cupped her face and held her so tight it was as if he was afraid she'd slip away again. He didn't have to worry. Leaving him was the last thing she desired.

He made tiny strokes with his tongue, drawing out every ounce of passion from her body, swamping her with the strongest of yearnings. She couldn't get enough of him. Devon had been in her dreams for months, and now that he was here in person, she never wanted to break the contact.

His hands left her face and found the button on her jeans. With amazing efficiency, he had the waistband undone and managed to tug down both her pants and panties without breaking their lip seal. Anticipation soared through her. They would finally make love, and she couldn't wait.

Devon was the one to move back. He then dropped to his knees. "Step out of these."

She held onto his shoulders and did as he asked. Now naked, she suddenly felt vulnerable. When sex had been a way to get what she wanted, being naked had meant nothing. Now that she wanted to please him, Vinea feared she would fail.

Chapter Fourteen

D EVON WAS BESIDE himself with lust and desire. He'd never met anyone as alluring and enticing as Vinea, and as much as he wanted to sink his cock into her, balls deep, he had to make her first experience more than just pleasurable. If she'd never climaxed, he had to take it slow. The problem was that he wasn't sure he could keep his damn wolf at bay.

Burying his face between her legs, his animal growled then scratched and kicked for release.

Don't you dare show your face, he warned. *If you want her in our lives, behave.*

All he received in response was a whine.

Vinea widened her legs and draped one leg over his shoulder, giving Devon better access. He inwardly groaned at the divine feast before him. One inhale sent him into a spiral of total bliss, and the first lick had his cock so hard and his balls so tight, he groaned in pain. Vinea grabbed his shoulder and responded with an equally powerful moan.

"That feels so amazing. Don't stop, please," she whispered.

Her breathless reply jacked up his libido even more. With each flick of her tiny nub, her sex perfumed the air, and her excited gasps pulsed pleasure through him.

"Do you want something bigger?" he asked.

Her fingernails dug into his shoulder. "Fuck yes I do."

When he slipped two fingers into her wet opening, she stood on her toes and cried out. Her leg nearly gave way, and Devon reached up, grabbing her waist to steady her. Once her leg slipped from his shoulder, he slowly lifted her back onto the table.

"Are you okay?" he asked.

Her eyelids fluttered. "What happened?"

He wasn't sure how to answer that. "What do you mean? Did you feel something?"

"One minute I was holding onto your shoulder and the next it was as if I was floating on a cloud."

Devon couldn't help but smile. "I think you might have had your first climax."

She stroked his face. "I've never felt anything so wonderful in my life."

"I hope I can transport you there again, many times over."

When Vinea wrapped her legs around his waist, he nearly shifted. Fuck, she felt so good. His cock throbbed and pulsed, but he didn't know if she was ready for him to plunge into her.

"Take me there, now," she begged.

She didn't have to ask twice. Making love with her on the table wouldn't be comfortable, so he slid her to the edge. "Drop your legs." As soon as Vinea obeyed, he twisted her around. "Grab onto the table and enjoy the ride."

Not only did she bend over, she widened her legs, clearly understanding what he planned to do. His wolf went wild, sprouting facial hair and cracking bones. Placing his dick at her entrance, he reached under her and massaged her pendulant breasts. Devon had to close his eyes to keep from shifting, and since his teeth were so sharp, he could mate with her with ease. But he wouldn't yet. They both needed time.

Don't you dare shift, he warned his wolf one more time.

Vinea pressed her hips back, and he concentrated on staying in his human form. "Don't move," he commanded.

"Why?"

"Because if you do, you might not like what happens."

Vinea stilled. "Okay, but hurry."

Thrilled she wanted to make love with him as much as he did with her, Devon slowly eased into her. With each inch, his need grew, until he had to grit his teeth to keep from coming.

"I want it hard," she begged.

Do it, his wolf urged.

Not yet. Exercising more control than he thought possible, Devon withdrew and pressed her breasts together as he lowered his head to her neck. The temptation to make her his own nearly toppled him, but he resisted.

Vinea moaned, and when she wiggled her rear, he finally gave in. With one long push, he thrust into her. Devon squeezed his eyes shut as he inhaled her delicate scent, which was a combination of lilac and lemon. Vinea might be a goddess, but she was more woman than he'd ever had in his life.

Because she's your mate! his wolf reminded him.

I know.

Vinea must have sensed that he'd mentally drifted, because she wiggled her hips. That did it. He pinched her nipples and pummeled into her again as he kept his lips on her neck. As they were both transported to another realm, they became one, her shoulders bunching as she met his thrusts stroke for stroke.

"Devon, yes."

Her plea was too much, and he had to fight to keep from coming. It was only after her scream signaled she'd finally climaxed that he unleashed his hot cum. Once his cock stopped pulsating, he held her tightly, relishing the feel of his skin on her smooth body. With his future mate in his arms, Devon never wanted to let her go.

It wasn't until Vinea dropped her head onto the table that he finally pulled out.

"I need to get something to clean us up. Stay here," he said.

"I couldn't move if I wanted to."

Devon trotted into the kitchen. He wet a towel, and when he returned, Vinea was lying on her back on the table, her eyes closed, and her mouth open. Never had he seen a more appealing sight.

As much as he wanted to take her again, he had to let her recuperate. Once he cleaned her up, he did the same for himself.

Devon then leaned over her and kissed her. That was a mistake. His cock throbbed, and Vinea's eyes flew open. "Give me five. Okay?"

He chuckled. "I think we both need to rest. How about getting dressed so I won't be tempted?"

She gave a small wave but nothing happened. "I think I'm broken."

"That's okay. I can help you dress."

Vinea sat up. "If you touch me, I'll have to have you again, and I'm quite confused right now."

That didn't sound good. "About what?" he asked.

"Why I have no energy, yet I want to fuck you till dawn."

Oh, boy. He'd been right. Vinea was a handful.

ONE OF THE hardest things Devon had to do was watch Vinea dress the next morning after she made a quick breakfast, only to disappear to go back to her house. Having her in his home seemed so right, but the fact remained that they both had jobs to do.

After she left, he headed off to work. He'd been there less than five minutes when Connor stepped in his office. "Did Vinea remember anything else about the upcoming robbery?"

"No." Though to be honest, Devon couldn't remember if they'd even talked about it.

"She's not planning to follow them on Saturday night is she?" Connor asked, sitting in the chair across from him.

"I told you that would be too dangerous. She's not even as powerful as Izzy. She might be able to disappear, but that's about all." He wasn't going to mention she could strip him naked with a wave of her hand.

His brother leaned back in his chair. "You might be right. If she did hover over them again and then reappeared by mistake, they'd probably try to kill her." His lips pressed together. "Can she be killed?"

"I asked her that, and she doesn't know, but I am not willing to take any chances that she could be."

Connor nodded. "Kalan alerted his boss about the potential robbery, and the place will be surrounded, ready to take them down. The department will set up roadblocks at every exit point. I asked Jackson to send his drone up to the hill throughout the day to see if there is any suspicious behavior going on at the Changeling's headquarters."

"That's great. Vinea and I will be holed up at my place, assuming I can convince her not to go off by herself and try to be some hero. We both know she's rather headstrong."

Connor stood. "Let me know if she learns anything else."

"You'll be the first person I call."

For much of the afternoon, Devon and Jackson conferred about the drone's timing and placement. Jackson said he would also be installing some cameras to overlook the parking lot before Saturday night.

Devon then touched base with Kalan about what his team was planning to do about the Lake Steakhouse robbery. Once Devon was convinced he'd done everything he could, he wanted to touch base with Finn. Being a bartender, his youngest brother probably knew better than anyone what was going on in town. It was time to pick his brain.

Even though it was cold, Devon decided to walk to the pub, needing the time to clear his head. The existing snow had already melted on the sidewalks and the sun was shining, making the day chilly but nice.

As he headed east, he realized that with the exception of the visit from John Ernst and Brother Jacob—who was posing as Vinea—the Changelings rarely visited the McKinnon pub—or at least that was what everyone believed. Except for Ainsley, no one could tell a

Changeling from a regular shifter, so perhaps more had stopped in the establishment than he'd been aware of.

After a brisk walk, Devon slipped into the bar then slid onto one of the bar stools. Finn finished up with a customer and came over. Fortunately, the bar was fairly empty this early in the afternoon.

"What's the occasion?" Finn asked. "I never see you here during the day."

"I came to ask you a few questions."

Finn grinned. "Ask away. Can I get you a drink first?"

"Coffee would be great."

Once his brother delivered the hot brew, Devon made sure no one else was within earshot. "Have you heard anything about a potential robbery in town?"

His brother's eyes widened. "A robbery? Fuck no. If I had, I would have notified Kalan. What do you know?"

Devon sipped his coffee, debating how much to tell him. The bar wasn't totally secure. "Vinea overheard someone talking about a robbery at the Lake Steakhouse this Saturday night."

"Holy shit." Finn stabbed a hand through his hair. "I'll be sure to pay more attention."

"That's all I can ask."

After they chatted a bit more, Devon tossed down three bucks and then headed out. As he neared his office, his cell rang. It was Vinea, and his wolf suddenly awoke. "Hey, what's up?"

She'd told him she rarely had a moment to talk during the day because the café kept her busy.

"The landlord called and said the heater arrived. His men are installing it now."

He couldn't tell if she was happy she wouldn't have to stay in his place, or if she wanted to spend a few more days with him at the guesthouse. A horn blared, and Devon realized he'd crossed the street without looking. Vinea was too much of a distraction. "That's great."

"I'm happy too. I wanted to let you know you can have your place to yourself again."

Ask her to stay, his wolf begged.

Don't worry. I plan to.

"Remember I suggested you stay at my place, at least for the next two nights, until after the robbery? I'm serious, Vinea. I don't trust anyone not to come after you."

She hesitated. "How about I come over Saturday? I have the day off, and I promise you can watch me all day if you like."

He chuckled. "I trust you, Vinea, and I don't need to watch you. I need to make sure you're safe."

"Thank you. I'm the first to admit that I have a tendency to meddle."

Devon appreciated her honesty. "Fair enough, but why not come over tonight?"

"I have a few things I need to take care of."

"Vinea?"

"Don't worry. I'm not going to visit the Changelings."

"I don't like it. They know what you look like. What if one of them spots you at the café?"

"They're not going to drag me out. There would be chaos, and someone would call the cops. Besides, as soon as they take me outside, I'll disappear."

She had a point. "Okay, but if you finish early, you know where to find me."

Someone called her name. "I gotta go. I'll see you tomorrow night then."

"I don't like it, but I guess I don't have a choice."

She chuckled, clearly knowing she'd won that battle of the wits. "No, you don't. Tomorrow then." With that she disconnected.

Damn, he was actually disappointed not to be with her tonight. Making love with Vinea last night had been the most amazing experience in his life, but he couldn't force her to do anything she didn't want to. At least it was only for one night.

We need to be with her, his wolf whined.

Don't get your tail in a twist. We'll survive. Maybe.

You'll be the one twisted. We need to mate!

Devon refused to respond. Damn wolf had too much control over him as it was. A sharp blast of cold air swept across the land and Devon picked up his pace. Something troubled him, but he wasn't sure what it was. His faith in Vinea was strong, so he had no reason to believe she'd double cross him. But Connor would say, she'd fooled him once and she could do it again.

Devon debated calling her back and asking her nicely to take off the next few days from work and stay in the office with him, but she'd never go for it. He only hoped her powers were as strong as she claimed.

Chapter Fifteen

W HEN VINEA ENTERED her trailer, she was met with wonderful warmth and sighed. To her surprise, being home actually calmed her. Staying with Devon had been wonderful—no, amazing actually—but it hurt her to see him withdraw, even if it was only for a few seconds at a time. Sure, the sex was mind-blowingly good, but whenever the topic of the Changelings came up, he'd hesitate. It was as if he still wasn't sure whether she was working with them or not, and that concept nearly sucked the breath out of her. Unfortunately, there didn't seem to be a damn thing she could do about it. Building trust took time.

As much as she wanted to spend tonight with him, Devon need-ed the time to understand his feelings. In truth, she could use a little internal contemplation too. The last thing she needed was to mess up now, just when things were looking up. At least Devon had his family and his Clan to confide in. Other than him, she only had EmmaLee.

Not that her friend could offer a lot of advice about how to handle the Changelings, but it was always nice to spend time talking with someone who wouldn't judge her.

Vinea took off her coat, made some hot coffee, and then settled down on the sofa. With her feet propped up on the coffee table, she called EmmaLee.

"Vinea?" Excitement laced her voice.

"Yes, it's me. How are you?"

EmmaLee hesitated. "Good, but I miss you."

"I miss you too." While Vinea should ask how things were going with Slater, knowing EmmaLee, she'd say they were fine, even if they weren't. Besides, just hearing his name grated on her nerves. If she got started about what a loser he was, EmmaLee would become upset, which meant Vinea needed to keep the topic on her favorite subject—Devon. "Guess what happened last night?" Vinea said.

"What? Were you with Devon again?" Vinea loved the hope in her voice.

"Boy was I." For the next half hour, Vinea filled her in, telling her about hovering over the Changelings one minute and then reappearing in Devon's office the next. That led to dinner and then to the amazing seduction.

"He sounds divine," EmmaLee said, dreamily.

"Devon McKinnon is a fine man." Vinea wasn't ready to talk about him being her mate until they made it final.

"I wish you didn't live so far away." EmmaLee sounded sad. Most likely it was because her life with Slater wasn't the fairytale she'd always dreamed of.

"Are you at home?" Vinea asked.

"Yes, why?"

"Are you alone?" Vinea didn't want to run into him.

"Yes."

"Be right there." Vinea giggled and then disconnected.

Picturing EmmaLee's house, she nodded and landed in her friend's backyard instead of in the living room. Shit. She needed to figure out why her internal system was off, but that would have to happen later. Right now, she needed to see her friend. Focusing on the brown plaid sofa and the dingy white walls, she tried again. This time, she arrived exactly where she'd pictured.

EmmaLee's eyes widened and she ran to Vinea. The hug that followed was wonderful. "I can't believe you came!"

"I don't like to make a habit of it. I imagine if Devon found out, he'd be upset, though I'm not sure why he should be. I'm probably safer in Billard than in Silver Lake."

"It doesn't matter what he thinks. You're here now."

Vinea leaned to the side to get a better look at her friend's face. "Is that a bruise?"

EmmaLee placed a palm over her cheek and averted her gaze. "I fell."

Vinea grabbed her friend's hand, led her over to the sofa, and sat next to her. "You don't need to lie to me."

"Fine, Slater was mad because I wanted to work on my research instead of going out. He took off and got drunk. At two in the morning, he came over looking for some action."

"And when you told him to get lost, he got mad."

EmmaLee nodded. Trying to convince her to leave the sorry sack always fell on deaf ears. "You could move to Silver Lake. I bet my boss could find a few shifts for you to work. You could even share my trailer if you don't mind sleeping on the sofa."

She shook her head. "You are so sweet, but I can't leave until I finish my master's thesis."

"Are you sure that's the only reason?"

She blew out a breath. "Fine, I like Slater, too. There's something about him that draws me in."

While Vinea felt the same way about Devon, at least her mate was noble. Even if he became angry, he'd never harm her. That level of confidence meant the world to her. "If you ever change your mind, let me know."

Vinea spent another hour there, but then it was time to go. "I need to get back. Remember, you can always call me, and I'll be here in a heartbeat."

EmmaLee's eyes shimmered. "Thank you. You don't know how much that means to me."

After one last hug, Vinea teleported back to Silver Lake. To her delight, she returned to her living room. Too often she bemoaned the fact that she'd lost most of her powers when the gods in the light realm had kicked her out. She should be thankful they'd left her with the ability to move about so freely.

DEVON PACED HIS living room. He should have insisted that Vinea stay with him. On the way home from the office, he'd stopped by her place, but she wasn't home. After checking the café, he was told that her shift had ended hours ago. So where the hell was she? If she decided to spy on the Changelings, he'd tan her ass. Putting herself in danger was plain stupid, especially since Brother Jacob and John Ernst could recognize her.

Even though she had agreed not to visit the Changelings, he wouldn't be surprised if she decided to scope out the Lake Steakhouse. Technically, she wouldn't be disobeying him if she went there.

He shook his head and couldn't help but smile. Her need to be useful seemed boundless. She might even have decided to hover over the restaurant patrons and listen in to their conversations to see if they were discussing anything of value. If Vinea reappeared by mistake, people would freak out.

Vinea, Vinea. Where are you? Yes, he understood she wouldn't answer, but someday she'd be able to.

The restaurant would be closing in a few minutes, which would be the perfect time for her to learn the exact movements of the manager. Devon wouldn't be surprised if she figured out how the Changelings plan to rob the place. Because she had the ability to fly above the restaurant and nearby establishments, she'd be able to find a good location for the Changelings to hide, or possibly to get off a quick shot.

Devon needed to stop her from investigating on her own. Believing that if she saw him, she'd make an appearance, Devon grabbed his jacket and headed out. When he arrived, the restaurant lights were out, enabling him to park directly in front.

Deciding to check out the back of the building, he trotted down the side alley. The light above the back parking lot flickered then dimmed. Man, the town really needed to keep up with maintenance. Despite his shifter eyesight, he still relied on lamps.

He was close to the rear entrance when he sensed three shifter signatures. He froze, his heart beating way too fast. The manager was human, so it was possible some Changelings were there to case the joint.

Devon debated turning around and checking the back from a different angle when the rear door creaked opened, and the manager exited alone. Part of him wanted to rush up and warn him, but if the Changelings were watching, it might cause an attack. Kalan and Connor had discussed with the team whether to warn the manager about the possible theft, and they decided it would be better if the man acted naturally. Tomorrow night, the cops would be surrounding the place, keeping the manager safe.

Two men appeared from out of nowhere wearing masks. Oh, shit. Had the date of the robbery been changed to tonight? He swept the area looking for Vinea, but if she were invisible, he wouldn't see her.

A shout sounded, drawing his attention back to the action. Devon was less than fifteen feet from the men, and it was only a matter of seconds before they sensed him. As carefully as he could, Devon slipped his phone out of his pocket, and just as he was about to text Kalan to send reinforcements, sharp teeth dug into his shoulder. His knees buckled, and the phone went sprawling. Fuck.

He'd not survive if he didn't shift. Without thinking of the consequences of showing himself to the manager, Devon fell forward the moment the wolf released his grip. With two feet between them, he shifted, spun around, and attacked.

A gunshot sounded and Devon waited for the pain to sear his body, but the only ache came from where his attacker had swiped a paw across his snout. Concentrate.

If he was going to win, he needed to conserve his energy. Out of the corner of his eye, the manager dropped to his hands and knees, crying out in agony. One of the two men ran off and the second one raised his weapon and took aim—right at Devon.

Another shot sounded, and this time the pain to his leg nearly immobilized him. The wound wouldn't kill him, but his inability to fight two wolves would.

AFTER SEEING EMMALEE and talking about how wonderful Devon was, it made her want to be with him even more. Devon McKinnon really was kind, focused, and gentle, if not a bit pigheaded. He was understandably troubled about her, but with time, she could help him find his own light.

She debated calling him to say she'd changed her mind about staying apart and asking if he would like some company for tonight? Wanting, or rather needing to see him, she decided to pay him a surprise visit instead. She quickly changed into black jeans and a white mohair sweater that hugged her body. Knowing how much Devon liked to remove her underwear, she picked a matching black lace set with extra bra padding that would drive his wolf crazy.

Not able to keep away from him any longer, she nodded and seconds later appeared in his living room. While she was happy with her success at landing in the right spot this time, she was dismayed to find his place dark. Damn. He wasn't there. Where could he be at eleven at night? He wasn't the type to party—unless he was trying to drown his sorrows at the pub. Was he missing her that much? For a brief moment, a shot of joy entered.

Focus. *Look for clues where he might be.* A quick check outside confirmed his truck was gone. The robbery wasn't until tomorrow, so he didn't need to be at the restaurant until then.

Needing some light to see if she could find something, she stepped toward the door to locate the light switch when a strong ache swept through her, nearly doubling her over. What the hell was that? Sure, she could feel someone else's pain, but only when she was touching them.

Devon's in trouble.

Vinea wasn't sure if someone communicated with her telepathically somehow or if she'd just thought those words, but right now, all that mattered was that it might be true. Vinea had to help him.

Not knowing for sure where he might be, she first teleported to McKinnon and Associates, landing in the hallway a few steps from his office.

The overhead lights flicked on, and she rushed toward his door. Not bothering to knock, she twisted the knob, but found it locked. Given the pervading silence in the building, no one else seemed to be around. Damn.

Next, she appeared about a block from McKinnon's Pub and Pool. If it wouldn't have caused a stir, she would have landed inside the main building. After becoming invisible again, she floated inside and searched both the main room and the poolroom. He wasn't there. Now what?

She couldn't imagine why he'd go to the Lake Steakhouse, but perhaps he wanted to check it out before tomorrow's robbery. Having exhausted all other options, she once more aimed for an area out of sight of people. One second, she was surrounded by music and laughter, and the next she was in the middle of a horrible wolf fight behind the restaurant.

She froze at the horror unfolding in front of her. Growls, coupled with gnashing teeth filled the air, and her stomach sickened. While she'd never seen Devon in his wolf form, she had no doubt which one he was. The two wolves attacking the lone wolf had red glowing eyes—Changeling eyes. But the most disturbing difference was that Devon was covered in blood.

Her protective mechanism shot into gear. "Stop!" she screamed.

Both attackers halted their assault and glanced up at her, giving Devon a few seconds breather. He darted out from between both of the wolves, turned around, and charged. She wasn't even certain he'd noticed she'd arrived.

As he tore at the black and gray wolf, her breath lodged in her throat. Vinea had to help. But how?

She searched her limited talents. Just as she was about to disap-pear and smash a rock over one of the attacker's head, she spotted a gun on the ground. While she'd never shot anyone before, she figured if she hovered close enough she wouldn't miss.

Vinea rushed over to the weapon and as she bent down to pick it up, one of the wolves charged her! Crap. One second she was visible, and the next she wasn't. The wolf froze and looked around, justifiably confused.

Move!

She grabbed the gun, aimed, and when she pulled the trigger, she swore her heart stopped. The wolf that'd come after her jerked, stuttered backward, and dropped onto his haunches, blood dripping down its side. Even if she unloaded the whole clip into him, he probably wouldn't die, but it would slow him down. Only then did she notice a man lying in a pool of blood on the steps hidden by the shadows. He wasn't moving. Devon yelped as the second wolf clawed at him. As much as she wanted to help the poor man, Devon needed her more.

Her heart lurched. Devon's right hind leg appeared broken and his snout was a bloody mess, but now the other wolf wasn't in much better shape. She raised her arm again to take aim, but the two of them were twisting around too much for her to be sure she'd hit her mark.

Vinea might never have killed a shifter before, but she knew that the neck was the most vulnerable spot. More snarls and grunts rent the air and she floated closer. She pressed the weapon against the second wolf's neck, but her finger wouldn't move. Before she'd been cleansed, she never thought twice about killing. Now she was different, making the decision a difficult, but not impossible one.

Devon needs me.

She closed her eyes and pulled the trigger. Her stomach soured, and the shock caused her to instantly return to her visible body.

When she opened her eyes, both Devon and the wolf she'd just shot had collapsed on the ground. Vinea dropped the gun and knelt next to the man she was fast falling in love with. The first wolf she'd shot lay quivering on the ground, no doubt trying to heal, but she'd shoot him again if he tried to harm Devon.

She placed a hand on Devon's flank. "Devon, are you okay?"

She knew he wasn't able to answer, but she had to ask. Sirens sounded in the background. Oh, shit. Having no time to think through the options, she slipped her hands under his body and lifted him up. He was heavy, but she was strong. She hadn't figured out exactly what to do, but she was convinced their best option was to get out of there.

With Devon's wolf pressed against her body, she ran down the alley, keeping as close to the building as possible to avoid being spotted. When she neared the street, she set him down the moment she saw his truck. Damn. She needed his keys. "Stay here."

Given his condition, he wouldn't be moving. Once more she disappeared, located his clothes and keys, and returned with them. Thankfully, due to the late hour, few cars were on the street. Once the coast was clear, she rushed to his truck and opened the door. Her white sweater was coated in blood, but she hoped no one would stop and ask her questions.

With the sirens fast approaching, she returned for Devon, gathered him in her arms, and rushed him to the truck. Not wanting him to move about during the drive back to his place, she put him on the floor and then jumped into the front seat.

No sooner had she taken off than two police cars stopped in front of the restaurant. Most likely someone had heard the shots and called it in.

As Vinea turned out of sight, she glanced over at Devon, who didn't appear to be breathing. *Dear goddess, please let me help him.*

Chapter Sixteen

W HEN DEVON ROUSED, the first thing he noticed was that his pain was gone, which made no sense. The second was that his opponent wasn't trying to kill him. What the hell had happened? He opened his eyes and recognized the dark outline of his bedroom. Confusion assaulted him. How had he ended up here if he was still in his wolf form?

Vinea! A soft snore erupted beside him, and he rolled over. Her breath was shallow and rapid. Oh, shit. She'd healed him, but at what cost to herself?

Heart pounding, he changed into his human form and gently nudged her. "Vinea?"

He didn't like that she'd made such a sacrifice. She might have died—and still might. Acid burned in his gut at that terrible thought. Maybe she didn't know that given enough time his wolf would have taken care of his injuries.

The memory of the fight flitted in his head, and he vaguely recalled seeing someone arrive just as the two of the Changelings were attempting to tear him apart. It must have been her. One moment she was visible, and the next she was not. A second later, a shot sounded, and the stronger of the two wolves dropped to the ground. After that, he remembered nothing, other than the incredible weakness and violent pain.

Devon stilled for a moment, trying to detect if anyone else was in the house. Had she carried him to his truck by herself? She must have since he doubted he would have been capable of moving on his own.

There was a lot more to Vinea Summer than he realized—strength, determination, and loyalty.

He nudged her once more, but when she didn't respond, his adrenaline surged. Devon had to find help for her. Needing to call Missy, he eased out of bed. Crap. When he shifted, all of his possessions, including his cell, were strewn behind the restaurant. Guess he'd have to go over to his parents' house and call from there.

Vinea must have cleaned him up because only small patches of blood remained on his chest and arms. After dressing, he rushed out of the bedroom. On the dining room table sat his torn clothes—and his phone. Thank goddess for Vinea.

Fortunately, Lexi had insisted on adding every phone number he'd ever need in his phone—including that of the local healer, Missy Berta. Just as he was about to call her, Vinea moaned, and his protective instincts shot into high gear. Devon rushed back into the room and flicked on the light next to the bed. Her eyes were open, and she was trying to sit up.

"You need to rest," he said, sliding onto the bed next to her.

"Are you okay?" she asked.

Was he okay? "Don't I look good?" He smiled, hoping to calm her fears.

"Yes, and I'm glad." She closed her eyes again.

He placed a hand on her forehead, and the heat nearly burned him. While he didn't know much about medicine since his wolf did all the healing, he knew enough to know that he needed to cool her off. Once she was strong enough, they would talk.

No sooner had he placed an ice pack on her forehead than his cell rang. It was Kalan. He dreaded learning how much he'd fucked things up by going over to the restaurant. The owner might not have been shot if Devon hadn't shown.

While he wasn't sure if the two wolves had lived or died, he could only hope that shifters happened upon them. No telling what the humans would think.

"Hey," Devon said.

"It's Kalan. Sorry to bother you, but I wanted to let you know that the Lake Steakhouse robbery went down a few hours ago. Apparently, the Changelings had a change of plans."

So he hadn't learned what had happened exactly. "I know."

Devon explained why he'd been there. He also told Kalan how he'd seen one of the three masked men shoot the owner and run away with the cash.

"Why the fuck didn't you call me?"

"Because I just woke up a minute ago after nearly dying in the attack." Devon explained how one wolf had attacked him from behind, and then the second man shifted after shooting him. "I was in a fight for my life."

"Are you okay?"

"Now I am. Vinea healed me, but she's in bad shape."

"They attacked her?"

He didn't have time to discuss her abilities and what she'd done. "No. She healed me by taking away my pain as her own."

"I'd heard she'd healed Rye's son."

"Yes."

"What happened to the other two wolves?" Kalan asked.

"The men weren't there when you arrived?"

"No. Only the owner was there. He's in the hospital now in critical condition, but we doubt he'll make it."

Damn. "Did you see any sign of a fight?"

"Hell, yeah! It looked like several men had bled out."

Devon explained to the best of his ability what Vinea had done. Only then did Devon realize that both of the men could now identify her as someone who had tried to kill them—assuming they were still alive. He wasn't worried about himself. The McKinnons and the Changelings had gone head to head many times, and everyone was still healthy. It was Vinea who was in danger because of him.

"Can I speak with her?" Kalan asked.

"She's still too weak. When she is feeling better, you can, though it's not like she can give a statement."

"No, I suppose not, especially if she became invisible, but she might be able to identify someone."

"Let's hope."

"Did you call Missy?" Kalan asked.

"I plan to."

"Good. Keep me in the loop," Kalan said.

"Have you spoken with Connor?"

"I just did, but he knew nothing. I'll call him back and let him know what you said."

That worked for him. "Thanks."

VINEA HEARD ONLY one side of the conversation, but it was enough to know that she'd messed up, royally. Both of the men she'd shot might still be alive, which meant they could identify her—and Devon. Now they were both targets. Damn.

Once he hung up, she reached out her hand. "Devon?"

He tossed the cell on the bed and was by her side in a flash. "How are you feeling?"

"I feel like I've been bitten and clawed to death."

His face paled. "Did a wolf attack you?"

Her smile came out weak. "No, but they attacked you. Don't worry, I'll live." She squeezed his hand. "I'm sorry."

"For what? You saved my life."

This time. "Those men lived. They saw me."

"We don't know that. The man who ran away with the cash saw me before you even showed up, but why didn't you remain invisible?"

"When I teleported there, I didn't expect to find anyone behind the building. I aimed for the back of the restaurant, and when I appeared, there you were along with those men—or rather those two wolves."

"My memory is a little faulty. Can you fill me in?"

She told him how she wanted to stop those wolves, but she didn't know how. "My best option was to shoot them."

"So that's why one of the men collapsed. And the other one?"

"I shot him too. It was horrible. I didn't want to pull the trigger, but I had to. You would have died."

He nodded. "The bullet to my leg wouldn't have been fatal, but sooner or later they would have torn out my throat."

Her stomach nearly revolted. "Why did you put yourself in harm's way like that?"

"This time, it wasn't intentional." He explained why he was there.

"So it was my fault. You were looking for me."

"It wasn't your fault," he said.

She rested her head, and when she closed her eyes, it was clear fatigue was about to claim her again.

"I should have guessed they'd change their plans," she said, her words slightly indistinct from exhaustion.

"Our team should have been prepared for that possibility."

"Next time."

Devon stroked his hand over her forehead and she sighed. "There won't be a next time."

Sleep claimed her before she could argue. No doubt they'd never agree on how to handle the Changelings.

SOMETIME DURING THE night, in between bouts of waking, Vinea had made up her mind. Being around Devon was bad for his health. She had no doubt that the Changelings would come after her, and she didn't want Devon to be caught in the middle of it.

When she finally returned to consciousness the next morning, light was streaming through the slit in the curtain and a pretty woman with long auburn hair was waving a hand over her. It was

Missy, Zane's mate.

"What are you doing here?" Vinea asked, her mouth dryer than sand.

"Devon asked that I give you a helping hand in healing."

Vinea wet her lips. "Why would you want to help me? I tried to kill your mate."

"But you didn't. You stopped, remember?"

That was true, but everyone always assumed the worst of her. Had Devon finally convinced his family and friends that she could be trusted? "Thank you for putting aside your hatred."

"I'm a healer. I don't like to judge."

What a wonderful woman. "How is Zane?"

Missy looked off and smiled as she patted her rather pregnant stomach. "Happy."

What Vinea wouldn't give to be carrying Devon's child. "How is Zane adapting to this world?" Vinea hoped he was doing well, as there were many challenges. Having been asleep for one hundred years, he had a harder road than even she did.

"Things were tough for a while, but then out of the blue he received a birth certificate and social security card in the mail, which enabled him to get his driver's license and apply for a job. Since then he's thrived."

Relief washed through her. "I'm glad they arrived and that they worked."

Missy stopped her candle waving and sat on the edge of the bed. "What do you mean?"

"Did Devon tell you how he'd cleansed me at the lake right before I lured you to the cave?"

"Yes."

"The cleansing took a while to take effect. The evil in me didn't start to disappear until I held that knife in my hand and was ready to kill Zane. Somehow it hit me out of nowhere what evil I was about to inflict, and I stopped. Frightened and horrified, I ran away."

"I've wondered why you didn't follow through. While I was very confused, at the same time, I was quite grateful that you'd had a change of heart."

"I didn't think you'd ever forgive me. I mean, why should you?" Vinea waved a hand. "It doesn't matter now. I wanted to make up for what I did—even if it was something small. I totally understood how necessary it is to have the proper paperwork, so I created a birth certificate and social security card for Zane."

"You did that? How?"

She wasn't proud of her actions, but it had to be done. "I paid someone to hack into a few different government offices and make the changes. I don't like breaking the law, but I didn't know how else to help."

Missy leaned over and hugged her gently. "Thank you. We never knew."

Devon entered the room, unshaven and with dark shadows under his eyes. Despite his weary appearance, he still got her motor revving.

"How are you feeling?" He glanced over at Missy and then back at her.

"Doing better. I should be back to work in a day or two." Vinea didn't want him to worry. He had enough on his mind.

Missy stood. "Vinea is healing rather well, but if you see a turn for the worse, call me."

"Thank you," she said to Missy. "I know it had to have been hard to treat me—someone who you believed was your enemy."

"You aren't my enemy or even Zane's enemy, at least not any longer. Devon vouched for you, and that's good enough for us."

Vinea could feel the tears well up, and she had to fight to keep them from falling. Missy's words meant the world to her. Once the healer gathered her gear, Devon escorted her out and then returned.

"I've been thinking," he said. "I think you should move into the safe house at McKinnon and Associates. Your trailer is not secure. You're too vulnerable there."

If Vinea had had more energy, she'd have laughed. "While Lexi seemed to do okay holed up there, that's not who I am. It would drive me crazy being confined."

He dropped down onto the bed. "I don't think you understand. There aren't many five foot-ten women in Silver Lake who are curvy and gorgeous. You'll be easy to spot, and no telling what the Changelings will do when they find you."

She raised her brows, trying to act nonchalant. "Let them try. I do have my powers."

"Yes, you can disappear, but can you shift into a wolf or a bear and fight them?"

He was being protective, and it warmed her heart. "No, but if you recall, I was able to pick up a gun and shoot it, even in my invisible form. Since the gun disappeared as soon as I touched it, the Changelings didn't know who was responsible."

"I thought you didn't like to kill."

"I don't, but if my life is threatened—or yours—I will take action."

Devon stabbed a hand through his hair. "Is there anything I can say that will convince you to at least not go to work? Brother Jacob and John Ernst eat there—at least they did that one time."

Poor Devon. Her presence was causing him added stress. "No. Now stop worrying."

"Then how about moving in here with me? For good?"

Really? She smiled. "Now that I'd agree to."

Chapter Seventeen

"**W**HAT DID YOU learn?" Devon asked Kalan.

Because of the sensitive nature of the robbery, and the fact the store owner might have witnessed some strange happenings in the form of humans shifting into wolves, Kalan suggested they once more return to one of the department's interrogation rooms to have their conversation in private.

"Other than blood, nothing was left behind at the scene, and we've yet to locate the money. We figure either the men shifted back and grabbed their stuff, or the first man came back for them and cleaned up. We may never know if the men lived or died."

"Vinea said that she held the gun to the one wolf's neck and pulled the trigger."

Kalan lifted one shoulder. "She might have killed him then."

Wounds to the neck were often fatal. "It really shook her up." Devon had been surprised by how much.

Kalan's brows rose. "After hundreds of years being evil?"

"Apparently, the cleansing has really changed her."

"That's good to know."

"Here's what has me really worried," Devon said. "If either of the wolves lived, they'll be able to identify her. And if one of the men died, the Changelings will be out for revenge."

"What are you going to do? I doubt you can keep her cooped up for the rest of her life."

He chuckled, but it held little mirth. "I suggested that, but she refuses to quit her job or keep a low profile. She did however agree to stay with me. At least at night, she'll be safe."

"What about your Pittsburgh office. Do you think she'd be willing to relocate?"

Devon would have to return at some point. "I'm hoping, but we need more time together before she's ready to say yes."

"I understand." Kalan leaned back in his seat. "I can't say I blame her for not wanting to hide. If everyone who feared for their life quit their job in order to stay safe, there would be no sheriff's department."

"True, but it doesn't mean I have to like it. She says she can stay safe by disappearing, but I can smell trouble coming."

"How about asking Finn to keep an ear out for any rumors about either a sardonyx sale or someone buying one of the local stores?" Kalan asked.

"I can do that, but I doubt a Changeling would be stupid enough to mention something like that."

"I know, but short of bugging the Changelings' headquarters, I have no other ideas."

"Hell, maybe you should do that!" Devon said.

"The only person or people capable of not getting caught are Vinea or Ainsley. Even then, there is a risk."

"I agree. Besides, Brother Jacob is probably paranoid enough to have the place swept on a regular basis." Devon blew out a breath. "So now what do we do?"

Kalan tossed down the pen he was holding. "Dalton volunteered to snoop around their compound since he's capable of taking down two or three wolves at a time, but I don't want to chance him getting caught. Other than pissing off the Changelings, I don't see how we can learn anything more."

"Then our only option is to wait for their next move."

WHEN DEVON RETURNED home that night, the fire was going and

Vinea was in the kitchen. He rushed up to her. "What are you doing up?"

She spun around and placed her hands on his shoulders. "I'm fine. Missy is a miracle worker."

"You're the miracle worker." He ran his gaze up and down her body, detecting no ill effects.

"I'm making us some dinner. I hope you like it."

"Where did you get the food?" His heart raced. "You didn't go out, did you?"

She chuckled. "No. I could have changed my appearance and hoped for the best, but instead I asked one of the servers at work if she wouldn't mind picking up a few things for me. I told her I was sick."

"That was good thinking, but make sure you remain vigilant."

Vinea stroked his arms. "You have to stop worrying about me. I'm not going to put my life on hold because of a threat. Hell, if I did that, I'd never go out."

She was stubborn, yet brave at the same time. "I have an idea, assuming the dinner won't burn."

"It's ready now. How about we eat first, and then have some fun?"

He laughed. Her idea of fun would involve having wild sex, but before they did, he wanted to be convinced that she could handle herself. "Deal."

Together they served up the baked chicken, green beans, and a salad. "I hope you'll like this," she said. "I really don't know what you like to eat."

Vinea was trying so hard to please him, and his heart squeezed while his wolf yipped with joy.

You love her! his wolf howled with happiness.

Love? Devon wasn't sure he would recognize the feeling if it bit him in the ass, but he knew he had this intense need to protect her. And hold her. And make love with her.

"Devon?"

"Oh, I eat almost everything. This looks amazing."

She gave him a sly smile as if she could read his mind. If she possessed the ability to know his thoughts, he'd be in real trouble.

"Did you learn anything more about the robbery?" she asked.

"No. The owner hasn't regained consciousness, and Kalan has no leads."

"So he doesn't know if I killed those wolves?"

"No."

She let out a breath, as if relieved he didn't have confirmation. "What about the owner? If he wakes up, what will he say?"

Devon shook his head. "I don't know. The owner was shot and then collapsed just as I arrived on the scene. He might not have seen much of anything. At least I hope that's true."

"Bottom line, my lead about the robbery backfired." Vinea looked off to the side, and Devon's heart went out to her.

"No, it didn't. At least I saw the three robbers—kind of. If I ran into either of the wolves I fought with again, I'd recognize them."

Light returned to her eyes. "I hope you never see them."

Once they finished their meal, he pushed back his chair. "I want you to do something for me."

"What is it?"

He held out his hands. "Come here."

Vinea pushed back her chair and stepped in between his outstretched arms. "Make love with you?"

He laughed. "Behave. No, at least not yet. I want you to show me how you could defend against an attack."

Her brows scrunched. "What do you mean?"

"Let's say I attacked you. What would you do?"

"Disappear."

"Show me, but don't do anything too drastic."

She smiled. "Okay, I'll play along."

"I'll pretend to kidnap you, and then you do your thing."

She nodded. Devon reached out and grabbed her arm. A second later she was nowhere to be seen. Devon twisted around and held up his hands in a protective stance. The kitchen drawer that held the knives opened. "I said nothing drastic. Don't cut me, okay?"

She might have answered, but he couldn't hear her. Without warning, she pressed a sharp knife against his throat. Even though he believed she wouldn't harm him, he needed to fend her off. Besides, Devon wanted to understand what she was capable of. He reached out to where he thought her wrist might be, but all he found was air. Dang. She just might be able to do a sneak attack on the Change-lings.

He held up his hands. "Okay, that was good."

Vinea appeared in front of him with a grin on her face, waving the knife. "See?"

"Got any other talents I should know about? I will admit the ability to strangle, cut, shoot, or hit someone when they can't see you, is good."

"Hmm." She paced in front of him. "I used to be able to freeze time."

"Freeze time? I don't understand."

Vinea set down the knife on the dining room table and returned. "Come at me," she said, holding up her hands in a mock boxer's pose.

Without asking what she planned to do, he ran toward her, but he wasn't able to reach her somehow. How was that possible? Even though Devon was totally aware of his thoughts, the world seemed to have stopped. Then as if she'd flipped a switch, he was moving again, only Vinea wasn't there.

"Over here," she said waving and smiling.

"That was the strangest thing that has ever happened to me."

She clapped. "I can't believe I did that. I wasn't even sure I could anymore."

"You really stopped time?"

"Yes!"

"For how long?" His mind spun.

"Five seconds, maybe? It's really hard to do. I have to keep focused on everything around me."

"There have to be consequences." Even if she'd stopped time during the fight with those two wolves, he wasn't sure how much time it would have gained him.

She shrugged. "I can't say as I haven't tried it in years. I honestly didn't think I had the power anymore."

"Did everyone in the world lose those few seconds?"

"No. Just those I focus on."

He wanted to understand the scope of her talent. "So if two people are next to each other, could you stop time for one and not the other?"

"I don't know, but if they were right next to each other, probably not."

"Regardless of your accuracy, I have to say I'm impressed." Devon was quite satisfied that Vinea would be safe against the Changelings.

She moved closer and dragged a finger down his chest. "How impressed?"

He tapped her nose. "Very, but not enough to say you can let your guard down."

"Don't worry. Nothing will happen to me."

"I hope not."

"Would you miss me if something did?" She sucked in her bottom lip, and his wolf went wild. His balls drew up, and his pulse sped.

Then at the thought of losing her, a strong ache nearly crushed him. "I'd more than miss you. I'd be tormented for the rest of my life."

She grinned. "You don't have to go that far. Being sad is good enough." Vinea winked, and his cock hardened further.

When she looked up at him with her gorgeous green eyes, he could no longer hold back. Devon pulled her so close the pressure from her breasts heated him up from the inside out. Between the relief at her having lived, to knowing she could take care of herself, the tension that had been building all day finally let go.

He ran his fingers across her jaw and then tucked a loose strand of hair behind her ear. Cupping her neck, he leaned in close and whispered, "I want you, Vinea."

She turned her face and brushed her lips against his. Devon's cock was on full alert, and it nearly exploded as their kiss became more heated and passionate.

"I'm going to rock your world, Devon McKinnon."

"Show me what you got, beautiful."

"GET READY," SHE said. "This time, I'm going to use my powers."

His brows furrowed. When she swept a hand over her body and removed all her clothes, his eyes widened. Devon reached out to touch her, but she shook her head.

"What's wrong?" he asked, obviously upset.

"Don't move."

He cocked a brow. "Or what?"

She gave him a sly grin. "Or I'll put my clothes back on before you can even touch me."

Devon laughed. "I accept that challenge."

One minute she was three feet from him and the next, she was over his shoulder in a fireman's hold. Vinea beat on his back and giggled. "Let me down. I wanted to suck on your cock."

With a quick swat to her ass, he growled. "Oh, you will definitely get to do that, but first I want to see you try to keep those screams, moans, and adorable little quick breaths to yourself."

He pushed open the bedroom door and dropped her on her back onto the bed.

She propped herself on her elbows. "Try me."

"Don't you worry, my little goddess, I promise I'm not stopping until you scream my name in pure ecstasy."

Vinea couldn't wait. Devon toed off his shoes and removed his socks. As if he wasn't interested in her naked body, he placed the items in the closet. Her mouth drooled in anticipation. He slowly unbuttoned his blue chambray shirt, and his stall tactics only served to make her hornier.

She ran a finger around her nipple. "Need help moving along a little faster?"

"Nope."

Spoilsport. Once his shirt was open, he unbuttoned his jeans, turned around, and dropped his pants down over his delicious ass. She so wanted to jump off the bed and bite him, but she didn't.

After he stepped out of his jeans, he eased his briefs down over his finer than fine butt.

Okay. That was it. She couldn't take the teasing any longer and had to finger herself in order to get some satisfaction. Wiggling her digit around, she searched for that spot Devon had discovered. She failed, but it was better than doing nothing. Damn man needed to hurry.

When he was naked, he kicked his jeans and briefs closer to the door then turned around. "You're an impatient little minx!"

He stalked toward her with pure desire in his eyes. "What? I thought you forgot about me over here," she said with a pout.

"Oh I could never forget about you, but by all means continue." He crossed his arms.

"Like this?" she asked, pretending she wasn't sure what he meant.

Vinea removed her finger and dragged her juices over each of her nipples. His eyes turned amber, and the hair on his arms thickened. Keeping his gaze on her face, he placed one knee on the bed and leaned close.

"Exactly like that, and now you will see how I do things." He bent down and sucked her nipple so hard that her body arched up uncontrollably.

Oh, she was so ready for that.

Chapter Eighteen

"I CAN'T TAKE it any longer," Devon said.

"What are you going to do?"

"This." Devon ducked his head and sucked on her other nipple, sending spikes of heated pleasure through her.

Never in all the years she'd lived, had she known sex could be this wonderful. Perhaps she hadn't been the right person to mate others, when she herself had no idea what love and sensuality was about.

Love? Is that what this delirious feeling was?

It just might be.

Vinea wrapped her legs around Devon's waist and held him tight. She then grabbed his shoulders, dug her nails into his skin to make sure he was real, and dropped back her head. "Yes!"

"You like that?" he asked in between tugs and sucks.

She could no more deny it than she could turn to stone. "I more than like it. I'm ready now. Please Devon, I need you inside me."

"In due time."

So now he was going to torment her? Fine. If she had the chance to touch him, he'd be sorry. Vinea tried to reach between the two of them to grab his cock, but all she managed was to touch the tip.

Devon brushed her hand away. The man was so controlling. With one strong nip of her nipple, he slipped downward, breaking her hold on him. She had no doubt that once he licked her, she'd crumble. Devon grabbed her knees and spread them apart, then swiped a tongue across her opening. She bucked up and clutched the sheets. Maybe it was from almost seeing him die that Vinea wanted to clutch every morsel of joy he threw her way.

The next lick had her moaning with overwhelming pleasure. She so wanted to suck on his cock, but she was enjoying this too much to beg him to stop. It was when he slipped two fingers inside her and arched them up to that sweet spot that she couldn't hold back any longer. An intense wave of erotic bliss swamped her, forcing her to gulp in more air in order to breathe. Then when he drew her clit into his mouth, her climax finally claimed her hard. Stars burst on the back of her lids, causing her to nearly black out.

The bed bounced, and when she opened her eyes, Devon had twisted around, placing his cock close to her mouth while his lips were centered over her damp curls. Just as she was about to grab his thick shaft, he lifted her up and positioned her onto her elbows and knees so that she was straddling him, giving her better access to his large dick. Now that he was offering himself to her, she wasn't going to waste this chance. It didn't matter that her bones had almost melted after that last orgasm.

Vinea grabbed his thick length again and drew him deep into her mouth. As much as she wanted to take her time and drive him crazy, her next climax happened a minute later. When she was around Devon McKinnon, Vinea had no willpower.

Once she regained some strength after her powerful release, she swirled her tongue around his hard dick and bobbed her head, tightening her hold with each stroke.

"Goddess that feels so good," Devon panted.

As if he wanted her to be as excited as he was, Devon flicked her sensitive nub back and forth, causing sparks of need to shoot through her, sending her into a spiral. For those few seconds, she lost focus and stopped moving. When he grunted, Vinea jerked back to the present and continued. Her pumping fist, along with her moans, seemed to encourage him even more. Not only did she want to swallow him whole, when he pressed on her most sensitive spot, he lit her up. Unable to keep from coming again, she lifted her head and sucked in a breath, letting the waves of passion wash over her.

Devon chuckled. "Don't think you're done yet."

She hoped not. "Can I have your cock inside me now?" She truly had no idea how these many climaxes would effect her. Would she be in a permanent state of arousal?

"If I weren't on the brink of shifting, I'd hold out for hours."

As if he could, though she kept that comment to herself. Devon twisted around, pressed his body against hers, and kissed her like she was the most important person in his life. A large chunk of her heart melted.

"How about I get on top?" she asked. Vinea hoped that if she controlled the speed, she might be able to last longer.

"If you think you can handle it."

She loved that Devon liked to play the macho man. Before he changed his mind, Vinea faced him and then straddled him. She grabbed his cock and placed it at her entrance. Before she slid down on him, she leaned over to kiss him, nice and slow and easy.

Devon groaned and slid his fingers through her hair and tugged. His possessive attitude ratcheted her desires to the point where she might come again before she'd taken in all of him—and that wouldn't do. She'd never live it down.

When he demanded entrance to her mouth, she willingly opened up. The first taste swamped her, confirming that she had to have more. Then when Devon's hands clasped her hips and coaxed her down onto his cock, Vinea let herself drop. Even though her slick juices eased the way, his width was almost too much for her. Pressing her breasts against his chest caused the slight change in angle, allowing him to enter her fully. Holy fuck, his cock was huge, but it felt so fucking good.

"My turn," he announced as he tightened his hold on one of her hips. "Stay still."

What—and not move? He had to be kidding. When he drove up into her, the heat was so intense that she wasn't able to move even if she wanted to. Devon cupped the back of her head with his other hand and kissed her as if there was no tomorrow, and the thrust that followed nearly toppled her over the edge.

His teeth sharpened, nearly cutting her tongue, but she didn't care. She wanted him and that included his wolf too.

"Vinea, Vinea." He closed his eyes and drove into her so deep she nearly lost her mind.

When his hot seed burned her insides, her orgasm swept in. She lifted her head and screamed his name. Minutes later, his grip slipped to her waist, and then he wrapped his arms around her.

Stretching out next to him, she rested her head on his shoulder where they stayed cocooned in each other's arms for a long time. "That was amazing," she whispered.

"I told you I would get you to scream my name."

Vinea giggled and nipped at his shoulder. "Don't go getting a swelled head, mister."

"I'll show you a swelled head, minx." Devon arched his hips and nudged at her entrance again, causing her to moan.

"I can't get enough of you, Vinea."

"That's a good thing, right?"

Devon rolled on top of her, and with one strong thrust of his hips was fully buried back inside her. As they moved together, he licked the shell of her ear. "Yes, that's a very good thing," he whispered.

Despite the euphoria racing through her veins, Vinea couldn't stop that niggle of worry from pricking her heart that she had brought more danger to him. Perhaps she should stay away from Devon or maybe even leave altogether. She had come too close to losing him already. Whatever it took, she would make sure he was safe.

Just as she was losing herself in her thoughts, Devon sucked on her nipple and brought her back to the present. He reared up onto his knees and grabbed her ass, pulling her up onto his thighs causing him to go even deeper. As he started to pound into her, Vinea forgot about everything as they became swept away in their passion for each other once more.

FOR THE NEXT few days after the robbery at the Lake Steakhouse, Vinea was having a hard time concentrating at work, and that was bad. She was worried about Devon. He seemed determined—no possessed—to find out as much about the attack and robbery as possible. He'd told her he felt responsible for not doing more to solve these crimes. She tried to explain that if he hadn't shown up at the restaurant when he did, the owner might have died. The police had shown up in time to save the man. Despite her logic, she failed to convince Devon he wasn't to blame.

Even though their lovemaking sessions at night were becoming increasingly more intense and sensual, no amount of prompting would get him to tell her what was truly on his mind. She suspected it had to do with his desire to return to Pittsburgh where his office was located, but she also believed he didn't want to leave her alone in Silver Lake. Vinea had thought about suggesting she move to Pittsburgh with him, but there had been no mention of mating since that one discussion, so all Vinea could do was wait it out.

At least until the Changelings made their move—if they ever did—she doubted he'd leave town.

Last night, Devon didn't come back to the guesthouse until after ten, and Vinea was a bit frightened. When he finally arrived, he told her there were some rumors about the Changelings shaking up some things, and he feared something bad would happen to her.

If it were true that the Changelings planned to take out their revenge on her, being at Devon's house might bring those beasts to him, even though he'd said they didn't like being anywhere near the lake.

"Vinea?" the cook at the café said. "You've been staring at the meatloaf for thirty seconds. Is something wrong with it?"

She shook herself out of her malaise and smiled. "Not a thing! It looks mouthwateringly good."

The cook smiled and went back to flipping the burgers. Perhaps she should just move back to her trailer to give Devon some relief, but then she decided he'd worry about her even more.

Dang. There just didn't seem to be a solution.

Needing to see a friendly face, she quickly finished her late lunch, and then went in search of Mr. Sanford, her favorite customer. Each week he came in on Wednesday and Friday around eleven for a late breakfast and would order a coffee and Danish every time. But on Mondays, he would show up promptly at four, and if she had a spare moment, she'd sit with him and shoot the breeze. It was nice to interact with someone who only judged her on her current actions and not on her past.

Only today, he hadn't shown up and that worried her. But he might have had a doctor's appointment, so she didn't think there was a need to panic, yet.

When four thirty rolled around and Mr. Sanford still hadn't come in, Vinea asked Marissa if she'd seen him, as they shared neighboring stations.

"Not today, but two days ago he said he wasn't feeling all that well."

The tension in Vinea's shoulders increased. "Oh, I'm sorry to hear that. I'd call him if I knew his number."

Marissa rubbed her arm. "He probably just lost track of time."

"Let's hope."

Another customer, about sixty who she'd never seen before, sat down at one of her tables. "I gotta go," she told Marissa. Vinea stepped over to him. "What can I get you?"

"A coffee and a menu."

"Coming right up." Once she delivered his drink, she was about to check on another table, when the man stopped her.

"Miss, can I ask you something?"

"Sure."

"I was supposed to meet Bill Sanford here at four, but I got tied up. He's about five foot seven, short gray hair, and about seventy—"

"I know him. In fact, he always comes in around this time."

"But he hasn't been in today?"

"No."

The man leaned back in his seat. "I'm worried about him."

"So am I." She wondered how well he knew Mr. Sanford. "He comes in three days a week, and never misses his café time—until today that is."

The man sipped his coffee. "Maybe I'll go over to his house and check up on him. We need to go over some paperwork." The man nodded at his briefcase.

"If you have no objections, I'd love to go with you to make sure he's okay, but I don't get off work for another hour."

"I can wait. I'll chew slowly." The man winked.

"I'd appreciate it."

Right before Vinea's shift was over, she called Devon and explained that she might not be home until closer to seven because one of her regular customers, Mr. Sanford, hadn't shown up at the café despite having an appointment with someone. She feared he might be ill. Even though Devon rarely came home that early, she didn't need him to worry.

"Be careful," he said.

"Mr. Sanford is seventy. Nothing will happen."

"Okay. I'll see you soon," he said with a fair amount of cheer in his voice.

"I can't wait." She meant that. Devon had gotten under her skin, and after they made love the first time, her body hadn't stopped vibrating with a constant need.

When her shift finished, she found the kind stranger. "I'm ready," she said.

"Do you want to follow me in your car?" he asked.

"I would if I had one." Darn. If he had business with Mr. Sanford, perhaps she shouldn't interfere. And if he lived too far out of town, she could always say she'd walk home and then find a hiding spot before teleporting the rest of the way.

"I'll drive you."

"Great."

He drove a fairly new black SUV. Before she slid in, she wanted to exchange at least one pleasantry. "I'm Vinea Summer by the way."

"Chad Acres." He held out his hand, and she shook it.

"Nice to meet you." Once inside the car, she twisted toward him. "How do you know Mr. Sanford?"

"I'm his lawyer."

It wouldn't be polite to ask what Mr. Sanford needed legal advice about, so she kept quiet. Maybe there had been an issue with his wife's death. Mr. Acres headed west, and when he drove past McKinnon and Associates, her body actually had a visceral reaction to being so close to Devon.

"Are you from Silver Lake?" Chad asked.

While she really wasn't in the mood for small talk, it would have been rude not to answer. "No, I just moved here from Billard, Georgia a short while ago." Vinea added an extra amount of southern twang to sound more convincing. "You?"

"I'm over in Andersonville, about a half hour from here."

Mr. Acres turned down a side street where the homes were modest but clean and parked in front of a green cement home. The landscaping was sparse, which surprised her since Mr. Sanford often talked about Marie's fondness for gardens. Then again, it was winter, and his wife had died two years ago.

Mr. Acres opened the door. "Let's hope Bill is home and just forgot our appointment."

Vinea followed him to the front door. He knocked, and when the door opened, something very heavy crashed down on the back of her head, buckling her knees. An ache as strong as the one she'd received when taking Devon's pain filled her. She tried to engage her cloak of invisibility, but she lost focus before she succeeded. A second after her face met the front entrance way, something stabbed her arm, and then a burning sensation coursed through her veins. Oh, shit.

Chapter Nineteen

D EVON HAD A rather frustrating day at work. He'd spoken with
Finn a few times, but he hadn't heard anything about who
might have been behind the attack or if any of the robbers had died.
Coming up empty-handed was rather unusual for his brother;
everyone chatted with a bartender. The only good news he'd learned
was the Lake Steakhouse owner would live. He was too drugged up
on pain meds at the moment to talk—but he would be alert and able
to speak soon enough.

When Devon walked into his house at seven thirty, he was surprised Vinea hadn't returned from visiting her friend. She'd said the
older gentleman was a regular, so maybe they had a lot to chat about.
Devon just hoped the man hadn't taken ill and Vinea hadn't seen fit
to take away his pain. At some point, her healings might be lethal to
her, or at the least cause her great discomfort.

Thinking she'd be exhausted when she returned home, he
washed up and then scrounged around for something to cook. To his
dismay, he'd been so focused on this case that he hadn't taken the
time to shop. The best he could come up with was rather old package
of spaghetti and a jar of meat sauce.

Since he wasn't sure when she would return, he set out the in-
gredients, ready to cook them once she arrived. By eight fifteen,
Devon was becoming increasingly concerned. He figured she
wouldn't mind if he called to check on her. If nothing else, he could
ask her what time she would like dinner.

He dialed her number, but when she didn't answer, his sixth sense shot into high gear.

Her phone went to voicemail. "Vinea, when you get this, call me back immediately." Devon disconnected and paced, trying to figure out his next move.

She could take care of herself, unless she was too ill to help herself. The best thing to do was to find out where Mr. Sanford lived and head on over there. If she was deep in conversation with her friend, Devon would leave.

The problem was that he had no idea where the man lived, but maybe someone at the Silver Lake Café would know. In case Vinea returned while he was out, he left her a message and placed it on the dining room table.

When he arrived at the café, the inside was dark. Fuck. The sign on the front stated the hours. They closed at six on Monday. Well, damn. How did he not know that? Some investigator he was. Devon would have contacted one of the waitresses if he could remember any of their names. Whenever he came into town, he'd been too busy to pay much attention to what or where he ate.

Sitting in his truck with the heat on medium, he called Jackson. As much as he didn't like disturbing him, this was important. Jackson could track down anyone.

"Hey, Dev. What's up?"

"I think Vinea is missing." That sounded lame, but he didn't know how else to word it.

"What do you mean she's missing? Are you sure she didn't teleport somewhere without telling you?"

He explained that she'd called a little before six saying she was going over to the house of one of her regular customers. Apparently, he hadn't shown up at his usual time, even though he was to meet a friend there. Worried, Vinea wanted to check on him.

"What do you need from me?" Jackson asked.

"I went to the café to see if anyone knew where he lived, but the place was closed. Do you think you can track him down? His last name is Sanford."

"Do you know his first name?"

Shit. What kind of mate would he make if he didn't even take the time to ask Vinea about her work? "No, but she said he's around seventy."

"That might narrow it down. Let me check, and I'll get back to you."

"Appreciate it."

Devon put the truck in gear and headed back home. He slammed his hand on the steering wheel. If the robbery hadn't occurred a few days ago, he wouldn't have thought anything about her visiting a friend. Vinea had taken the time to call and tell him where she was going, so how bad could it be? She didn't sound under duress, and from the background noise, she'd been at the restaurant when she'd called.

After a few hours at the man's house, he would have thought she'd at least touch base with him again. So why hadn't she? His gut said something was wrong.

No sooner had he entered his dark house than his cell rang, jacking up his pulse. It was Jackson. "What did you find?" Devon asked.

"I have an address for a Bill Sanford, aged seventy-one. He lives over on 721 Pine Avenue."

"Thanks."

"Do you want me and Ainsley to meet you there?"

Devon's heart nearly stopped. "Why? What are you thinking?"

"Not much, but given the recent events, we should be careful. Safety in numbers, you know."

Smart. If they drove separately, and nothing sinister had occurred, he'd wave them off. If something had happened, he'd appreciate the backup. "Sounds good. I'll jump in my truck and head on over now."

"Meet you there."

Devon tried to tell himself that nothing had happened to her; he was being overly protective, but until he spoke with Vinea, he couldn't relax. Surely, if she'd been threatened in any way, she'd just become invisible and return home. His imagination had to be out of control.

Ten minutes later, he approached Mr. Sanford's house. It sat on a wooded lot with one car in the drive. While winter had taken its toll on the landscaping, many of the bushes leading up to the front door were green. He let out a breath seeing the inside of the home was well lit. Not having the patience to wait for Jackson and Ainsley, Devon jumped out of his truck, rushed up to the front, and knocked.

Thirty long seconds went by before the door opened. The dapper older man was dressed in a beige button down sweater and baggy pants. "Yes?"

"Mr. Sanford?"

"I am. How can I help you?"

"I'm Devon McKinnon and my girlfriend, Vinea Summer, stopped over here tonight, and I was wondering what time—"

The old man held up a hand. "Vinea? I haven't seen her in days. I heard she was ill."

Devon's heart sank, and his wolf began to claw at his insides. The man appeared sharp, and his eye contact was straightforward. "She didn't stop by tonight?"

"No. I always go to the café every Monday, but someone called and said they had to close early. Something about a gas leak."

When his teeth began to sharpen, Devon looked away. His wolf was angry and wanted to be released. "If she does stop by, will you tell her to call me?"

"Devon McKinnon, you say?"

"Yes."

"I sure will."

As he headed back to his car, Jackson and Ainsley pulled down the driveway. He rushed over to them. "Mr. Sanford said Vinea's not here, nor did she stop by."

"I don't like it. What are you thinking?" Jackson asked.

"The Changelings must have her."

"Do you have any evidence that they took her?"

"No, but they must have drugged her or something, or else she would have teleported home. Fuck."

"Call her."

"I already did," Devon shot back.

"Try again. Maybe she's at your house already and you just missed each other."

He dialed her number, but it went to voicemail again. "Vinea, I'm worried. Really worried. Call me."

WHEN VINEA OPENED her eyes, it was so dark she could barely see anything. Wherever she was, it was cold, and the floor was hard. She wet her lips and then tried to sit up. Her head throbbed like a bitch, and her back was stiff. When she tried to touch her face to check why her cheek hurt so much, she found her hands tied behind her back. Acid burned in her gut at the constraint. Whoever did this would pay.

The first thing she needed to do was get out of this hellhole. Picturing Devon's front living room as her destination, she nodded to transport out of there.

But nothing happened.

What the hell? Why hadn't she teleported? Or become invisible for that matter?

The door creaked open, flooding the room with ambient light. "Well, well. You're awake."

That voice was familiar. It belonged to Brother Jacob. Well, fuck. Vinea had to figure out how to play this. Acting scared would only cause more problems, but she could only bluff so much. With her hands and feet tied, she didn't have much to bargain with. As for her other talents, she couldn't even change clothes without her hands.

"Why did you bring me here?" she asked.

"Because you are a menace. That little stunt you pulled in my office was very dangerous. I'm beginning to suspect you had something to do with the stolen sardonyx too."

Did he really think she'd cop to that? "What's sardonyx?"

The slap across her face had her falling backward, slamming her head against the wall. Ouch.

"I saw you in my office. If you can appear and disappear, I'm thinking you followed me to California."

"Did you see me there?" A bit of the old goddess surfaced.

"How would I if you were invisible?" He kicked her hard in the side and knocked the breath out of her. "I want my sardonyx."

She would not cry. The problem was that Vinea was not built for abuse. "Fine, I did take it, but I took it to the sheriff's department for safe keeping."

Telling him that was probably the stupidest thing she'd ever done, but maybe he'd realize how talented she was and want to make her a deal. Not that she'd take it, but she needed to stall.

"Who did you give it to, exactly?"

She wasn't giving up any names. Other than Kalan Murdoch, she didn't know anyone. "Whoever was at the front desk. I told him I found it and was turning it in. I said I didn't want any reward, but since it looked valuable, someone must want it."

That had Brother Jacob looking off to the side. "I have to admit, I didn't take you for someone who was that stupid."

What was that supposed to mean? "Did you think I'd try to sell it back to you?"

He huffed out a laugh. "As a matter of fact I did."

At least he must believe she was still bad. Let him think that. "Now that you know what I'm capable of, why not let me go?"

"Because you're bait."

Her stomach clenched. She struggled, but that caused the ropes to dig deeper into her wrists. Even if she could stand, she couldn't get far with her hands and feet bound.

"Oh, and if you're wondering," he said. "I had a witch put a spell on you. You won't be able to become invisible ever again—or teleport—no matter how hard you try." He laughed, spun on his heels, and left.

The room became dark once more, sending her soul into despair.

DEVON DRUMMED HIS fingers on the conference room table. He hadn't been able to sleep last night trying to figure out where Vinea could be. Her boss at work said she didn't tell him she was taking time off. Vinea had mentioned a friend in Billard, but Devon didn't remember her name either. When he had her in his arms again, things would change.

Connor looked at each of the members of the team. Because Ainsley had come with Jackson last night, she'd insisted on helping. Lexi sat next to Sam, taking notes.

"What do we know?" Connor asked.

"Nothing," Devon said. "Vinea isn't answering her phone, and there have been no demands. I get the sense they—meaning the Changelings—will contact us and insist I meet them alone."

"Why you?" Jackson said. "We've all been involved in their demise. You only came onto the scene recently."

"They might have figured out that Vinea took the sardonyx. If they don't want me, they might insist that we exchange her for the stone."

Everyone around the room nodded.

"So now what?" Connor asked to no one in particular.

"I think I should go over to the café and see if anyone knows who called Mr. Sanford and told him the café was closed yesterday afternoon," Devon said. "That would let us know who has Vinea."

Connor tossed the pencil he'd been holding onto the table. "The call didn't come from an employee of the cafe. Jackson already asked. No, the call was really about luring Vinea to a place she thought was safe."

Connor was right. "Then what do you suggest?" Devon asked.

"I wish I knew."

Devon looked at Jackson. "How about flying your drone over the Changeling compound with the heat signature equipment attachment?"

"I can do that but it will show hundreds of people moving about. I can't detect one person from another."

Devon slammed his hand on the table. "Sorry. It's just that it's so frustrating. Why doesn't she disappear and return home?"

"Maybe she can't," Ainsley said. "Even when I'm invisible, you can still touch me. If someone tied me up, even if I became invisible, I couldn't move."

Devon shook his head. "Vinea is a goddess. She's different." He explained how when they were playacting, she'd held a knife to his throat. "I tried to grab her wrists, but I felt nothing."

"We don't have any choice but to storm the place," Sam said.

He might be a military man, but that could get Vinea killed. "I'd like to try that only as a last resort," Devon said.

"And do what in the meantime?" Sam shot back.

Devon appreciated that Sam was willing to help, especially considering what Vinea had tried to do to him, but Devon feared his method might not work. "Look, I want to go after her more than any of you, but we need something to go on. We know she's been in Brother Jacob's home, so I doubt they'd keep her there. Jackson can send the drone over that house to see if there's only one signature inside, assuming the man isn't married, but I'm not confident he'll find her."

"Brother Jacob, married? No woman would be committed to that ass," Sam said with way too much bitterness.

"I'm game to try the drone," Jackson said.

Connor nodded. "Do it, and let us know what you find. In the meantime, I'll ask Rye to send out a call for help. If we have the entire shifter community looking for her, we should learn something." He turned to Devon. "In the meantime, go home in case Vinea returns."

As much as he didn't want to, there was a chance she'd be there. "I will, but first I want to speak with someone at the café to alert us if she shows up."

Connor nodded. "Let us know."

Now came the hardest part—the wait.

Chapter Twenty

VINEA WAS BOUND and determined to get the hell out of there—wherever *there* was. The house could belong to anyone, making her location harder to determine. Given there was no furniture in the ten by fifteen foot room, it was probably some old, abandoned house. Shouting or pounding the walls would fall on deaf ears. Damn.

Normally, she would just teleport to Devon's house. He'd untie her and all would be well. The problem was she couldn't become invisible no matter how hard she tried. If what Brother Jacob said was true about the curse, then she was doomed forever. Though knowing that ass, he was lying. Her best hope was that Devon would round up help. How they'd find her was anyone's guess. Jackson's drone wouldn't be of any help unless Brother Jacob had ten guards surrounding the place, all spaced evenly apart and standing still.

Once more the door opened, and this time both John Ernst and Brother Jacob came in. Ernst stood over her. Great. Two egotistical goons—and a type she was very familiar with. "Hi ya, boys," she said, emphasizing the last word.

Brother Jacob loomed over her. "How did you and Devon McKinnon know to go to the Lake Steakhouse the night of the robbery?"

Her heart squeezed tight. So they were responsible for that crime. Now that they'd basically admitted it, they'd never let her go. Her stomach nearly revolted. Whether they could actually kill her was something she didn't want to find out. Dying without telling Devon she loved him was a thought too horrible to imagine.

"I had no idea there would be a robbery. Devon said he'd lost his wallet and went to look for it. Since he'd just picked up dinner for us there an hour before, it made sense to go back and look." Vinea was pleased she still had the ability to weave a tale.

"I don't believe you. The restaurant was closed."

Her heart skipped a beat as adrenaline soared through her. "Which was why he went to the back, to see if that door was open. That's the truth, I swear. He had no idea you'd be robbing the place." She was able to sound convincing since neither of them knew the robbery would occur that night.

Ernst looked over at Brother Jacob, probably wondering if his friend believed her. "One of the men died. We think you were responsible."

Only one of them died? Damn. She opened her mouth to show her surprise. "Me? You think little old me was responsible? How could I harm a werewolf? I'm helpless when it comes to fighting. When I saw Devon in that bloody battle, I freaking ran."

She'd freaked all right, but thankfully she'd had the presence of mind to find something to help him.

He shook his head. "Then how do you explain that both of my men were shot?"

"I can't. What did they say happened?"

"One of them can't say anything, but the other one said that when he went to attack you, you disappeared. Then he was shot."

"Seems to me if I had shot him—which I didn't—it would have been self-defense." She crossed her fingers. Sure she felt bad for lying, but with both her life and Devon's on the line, this kind of lie was for the greater good.

"Where did you run off to?"

Since she'd returned to her human form in order to speak with Devon before carrying him back down the alley, she couldn't say she'd gone home. "I waited at the far end of the alley, out of harm's way."

"My man saw you return after you shot him."

"I didn't shoot him." It was his word against hers. "Once the growling stopped, I came back to help Devon."

For some reason, they seemed to believe her this time—or else they weren't sure how to proceed. Vinea struggled with the ropes tying her hands, but she failed to loosen them. Never had she been this helpless.

"We're not finished with you yet."

Ooh, I'm scared. Or at least she told herself that. Except, she really was scared and just hoped she could keep that hidden from these assholes. The last thing she wanted was for them to use it against her.

No sooner had the two men left than Androf appeared before her, startling her. Vinea had to blink a few times to make sure she wasn't hallucinating.

"Well, well. I see you've gotten yourself into a bind." He laughed. "Bind. Get it?"

What an ass.

"Why in the hell are you here?" she snarled. She didn't need more horror dumped on her.

Androf folded his hulking arms across his chest, looking like Mr. Clean—only the two had nothing in common except for the bald head and broad chest.

"Thought we could strike a deal."

He was delusional. One of his deals would only serve him. "I'm listening."

Normally, she'd tell him to go fuck off, but given her rather precarious situation, Vinea wouldn't mind trying to trick him into helping her.

"I can get you out of here."

Her traitorous heart lurched. Too bad the cost would be inordinately high. "How about untying me first so we can talk?"

"I will if you agree to undergo reversion therapy."

No way. She'd seen how he'd recruited one unsuspecting goddess over to the dark side. To complete the reversion process, he had to remove her light, and it wasn't a pretty sight. "I'll take my chances here. That part of my life has died, and I have no intention of resurrecting it. Thanks anyway." She stretched out her bound legs and leaned back against the wall, pretending to look comfortable.

"You're a fool." Androf lowered his arms and peered down at her. "Surely, you don't think you'll get out of here alive? You need me."

Acid burned inside her. So it was true. She could die. Or was he bluffing? "As I just told you, I'll take my chances. I don't think these men really want me anyway. They're trying to lure my mate here."

Telling him that she and Devon had mated was a calculated risk. However, she didn't need Androf to gather her up and speed her back to the dark realm where she might never escape. The thought of not seeing Devon again sickened her. Her vision blurred for a moment as bile raced up her throat.

"You aren't mated to anyone."

Had he been spying on her? Oh, yeah. He was a god. He knew things. "Does it matter? Besides, it's none of your business." She nodded to the door. "If you don't leave, I'll yell for my captors to take you down."

His boisterous laugh had to have alerted them of his presence—just what she wanted. Though, if Androf killed Brother Jacob and John Ernst, the world would be a better place.

"Very well," he said. "I hope you die a painful death." With those less than gracious last words, he disappeared.

The door burst open, and two men she'd never seen before barged in. The tall one with the unibrow and pointed chin looked around. "Who were you talking to?"

Telling them the truth might help keep her safe for a few more hours. "My old boss came to check up on me."

They glanced at each other. "Is that so? Then where is he?"

She chuckled. "I'm a goddess, which means my boss is a god. He can appear and disappear as he wishes. Since he's from the dark realm, he can kill all of you with a sweep of a hand." Sure, that was a slight exaggeration, but they didn't need to know that.

"Sure he is. Do you actually think talking to yourself will trick us into untying you?" the tall one asked, still checking out the room. He probably thought Androf was invisible, ready to take them down. Vinea scratched her nails on the wall behind her, and then smiled at the look of sheer terror on their faces.

They spun around and ran out of there, their footsteps pounding down the hall. At least Androf was good for something. Perhaps the news of his appearance would get back to Brother Jacob and keep him scared enough to stay away. Then again, he might decide she could be useful and try to court her to join his evil side. While it would bide her time, she didn't think she was that good of an actress anymore.

DEVON WAS FREAKING out. So far none of the leads to locate Vinea had panned out. She'd been gone two days, and the longer she was missing, the more frantic he became. His wolf wasn't any better, pacing, growling, and snapping. He was pretty sure if he shifted, the beast would go ballistic, destroying everything in his path.

She couldn't be dead. He'd know it! But if she were alive, why hadn't she shown up? Hadn't she said that even if she'd been tied down she could become invisible and float away? So why hadn't she? Asking the same question over and over again, however, wouldn't help him find her.

Connor knocked on his office door and entered, his brows furrowed and evidence of a sleepless night resided under his eyes.

"Anything yet?" Devon asked.

"No."

"I'm guessing Jackson hasn't found anything either?"

"No, but he's looking for a room or building where a person is fairly stationary."

"Is he thinking Vinea has been drugged or restrained?" Devon asked.

"He's not speculating. If they have her, and she can't reappear elsewhere, then that would seem to be the logical answer."

"That does make sense." Devon didn't like that scenario, but at least it meant they were keeping her alive for a reason.

"If anyone can find her, it'll be him."

Devon's cell rang, but he didn't recognize the number. He held up a finger for his brother to stay. "Devon McKinnon."

"Mr. McKinnon this is Charles DuPree, the owner of the Silver Lake Café."

Devon sat up straighter. This had to be about Vinea. "Can I put you on speaker?'

"Sure."

He pressed the button and motioned for Connor to take a seat. "Go ahead."

"Before you ask, Vinea has not shown up for work. One of my servers said she overheard there was going to be a big party tonight up on the hill, and Vinea's name was mentioned."

His heart nearly stopped. "Mentioned in what way?"

"Just that she was being honored. If she is attending a party, why didn't she let me know?"

Devon fisted his hands. This had to be a lie—a rumor—spread by the Changelings. "Did they say where this *party* was taking place?"

"Marissa thought it was in their community center."

"Tell Marissa thank you. When I find Vinea, I'll have her call you." Devon disconnected. "What do you think?" he asked his brother.

Connor frowned. "Do you really want to know?"

Fuck. "Don't say she's colluding with the Changelings. She's not."

He held up his hand. "I would like nothing more than to agree, but why else would they honor her?"

Was he serious? "It's a hoax to get me to go up there. They want to get back at the McKinnons. We do have a good track record for ruining their plans."

"We do, but I don't understand why they'd want you. I've been a bigger pain in their ass than you."

"True, but you don't have a mate—someone to draw you there."

Connor's shoulders slumped. "Maybe you're right."

"How about asking Jackson to find this community center and fly his drone over the building?" Devon asked.

Connor slapped his thighs and stood. "I'll ask him. I just hope you aren't crushed if we find out she really has pulled the wool over your eyes once more."

"Don't worry. I trust Vinea."

"That's precisely what worries me."

Connor spun around and left. Devon refused to be swayed by his brother's harsh words. Connor didn't know Vinea like he did. She had changed. He was sure of it.

Less than a half hour later, Connor pushed open his door, his eyes brighter. "Jackson thinks he may have found something. We all need to head to the auditorium."

Heart pounding, Devon jumped up and jogged after Connor, who'd taken off down the hallway. Inside the large room, Jackson had images from the drone up on the large screen. Kip and Sam were already seated, and Connor moved to the front.

"Tell them what you found," Connor said.

Jackson remained on the platform behind the table that held his computer. "I've spent countless hours studying each of the thermal images to learn which ones haven't moved in over a day. I had several ideas, but when Devon found out about a possible party up on the hill at their convention center, I looked closer. I didn't see anything at their large assembly hall, but there is a house nearby that previously had been abandoned. Since I have hundreds of hours of footage from that area I've been collecting for months, I compared the activity between now and a month ago. Before, no one had bothered with the place. Now, the building has several people milling about in an orderly fashion around the perimeter."

"Like they are guarding it," Devon said, his heart banging

against his ribs.

"Yes. There is one room where a relatively stationary person resides."

As much as Devon wanted to demand the location so that he could rush to her rescue, they needed a plan. He wasn't that foolish.

Connor looked around. "Any ideas?"

"While I think they are looking for a confrontation with us, and as much as I hate to suggest it, we can't just charge in," Sam said. "Since this is a recent feed, the number of men would be fairly accurate.

"I agree with Sam," Devon said.

Sam nodded. "Furthermore, I don't advise calling in half our Clan to take out the guards. A widespread slaughter would only make things worse."

"I think we can handle a few guards if we're careful," Devon said. He then turned to Kip. "If there is power to that building, could you disable it? We don't need to have alarms going off."

"No problem," Kip said.

Devon turned back to Sam. "Thoughts?"

"I can do a mind bending trick on the guards. I'll convince them that Vinea has been moved to a different venue, and they are needed there."

His pulse sped up at the possibilities. "Sounds good, but what are we missing? Unexpected things always pop up."

"How about asking Dalton to join us?" Jackson said. "There seems to be two to three people in the house with Vinea at all times. Having a tiger shifter would throw the odds in our favor."

Devon nodded. "Let's ask him."

"I'll text him now and request that he come help," Sam said, pulling out his phone.

"Good. Anything else we should consider?" Devon asked.

"What if Brother Jacob shows up?" Kip asked.

Devon smiled. "If he attacks, I'd love nothing more than to kill the sorry son of a bitch myself."

Chapter Twenty-One

I T WAS AFTER five by the time Dalton was available to help them swarm the Changeling outpost for Vinea. In that time, Rye and Kalan had rallied the Clan, who were ready to jump in should things go south.

And while Devon understood the need for caution, his wolf didn't.

If those Changelings harm her in any way, no telling what I might do, his wolf warned.

Cool it. We have to stick to the plan, Devon threw back. So what if his stomach had already turned into a roiling acid pit. *One false move could cause Vinea her life—and ours.*

Fine, but I don't like it.

Even though Devon had nearly died when two Changelings had attacked him, with Vinea in their grasp, he could take on three wolves and win.

"Do we have a strategy if Vinea isn't there?" Sam asked.

Devon spun to face him. "Are you saying you don't think the Changelings have her?"

Sam held up his hands. "Not saying one way or the other, but I do think you need to decide what you'll do if she's elsewhere."

He was right. "I realize there hasn't been a ransom demand or any contact, but it's the only thing that makes sense."

"Sam's right," Connor said. "Preparation is the key to success."

"Fine," Devon said. "After Sam disables the guards, I'll go in alone to check. If they catch me, I'll be the only one they attack."

"Don't be stupid," Connor said. "That's too dangerous."

"It's better than all of us being slaughtered if this is a trap."

Sam placed a hand on his shoulder. "I know you need to do this, but if you're too emotional, it could cost Vinea her life. Trust me; I've seen it happen in my squad."

He didn't want to believe that. "I'll make sure my wolf keeps out of the way."

"We'll have your six," Sam shot back.

Connor nodded. "Good. Do we all know what we need to do?"

"Yes," they said in unison.

Jackson rushed in. "I flew the drone over once more and something's wrong."

Devon's heart stopped for a second. "What is it?"

"No one's in the house guarding Vinea."

Everyone looked at each other. "Why would they leave her alone? Even if they don't know we're coming, they wouldn't abandon her." Devon asked. "I don't want to think the stationary person is some plant to fool us into charging in."

"I don't like it either." Connor said. "I smell a trap."

Didn't I just say that? Devon kept his sarcastic response to himself.

Dalton piped up. "We have to go in and check things out—albeit carefully. You can be assured the guards will be somewhere close. Now that we're aware of them, it won't be a surprise.

Jackson shook his head. "How do you know they are close by?"

"It's the only logical course of action."

"I don't know where they could be," Jackson said. "I don't see a clump of heat signatures ready to pounce."

Sam snapped his fingers. "They might have heard your drone and hid under space blankets. That would block their infrared thermal imaging signature for at least a short time. Eventually, they'll overheat and you'll be able to detect them."

"Fuck, Sam's right," Jackson said, pressing his lips together, seemingly angry at himself for the oversight. "I wasn't thinking straight."

"So we proceed as if the guards will charge at any moment," Connor said. Everyone nodded his agreement.

In relative silence they piled into two vehicles and headed up to the hill.

Hold tight, Vinea, we'll be there soon. She couldn't hear him, but he hoped the positive thoughts would reach her nonetheless.

THE DIM LIGHT in her room suddenly went out, bathing Vinea in total darkness. Her pulse soared as shades of her past surfaced, souring her gut. What was going on? If only she could float out and see what was happening, she'd know. Damn curse.

Wanting to hear something, she held her breath. A door creaked in the distance, breaking the death pall in the room, and she debated calling for help. If Devon and his men were here, she wanted to let them know her location. On the other hand, it could be the evil Changelings planning something.

No wait. They already knew where she was, so a shout out couldn't cause further harm.

"Hello? Anyone there?" Vinea's voice failed to project, forcing her to swallow in between words. They hadn't provided her with much water—or food for that matter—causing her throat to dry out. She tried again. "I'm in here!"

One set of footsteps sounded. Did they belong to Devon or to the creepy Brother Jacob? It had to be her captor coming to make sure she hadn't caused the power disruption—as if she could. Reason intruded. It couldn't be Devon. He'd never come alone. The lack of food must be muddling her thought process.

The footsteps drew near, and then the door creaked open.

"Vinea?"

That one whispered word came from Devon, and her heartbeat jacked up. If she hadn't loved him before, she surely would have fallen in love with him then. "Yes. Over here," she said softly.

Tears brimmed. She wanted to tell him that he needed to be careful, but she trusted he understood the risks.

With his shifter sight, he found her right away. A flashlight clicked on, and he tapped his ear. "I found her. She's okay."

Relief weakened her muscles. "How did you get past the guards?" she asked.

"I'll tell you as soon as I get you out of here." With quick precision, he untied her wrists and ankles, and pain flowed to the stiff muscles. "Why didn't you just disappear to escape?"

"They had a witch put a curse on me. I couldn't become invisible." The thought once more sickened her.

"We'll deal with that later."

Once he helped her up, Vinea wrapped her arms around him and kissed him. "Thank you."

"We need to hurry. Did they hurt you?"

She'd received a few slaps, but nothing she couldn't handle. "Not much."

Before they could take a step, three red-eyed wolves with bared teeth rushed into the room, and her heart raced into overdrive. Devon dropped the flashlight, and the light cast eerie shadows on the walls, making the new arrivals larger than life.

"Vinea, stay back," Devon commanded. "When you can, run!"

Those were the last words Devon said before he shifted. The first wolf with a white spot on his forehead leapt in the air and landed on Devon. She cringed and clamped a hand over her mouth to keep from screaming. Just as the other two wolves crouched, ready to spring, she waved her hand, focusing all of her attention on freezing time.

A second later, both wolves became suspended in the air. Devon was safe from them for now, but she didn't know how long she could keep them at bay. He yelped when his attacker's teeth dug into his side, causing her to lose a bit of focus. Thankfully, the freeze remained in place.

After managing to throw the wolf off, Devon spun around and swiped a claw across the spotted wolf's nose. The animal retreated. Perhaps it was the rush of adrenaline from seeing the other two animals halted in mid air that gave him the energy to charge this wolf. With a lunge, he landed on the animal's back and took a huge bite out of his side. The spotted wolf cried out and dropped to his haunches.

Scraping paws from down the hallway charged toward them. Just as they reached the doorway, Vinea's ability to hold the freeze broke. The two wolves that had been suspended dropped to the ground and came at Devon. But before they reached him, the most beautiful white tiger raced in and sped toward those two. Behind him came another wolf, one that was dark gray with sand colors woven in.

Vinea pressed her back against the wall, not wanting to get in the way of the mayhem. The coppery stench of blood filled the small space, along with growls and whines. Slowly, the whimpers subsided and three dead men lay naked and broken on the cold floor. The fight was over before it had really started. The white tiger and both wolves shifted back. She recognized Connor but not the other man.

Heart pounding too fast, her muscles didn't unlock for a moment. When they finally did, she ran to Devon who was down on one knee, breathing fast. "Are you okay?"

"Yes." He rubbed his arm where teeth marks had left an impression.

Devon picked up something that he then placed in his ear. He eased to his feet and rose, clasping a hand on her arm. "We need to get out of here."

"I'd like nothing more."

A bit hunched over, Devon wrapped an arm around her waist and led her out the door. Connor and the other man followed. They were halfway down the hall when the lights clicked on, and all three men stopped. Devon tapped his ear bud. "Kip, did you turn on the lights? Then what's going on? Gotcha."

Devon tapped his ear once more and then faced his men. "Two

Changelings just entered through the back. Sam was able to incapacitate the rest, but these two came from a different direction."

The white tiger shifter nodded. "If there are only two, I can take them. You get Vinea to safety."

"I'll help you," Connor said to the tall man.

Before Devon could lead her away, angry voices sounded, and suddenly Brother Jacob appeared with a man she didn't recognize. Jacob stopped and held out a hand for the man to halt. Jacob's lips twisted, and the hair on his face darkened. "What are you doing here?" he said with a sneer on his face.

She thought the answer was obvious.

"Vinea, go out to the front," Devon commanded through gritted teeth. "Our men are out there. You'll be safe."

No way in hell was she going to leave Devon with Brother Jacob and that other man. It didn't matter that Sam had incapacitated all the other men or that Connor and the other weretiger could help. She might be able to do something. "No."

"Don't argue with me, just do it!" Devon practically shouted.

Not wanting to distract him, she turned toward the main entrance and pretended to leave, though she had no intention of actually doing so.

Without warning, Brother Jacob and his sidekick shifted, forcing her to look in their direction. The man who had been the white tiger stepped forward, but Devon held up his hand. "Dalton, Brother Jacob is mine."

Vinea wanted to shout at him to let his friend help, that he didn't need to be some hero to prove something to her, but the stubborn man never listened.

All three men shifted again. This time Connor and Dalton stalked Brother Jacob's sidekick while Devon crouched low in front of the black and tan wolf. She had thought Devon was a large wolf, but Brother Jacob was even bigger. His genetically defective genes seemed to have imbued him with extra weight and muscle. She could only hope that Dalton and Connor would kill the sidekick and then come back to help Devon with his foe.

Brother Jacob snarled and charged, aiming for Devon's hind leg. He hit the mark, biting down on Devon's upper thigh, and when he yelped, her breath hitched. Yes, she could freeze time again, and maybe even interfere somehow, but Devon would never forgive her if she did. He needed to battle with this man—whether it was to prove something to her, to himself, or to his family.

Part of her didn't want to watch the fight-to-the-death, but her love for Devon made her stay put. The sidekick howled, and the tiger and wolf stepped back as he transformed into a dead human. Yes! One down. Only one more to go.

She expected both friends to jump into the fray, but they merely surrounded the two fighters, honoring Devon's wish. Keeping out of sight, Vinea held her breath, wincing every time Brother Jacob got in a good scratch or bite. Devon growled. Keeping his eyes on the red-eyed devil, he circled him, while Dalton and Connor moved back to give them room. As if the two fighters heard a shotgun go off, they both launched themselves into the air. Teeth collided, and they pawed at each other, jockeying for the best position. When they landed, Brother Jacob had a hold of Devon's throat.

No! Vinea's knees nearly buckled. Her mind swirled, trying to think of something she could do to save him. If she'd been able to become invisible, she could have rushed in and kicked Brother Jacob. He deserved all the pain she could give him for what he'd done.

When both Dalton and Connor moved closer, Devon's growl stopped them.

She couldn't watch, so she closed her eyes and prayed to her sister, to her mother, and to her father, begging them for forgiveness. When she opened her eyes a minute later, blood covered the floor, and the strong stench of copper stung her nostrils.

Both wolves stood facing each other, poised to charge. This time, Devon made the first move. Instead of leaping like he had before, he kept low. When he was close to Brother Jacob, Devon rolled onto his back and then latched onto Brother Jacob's neck.

Jacob's red eyes practically glowed, and then his legs gave way. Not until he collapsed on top of Devon, did Devon let go. When the man she loved didn't move, Vinea rushed to his side. No sooner had she knelt down than Jacob died, transforming into his human form.

She feared Devon's wound was too much for his wolf to handle. Without giving it a second thought, she placed her hands on his head and concentrated on drawing out all of the evil. Pain soared through her veins, but she would willingly take ten times that amount if it would help him heal. Her heart fluttered, and her body weakened.

When Devon opened his eyes, she let go and tried to smile, but she didn't have the energy. A set of hands grabbed her shoulders, and the last thing she remembered were her eyes rolling back in her head.

Chapter Twenty-Two

D EVON WAS BESIDE himself. He paced in front of his bed, watching Vinea's chest slowly rise and fall, willing her to open her eyes. He'd contacted Missy again, and after she performed her magic, she said while she couldn't make any promises, she was hopeful Vinea would recover. After all, Vinea had healed quickly the last time.

What had possessed Vinea to try to heal him again? If Missy hadn't been able to rush to the rescue, Vinea might have died. Why couldn't she understand that his wolf would have taken care of him?

Vinea's eyes slowly opened, and Devon immediately sat on the bed and picked up her hand. "How are you feeling?"

She took a moment to respond. Vinea glanced around, probably trying to figure out where she was. The last thing she would have remembered was being in that terrible house.

"Kind of weak, but okay."

He blew out a breath. "That was a pretty foolish thing for you to do," he said, keeping his tone light. "You know my wolf would have healed me. It just would have taken some time."

She glanced away. "You would have done the same thing if I'd been injured," Vinea said struggling to talk.

"Yes, I would have." This discussion seemed to be stressing her out. Her breath was quickening. "You need to rest now. We'll talk later."

"I've rested enough."

"Vinea," he said in the same voice his father used to use on the kids when he was young—stern but compassionate.

She grabbed his hand. "I need to find out about Mr. Sanford. He never showed up at the café, and I'm worried about him."

Devon remembered she was on her way to his house when she disappeared. "He's fine. I spoke with him. We'll talk about it later." A small smile flitted across her lips, and then she was out.

Confident that Vinea would heal, Devon returned to the living room. As soon as Dalton and Connor had helped them both home, they had gone back to headquarters to make sure things were ready when the shit hit the fan. The Changelings would need some time to regroup after losing their leader, but they would return with a vengeance. While killing Brother Jacob had been one of Devon's finer moments, it might have been his stupidest one. In the past, the Changelings hadn't come right out and attacked his Clan. Now, they might.

Needing to stay in the loop, he called Connor. "How's Vinea?" Connor asked without saying hello.

"She was awake for a little bit, but she's asleep again now."

"Is she going to be okay?"

Devon was pleased that his brother sounded so concerned. "I think so. It will take some time though."

"Look, I owe you an apology."

He sure did. "I'm listening."

"I misjudged Vinea."

That was all he needed to hear. "I get it. She hurt me the first time, and you didn't want it to happen again."

"Sorry, bro. I was an ass. I should have trusted your instincts."

"No, I was fooled by the evil Vinea the first time, and we both know it. You believed she was that same person. You were just trying to protect me, and I appreciate it," Devon shot back.

"So we're good?"

Devon could never stay mad at Connor for long. "We're good. Have you heard any scuttlebutt about the take down?"

"No. The Changelings are keeping everything quiet. I imagine it's not something they want to brag about. I figure it will take some time for them to take care of the mess and regroup. They'll need to find a new leader, though it will probably be John Ernst."

"He might be worse than Brother Jacob. Shit, maybe I made things worse." The door to the bedroom opened. "Look I gotta go. Vinea needs me."

"Tell her I'm sorry."

"I will." Devon hung up and rushed down the hallway. "You should be resting." Yes, he sounded like a broken record, but he couldn't help himself.

He reached out and wrapped his arms around her. She snuggled her head against his shoulder, and her scent shot his damn wolf to attention. "I'd rather rest out here with you."

He placed an arm around her waist for support and led her to the sofa. "Fine, I'll get you propped up on the couch, and then get you something to drink. Or are you hungry?"

"Do you have any hot chocolate? I've found that it relaxes me."

"Coming right up." Devon came back carrying the steaming cups. After placing them on the coffee table, he then pulled it closer so she could reach it easily. He lifted her legs and sat down, placing them over his lap.

"So tell me how you ended up in that house," he said. He hadn't wanted to discuss the tragic events until he was convinced she was strong enough, but she seemed on the mend.

She blew on the steaming mug then sipped her hot chocolate. "A man I'd never seen before came into the café around the time that Mr. Sanford usually shows up and asked if I'd seen him."

"And once you realized your regular customer was late, you began to worry."

"Yes. The man was supposedly Mr. Sanford's lawyer." She explained about the house he'd driven her to. "I remember thinking that it didn't look like how Mr. Sanford had described it, but I didn't say anything. I should have gone with my gut instinct and vanished."

He almost smiled at her answer to everything. "If you had disappeared, it might have made you a more valuable target."

"True, but in this case, they already knew who I was. To finish the story, just as we reached the door, someone came up behind me and hit me on the head, knocking me out. I felt a pinch and then the sting of being injected with a drug. I don't remember anything until I woke up in that room."

Anger at the attack once more stabbed him in the gut. "If I hadn't already killed Brother Jacob, I would rush up there now and tear him limb from limb."

She chuckled. "I don't think it would have been that easy. By the way, how did you get past the guards?"

"Sam incapacitated them."

"Wow. After what I tried to do to him, I'm surprised he was willing to help."

Devon smiled. "Everyone believes that you've changed. I think Sam has even forgiven you."

"I'll have to thank him."

Devon nodded. "What else do you remember?"

"When I came to, I was really mad at myself for not leaving when I had the chance. My lapse must have been because I had been worried about Mr. Sanford."

Devon looked off to the side. "The Changelings must have been planning this for a while. They knew just which of your buttons to push."

"I know."

Vinea was vulnerable. If anyone doubted the change in her, this would prove it. She was almost too kind. "If something like this ever happens again, we need to get something straight," he said after drinking some of his now-cooled hot chocolate.

"What's that?"

"You can't keep healing me."

She placed a hand on his arm. "What was I supposed to do? Let you die?"

"As I said, my wolf would have healed me."

She shook her head. "If you had seen yourself like I did, you too would have thought you had maybe an hour to live. Besides, when Naliana shot me with light, part of the process to rid my body of the evil was to give me the ability to heal. As I become a better person, my ability to draw the pain from others increases—or so I've found."

"I don't like it. If you keep doing that, people will learn of your abilities, and you'll have hoards of people flocking here to ask for your help. Some might even be Changelings."

Not that he and Vinea would be in Silver Lake for much longer, as he had his own office to run in Pittsburgh.

She looked off to the side. "I had wondered about that. I should probably restrict my healing only to those I love."

Devon stilled. "Love?"

"Yes, love. Like you."

"Me?"

"Yes, I love you, Devon McKinnon, and I have for a long time."

He lifted her legs, and she sat upright beside him. Devon leaned over, cupped her face, and then kissed her gently, not wanting to take advantage of her when she was still healing. Even that small touch caused his wolf to wake up and demand more. Devon had to work hard not to mate with her right then and there.

His breath came out too fast. "If I continue to touch you, I'll want to make love with you, which will lead to mating." Devon couldn't believe how far they had come since their first meeting. "You are the most important person in my life, Vinea. I love you."

She grinned. "Then show me."

"You aren't ready for that yet. You need to rest more. Actually, you should be in bed."

"With you, maybe, but geez, I've been in bed for almost a day now. Besides, Missy's magic worked."

He was so happy to hear that. "I think ever since she mated with Zane, she's become a stronger healer."

Vinea smiled. "Then I can recommend her to anyone who needs

help."

He stroked her face. "I like that idea better."

Vinea set down her drink and straddled him. "Oh, yeah?"

"Ahem," said a female voice in the direction of the kitchen.

Vinea's eyes widened, and she jumped off his lap. "What are you doing here?"

Devon twisted around, and they both shot to their feet. "Naliana?"

His tongue was barely able to say her name. He had forgotten that the white moon was tonight, the one night Naliana made her appearance. With everything going on, it also had slipped his mind about her being Vinea's sister.

Naliana smiled. "I came to congratulate you, my beautiful sister."

Vinea's eyes widened "For what?"

He could see the family resemblance. "Because you finally allowed your white light back inside you and are fully embracing it. As I've said before, I tried to help when you were sent to the dark side, but I was told that it wouldn't be for long. I'd just met James, and after I informed them that I wasn't ready to return, my punishment was to be kept away from you."

Vinea clasped Devon's hand. "I never did understand how you could defy our parents."

Naliana shrugged. "Think of it as letting my heart guide me. I figured if I was supposed to be the one to pair shifters and Wendayans, I needed to live among the mortals and learn about love."

Vinea staggered back, and Devon slipped his arm around her waist. "How about we all sit?" he suggested.

Naliana floated in front of them and then took the seat across from the sofa.

"So you really wanted to contact me all those years ago?" Vinea said to her sister.

"Yes. I knew deep inside you were a good person, albeit immature and rather impulsive. I'm happy to say that you've seasoned now, though I have to give credit to Devon for helping you."

A slight smile lifted Vinea's lips. "I'm seasoned. I like that."

Naliana looked down at her hands for a moment. "There are things you should know before you and Devon mate."

He planted a hand on Vinea's thigh. "What's that?" His voice came out harsher than he'd intended.

"Vinea is an immortal, but if she mates with you, she no longer will be."

Injustice slammed into him. "But you're mated to James and he's immortal. How is that any different from what Vinea and I have?"

"To save James's life and give him immortality, I had to return to the light realm for good. Do you want Vinea to do that?"

Conflicting emotions slammed into him. He looked over at her.

"No," she said before he could answer. "I want to stay here. With Devon."

"But we won't mate. I don't want her to make that sacrifice."

Vinea twisted toward him. "Like hell we won't. Why would I want to live any longer than you anyway? It would be a terrible and lonely life."

While seeming impossible, his love for her strengthened. "I guess that settles it." He faced Naliana. "Thank you for everything you have done to help both of us."

Naliana stood and opened her arms. "Can I get a hug before I go?"

Vinea choked out a sob. Slowly, she eased to her feet, stepped around the coffee table, and then flung herself into her sister's embrace. Her back heaved, and he hoped those tears were joyful ones.

Naliana stroked her sister's hair and rubbed her back. "Our parents wanted to let you know that you are welcome to visit any time you want."

Vinea leaned back, tears running down her cheeks. "Really?

They want to see me?"

"You are now the daughter they've always dreamed of having."

Vinea swiped a hand across her cheek. "I would love that, but I'd want them to meet Devon too."

"Perhaps that can be arranged." Naliana let go of Vinea. "I should get back to James. We have so little time together as it is. I will always love you, Vinea."

"Can I ask one more thing?"

"Of course."

Vinea looked at Devon and then back at Naliana. "Can a goddess and a shifter have children?"

"I can't honestly say, but I see no reason why not." She smiled and so did Vinea.

"I love you and thank you," Vinea said.

Not only had Naliana given her sister the wonderful gift of forgiveness, she'd given him much more. Devon stood. "Would it be totally inappropriate to ask for a hug too?"

Naliana opened her arms and smiled. The hug that followed filled him with hope and acceptance. A second later, she was gone.

Chapter Twenty-Three

DEVON GATHERED VINEA in his arms, his heart pounding. "What do you think?"

She looked up at him. "I'm kind of in shock. Here I thought she hated me, when in reality my sister was only trying to help me."

Devon leaned back and lifted her chin. "That's what life is about. Living and learning."

"I know your brother and friends thought I was evil for the longest time, but once I returned, you believed in me. Thank you."

He hadn't the whole time, but he trusted her now and that was all that mattered. He dragged a thumb down her cheek. "What's in the past should stay in the past. We need to discuss the here and now."

Vinea slipped out of his embrace and planted a hand on her hip, looking so adorable. "If you're asking me if I still want to mate with you, the answer is a resounding yes."

His heart soared. "You'll be giving up immortality if we mate."

She smiled. "Like I said, once you're gone, there will be no reason to live."

Devon picked her up and spun her around slowly. "You've made me the happiest man."

Needing her to rest, he returned her to the sofa. Vinea grinned then straddled him once more.

"Whoa. Let's not be hasty," he said. "You're not at full strength. You were at death's door a few hours ago."

"I'm a goddess, remember? I heal fast." When she rubbed her bottom against his crotch, his wolf growled.

"If you're positive you're healthy enough, I'd be happy to oblige."

Vinea swiped a hand down her front, and all of her clothes disappeared.

He moaned, positive his eyes were glowing a deep amber. "Goddess, I love that trick."

Vinea practically giggled; a sound that seemed so incongruent with the sophisticated woman he'd first seen in the bar in Vermont. He definitely liked this free-spirited version better.

"Really? I never would have guessed." She looked down at his erection that was ready to burst through his zipper.

Devon lightly slapped her ass. "Yes smartass, you make my body sing with pleasure. In fact, my wolf wants to eat you."

She laughed. "I'm no little red riding hood."

He wiggled his eyebrows suggestively. "You could be."

"I'm game." She leaned over, and when she nipped at his lips, any control he had disappeared.

Mate, mate, his bad boy wolf cheered.

This time Devon was in total agreement. He'd always lived the cautious life, often quick to judge others. Now, he could see what he'd missed. If Vinea loved him enough to give up eternal life, he'd make sure to keep her happy.

Vinea threaded her fingers through his hair, and when she grabbed hold, he couldn't help but growl. Vinea was feisty, disobedient, and totally delicious—the opposite of him—but that was what made them so perfect together. "Kiss me," he demanded.

She smiled. "I thought you'd never ask."

"Since when do you need an invitation?" He loved bantering with her.

"Are you giving me carte blanche?"

That sparkle in her eyes meant trouble. "I am."

She swiped a hand down his body, and a moment later, he was

naked too. "So much better."

He had to agree.

Kissing him, she pressed her tits against his chest, and Devon had to work to stay in control. Fortunately, his wolf seemed to enjoy the foreplay enough to keep from expressing himself more fully.

Devon's hands roamed down her slim back to her delicious ass, his cock throbbing and pulsing. A second later, he had her on her back on the sofa with him nestled between her legs. "I have to taste you. Mind you, it is merely to determine if you are healthy enough for sex."

She laughed. "You are so full of shit, but I love you nonetheless."

"Remember that when I'm tormenting you with my tongue."

"What are you waiting for?"

Devon didn't need any more encouragement. The first swipe had him sucking in a breath. Her sweet taste and lemony scent seeped deep into his soul. This was his mate, the woman he needed and wanted.

She grabbed his shoulders and lifted her hips. One thing he had to say about Vinea was that she wasn't shy. Devon slipped two fingers into her wet opening and then closed his eyes, needing to center himself for a moment. He wanted to sink his cock so deep into her she'd taste it, but he also needed to bring her to the brink first.

Vinea moaned and groaned, clawing at the sofa. "Please, Devon."

Wanting to please her, he stopped then stood up next to the sofa. Stepping close, he leaned over so that his cock was within her grasp. Vinea lifted up on her elbows and drew him deep within her mouth. Dear goddess in heaven, the woman would be his undoing.

Twisting around, Vinea pressed her shoulder against the sofa, freeing one hand. She grabbed the base of his cock, and when she pumped her fist, he had to grab her wrist. "Easy. I'm so ready."

"So am I!"

"Me too!" his wolf joined in.

ALL OF THE ill effects from healing Devon disappeared the moment their lips met. The man seemed to have a healing magic all his own—or else her body was so in tune with his that she was able to draw on his strength.

Devon grabbed her by the waist and lifted her off the sofa. Needing full body contact, Vinea wrapped her legs around his waist. As she pressed her opening against his hard cock, lust and total bliss blasted her. She held onto his shoulders and kissed him back—hard. Holy goddess. Lustful shards sizzled up and down her spine, igniting her core. What this man did to her! Here she'd spent hundreds of years in the dark realm, unaware of what real passion was all about. If only she'd listened to her sister early on and tried to reform, she might have had this sooner. Then again, if she had, she might never have met Devon.

With their tongues tangled, he walked forward until her back met the front door. The wood gave her enough support for her to use her arms to touch his delicious body. Devon moaned, and she increased the speed of their mingling. Her senses became so heightened that when her hard nipples rubbed against his chest, she nearly shattered.

Devon broke the kiss and moved back a half step. He then lowered his head and sucked on her tits. "I need these," he mumbled.

Joy. Bliss. Elation. That first lick had her nearly coming apart at the seams as endorphins mixed with hormones and zinged through her. "Don't stop," she begged.

She clawed his broad shoulders as he tugged and pulled on each of her sensitive nipples. Dropping her head back, she opened her mouth to suck in more air, needing the oxygen. On the next tug, she pressed her feet against his thighs and ground against his erection, the added pressure pushing her over the edge. Her fiery climax claimed her a second later. She gasped as she let the total bliss of pleasure wash over her.

He lifted his head and kissed her with more passion than she thought possible. Having someone as wonderful as Devon want her this much was almost more than she could comprehend.

Needing more of him, she plunged into his mouth, swirling her tongue around his faster and faster. He matched her fervor. Devon then slipped a hand between them and a second later his cock was at her entrance. Excitement soared. As soon as he let go, she lowered her hips and encompassed him, causing bolts of electricity to light her up from the inside. Devon grunted, and the hair on his face roughened.

"I need you, Vinea," he ground out.

"Not more than I need you."

Between his hands supporting her butt, and the door preventing her from falling backward, she fucked him with abandon. She might be giving up a lot by mating with him, but she was definitely coming out ahead.

Every thrust sent her higher, until she was in a frenzy of excitement. Fire burned deep inside her as Devon lowered his lips to her neck. The time had come for them to fully mate, and she exploded with ecstasy.

"Yes, Devon. Mate with me."

"Oh, Vinea." As he dragged his lips across her neck, his teeth sharpened, and she tried not to tense.

For hundreds of years, she had watched couples mate from afar. Now it was her turn to experience that wonder first hand. When he sunk his teeth into her, her world spun. Colors crisscrossed the back of her eyelids, the air seemed lighter, and every nerve ending caught fire. With the next thrust, his cock expanded, filling her so completely that her orgasm claimed her hard. Waves of erotic bliss swamped her, and she let out a high-pitched keen.

Devon lifted his mouth away from the area where her neck met her shoulder and licked away the drops of blood. He then clamped down on the sensitive shell of her ear, whispering words of love. As much as she never wanted to leave his embrace, eventually Vinea's legs slipped down to the floor. Weakened from the most powerful event of her life, Vinea held on tight.

"I don't ever want to let you go," he whispered into her ear.

"Then don't."

THE NEXT DAY, Vinea asked Devon to drive her to Mr. Sanford's house. She wanted to see for herself that the old man was okay. Before she went, she stopped at the café and bought him a cherry Danish—one of his favorite pastries.

The only difficult part was coming up with an explanation to her boss about her absence. She told him she hadn't been at a party up at the hill, but rather she'd been ill. Vinea told him that she'd agreed to housesit for someone who was on vacation. She must have eaten something that caused an allergic reaction and had passed out. It was why she hadn't called.

"That's why I was so frantic when she didn't return," Devon said. "She hadn't mentioned she would be at a friend's house."

Thankfully, Devon had agreed to go along with her story. Lying was distasteful, but there was no way she could explain about the Changelings wanting revenge!

"I'm so sorry," her boss said. "I'm just glad you're okay."

"Me too."

"Are you coming back to work?"

"I'll be here tomorrow." How long she'd stay in town, she didn't know. That conversation would have to wait until another time.

When they arrived at Mr. Sanford's house, she was thrilled he was home.

"Come in. What a nice surprise! I was worried when your fellow here came looking for you."

Unfortunately, she had to give him the same story she gave her boss about being ill. "But I'm fine now." She handed him the Danish. "I thought you might like this."

Mr. Sanford's face glowed. "You are too kind. Can I get you anything to drink?"

"We can't stay long, but a glass of tea would be wonderful."

AFTER A LOVING talk with Mr. Sanford, they returned home. Devon had contacted Izzy who had spoken with someone about possibly removing the curse, and she was on her way over now.

She was expected any moment, and Vinea was beside herself with worry. She had no reason to be. Mr. Sanford was alive and well, and yesterday's lovemaking had been nothing short of amazing. Then there was Naliana's visit. Topping that was mating with Devon. Never in her wildest dreams had she believed anything that wonderful was possible—especially given all the bad things she'd done in her life. Second chances truly existed.

She should be bouncing off the walls with joy, but meeting with this witch could alter her life. "Where is she?" Vinea asked, her voice shaking.

Devon stepped behind her and rubbed her shoulders. "Don't worry. Izzy said Ophelia will be here soon."

"Ophelia?"

Devon stilled. "Why? Do you know her?"

She glanced off to the side for a moment then shrugged. "I doubt it. It's just that I vaguely remember having an aunt Ophelia. That's all."

"Well, this woman is no goddess."

Vinea spun around. "Why is she coming here though? Izzy said that people always met with the town's most powerful witch in the woods near Izzy's old house."

He stroked her cheek. "She is coming here because you're special. I bet it's not every day that she gets to meet a goddess."

She didn't feel special. "At the moment, I'm hardly different from any other person on earth. I can't teleport or become invisible anymore." Not to mention she was no longer immortal. The concept of death, however, had yet to sink in.

"That's only temporary. Even if she can't remove the curse,

you're still a goddess to me—a very special and sexy one."

Vinea loved Devon for trying to cheer her up. "Yes, I can dress and undress both of us and yes, I am able to freeze time, but that's all."

Devon wrapped an arm around her waist. "You were a goddess last night in bed."

That made her smile. "I'm not talking about sex."

He leaned over and nibbled her neck, right where he'd bit her. "Why not? It was great, wasn't it?"

She wrapped her arms around his neck. "More than great, it was wonderful, fantastic, and stupendous."

Before she had the chance to enjoy him again, a knock sounded, and she stiffened.

"I'll get it," Devon said.

A moment later, a wizened old lady in a long black dress walked in. She was thin to the point of gauntness, yet seemed to possess great strength at the same time. A tightness vibrated in Vinea's chest, and it took her a moment to recognize it. "You are a goddess!" Vinea said with awe. Other than her sister, she hadn't run into anyone from the light realm.

Ophelia glanced toward Devon. "Yes, my dear, but I would appreciate it if you keep that secret to yourself. Only Izzy and her mother know of my heritage. No one else."

"Of course." There was something about this woman that almost looked familiar, but given that she appeared to be close to one hundred, it was probably just wishful thinking that she knew her.

Ophelia looked over at Devon and the light streaming in from the outside silhouetted her face. The strong nose and high cheekbones gave it away. Her pulse soared, and her heart pounded in her chest. "Aunt Ophelia?" Vinea blurted.

The older woman faced her. "You recognize me, dear?"

"Yes. You and Mom have the same heart-shaped face."

Vinea swore the older woman blushed. "Thank you. I hadn't wanted to say anything since you haven't seen your mom in so long."

Without another thought, she embraced her. "It's okay. Please sit down. We need to catch up."

Devon slipped into the kitchen, probably to make some coffee and to give them privacy. Vinea sat next to her and clasped her aunt's hands. "Tell me why you're on earth?" Vinea asked.

"It's a long story, I'm afraid."

"I could use a long story. I've been starved for family news for a long time—that is until Naliana visited me yesterday."

"Yes, she told me. Like your sister, I volunteered to come to earth when it was in need of some guidance."

"Guidance for what?" Vinea always believed the gods of the light realm were all-knowing and all-wise.

"Rumor had it there were more than the two realms hovering nearby, and some of the gods worried they might not be friendly."

"Really? I thought there were only two realms, Earth and Cargonia. At least that was what I was told."

"That was the prevailing opinion at one time." Ophelia slipped her hands out of Vinea's grasp and placed them on her lap. "It was believed that the two realms were made up of the gods who were at odds as to how to run this planet. A few hundred million years later, that realm had another split. They didn't contact us, so we didn't know much about them. However, it was thought that some of their gods had come to earth."

Vinea found it hard to absorb all of this. "Did you find evidence of this third realm when you came here?"

"I did. On my quest for answers, I met a man from there."

"Another god?"

She shook her head. "No, a shifter. Borin was his name."

From the way her head tilted and the slight smile that escaped, she cared deeply for him. "What happened?"

"He was on a fact finding mission just as I was, but we realized that if we went back to our realms and divulged what we'd learned, there might be a war. The philosophies of the two realms were quite different."

Vinea didn't like the sadness tingeing her voice. "So you both chose to stay here instead?"

"Yes. In fact, we mated, and it was glorious." Ophelia reached out and squeezed Vinea's hand. "I'm sure you know what that's like."

Heat raced up her face. "I do. What happened to Borin?"

Her aunt looked away. "He was killed in battle."

"Where? On Earth or back in his realm?"

She waved a hand. "It's not important, and enough about me. I don't need to dredge up painful memories."

"I'm sorry." Vinea had wanted to ask if her aunt lost her immortality after she mated with a shifter, but she didn't want to add to Ophelia's pain. Perhaps it didn't work the same if the shifter came from a different realm.

"So, I hear those damned Changelings put a curse on you." While she sounded upbeat, her voice held a year's worth of pain.

As much as she wanted to ask a ton of questions, Vinea didn't want to make her aunt more uncomfortable. "They did. Is there anything you can do about it?"

She smiled. "I'm not a goddess for nothing. Now give me your hands."

Devon placed the two cups of coffee on the table in front of them without saying a word and sat in the chair opposite them. Ophelia's warm hands began to shake as her breathing slowed and her lips thinned. "The evil is very powerful but not long lasting," she announced with her eyes closed.

Vinea's pulse soared. "How long before the curse is gone?" Damn the Changelings for telling her it would last forever.

"Be patient." Aunt Ophelia began to chant something that Vinea only barely remembered. It was an incantation her mother had tried to teach her so long ago.

Slowly the anxiety seeped away, and Vinea could feel her strength returning. Her aunt let go and opened her eyes. "Things will return to normal soon enough. You just need to give it some time."

"Thank you." Vinea leaned over and hugged her. "Do you ever see Mom?"

"Oh yes. I visit the light realm when I can but never for more than a few hours at a time. I don't want to get caught up in the politics of the place. I belong here in Silver Lake." Aunt Ophelia looked over at Devon and held out her hands. "Can you help me up?"

Vinea doubted she needed the aid, but perhaps she just wanted an excuse to touch him, to get a reading off of him. Once standing, she smiled. "It was wonderful to see you, Vinea. I have followed your journey, and I must say I'm very pleased with how it has progressed."

"Me too." She had to ask one more question. "When you were mated to Borin, were you able to shift?"

Butterflies beat against her stomach, awaiting the answer. Vinea so wanted to be able to share in Devon's experiences.

Ophelia shook her head. "I'm afraid not. While we look fully human, we still are goddesses. I'm afraid Devon won't be able to become invisible any more than you can change form."

Vinea tried not to show her disappointment. "I understand."

Ophelia opened her arms, and Vinea stepped into her embrace. "If you ever need me, just call."

Vinea doubted her aunt had a smart phone. She probably meant to contact her telepathically. "Thank you."

After she tossed a smile at Devon, she left. He stepped in front of Vinea and drew her into an embrace. "I'm sensing a feeling of loss. Care to tell me about it?" he asked.

"I don't think I've come to terms with my feelings yet."

"You sure? I would think you'd be disappointed that you can't shift."

Devon seemed to draw out the truth in her. "You're right. Shifting would have given us something to do together." Vinea slid her hands down his chest.

He kissed her nose and then looked deep into her eyes. "You can share your life with me. Isn't that enough?"

"Yes, but aren't you a little bummed that you won't inherit some of my abilities?"

He hugged her. "Would I like to be able to teleport? Sure. Become invisible? Hell yeah, but I really can't miss what I've never had." Devon leaned back. "Being with you is a huge win for me. Okay?"

She nodded. "Okay."

His cell rang. "Excuse me." He slipped his phone out of his pocket. "It's my mom."

"I thought she and your dad were still on vacation."

"I thought so too." He stepped back and answered. "How's Montana? You are? Did something happen?" His smile disappeared. "That figures." He walked over to the kitchen and continued to chat. About a minute later, he disconnected and returned.

"What did they say?"

"When Dad heard what happened with the Changelings, he insisted on cutting their vacation a couple of days short. He always has this burning desire to lend a hand when things get tense between the two clans."

Vinea wrapped her arms around his neck. "Your parents sound wonderful."

"They are, but I have a feeling they are returning to meet you."

"Well, I did kind of meet your father."

His brows pinched. "When?"

"That first day when I was eavesdropping about the armored car heist."

"Ah, yes. That seemed so long ago, I almost forgot."

"How do you think they'll react? Surely, they've heard all about the evil Vinea."

He smiled. "Don't worry. I'm sure Connor, or maybe even Rye, has filled them in on all your new good deeds."

"I hope so." Though usually, most parents are highly critical of their child's mate. "When will we be seeing them?"

"Mom has planned a big family get together this weekend."

"I can't wait."

He led her to the sofa. "There is something we need to discuss first."

She didn't like the sound of this. "What is it?" Devon could scare her more than Androf ever could.

"You do know I run the McKinnon and Associates office in Pittsburgh?"

"Yes." What was he going to say? That he no longer was willing to work remotely, and would only see her on occasion?

"I'll need to be returning now that things have temporarily calmed down here."

"I figured." Her pulse soared, waiting for the bad news.

"Are you okay moving there?"

Her muscles sagged with relief. "And stay with you?"

"Of course, silly. I'm never letting you out of my sight again."

"I feel the same way. I'd love to go to Pittsburgh." She ran her hands down his arms. "Were you worried that I might want to stay in Silver Lake?"

"Maybe, since you've made friends here. You told your boss you'd go to work tomorrow."

Devon was so kind. "I did. Now I'll have to break the news to him. While I really like the people here, it's safer for me if I'm not within sight of the Changelings. I don't think I'm their favorite person."

"You're right about that."

Chapter Twenty-Four

D EVON WOULDN'T DENY he was a little nervous about introducing Vinea to his parents. Given that his mom loved to be around happy people, he believed the two would get along famously. His father was a different story. The man tended to be a bit judgmental, especially when it came to his children's welfare. His mom always claimed that Devon took after his dad in that regard. It might not matter that Rye vouched for Vinea.

Thankfully, Vinea's ability to disappear had returned, just as her aunt had promised, along with Vinea's sense of excitement about life.

Vinea spun around in front of him. "How do I look?"

He had loved each of the last five outfits she'd tried on, but he had to admit these light blue jeans with the knee-high boots and black body-hugging sweater was the most striking of them all. "You'll fit in well."

"Thank you." Vinea slipped the scoop-necked sweater down her shoulder. "I should have worn something to make it easier to show off my newly acquired mark. I love the wolf's paw print," she said trying to look over her shoulder and, most likely, failing.

Devon smiled and moved closer. "We don't need everyone to be distracted. Distracting me is enough."

She smiled. "I just wish you'd been given something from me."

He rubbed her arm. "Stop worrying. I have you. I don't need another mark to convince my wolf that we are mated."

"I guess you're right."

"You okay?" he asked, worried about her.

"I'm nervous. I've never *met the parents* before."

He wanted to press her against the wall and make love with her again, but he didn't want to be late. "You'll do fine."

"I hope so." She inhaled deeply then picked up her warm wool coat and slipped it on. "I'm ready!"

Devon grabbed the bottle of wine and led her out. The worst of the bad weather was over, but spring had yet to arrive. Even the short walk to his parents' house would be chilly.

"Who else beside your family will be there?" she asked, threading her arm through his.

Devon really enjoyed the romantic gesture. "Besides the family, everyone from the firm I'm guessing."

"Will you tell them we've mated?" she asked, looking up with hopeful eyes.

"I will, though I wouldn't be surprised if everyone knows already. I mentioned it to Connor." Her lips pursed. "He's good. I told you he apologized."

"I know, but actions speak louder than words. I'll have to see how he treats me."

She was a cautious one. Living in this world still had some ups and downs for her. "I think you'll be pleased."

About ten cars were parked in front of the big house, meaning Vinea would be able to chat with Izzy and the other members of his team for much of the evening and not have to worry about being subjected to his mom's grilling questions the whole time. Vinea might even find Finn and Chelsea interesting.

When they stepped inside, the chatter was loud and full of excitement. The only ones not there yet seemed to be Sam and Lexi.

Devon squeezed her waist. "Ready to be introduced?"

Vinea inhaled. "I guess so."

He honestly hadn't expected Vinea to be so tentative. She was normally brash and outgoing. She must understand that this was the next step in their relationship.

"Devon!" His mom rushed over to them. She hugged him and then faced Vinea. "You must be my son's mate."

"Yes, I'm Vinea."

So Connor *had* spilled the beans. "I hope my son has been treating you well. He can be a little distant at times."

"Mom, what's that supposed to mean?" Connor was more distant than he was. Finn and Rye were the more emotional brothers, and Chelsea was always bubbly.

"You don't often express your feelings like you should."

And here he thought this evening would revolve around asking Vinea a lot of questions. "I take after Dad, remember?"

The front door opened, and Lexi and Sam entered, providing a nice distraction. He hoped there'd be no hard feelings between them and Vinea. Given how Sam had rushed to help find her when she'd been kidnapped, he seemed to have accepted her.

"Vinea, do you want to help me in the kitchen?" his mom asked before Sam and Lexi could reach them. "I'm about to serve dinner."

"Of course, I'd be happy to help."

He hoped she'd be okay. Once Vinea disappeared with his mom, Devon wandered over to the large dining room table full of hors d'oeuvres. His dad slipped next to him and clamped a hand on his shoulder. "I heard you took down the leader of the Changelings."

Pride filled him, but only for a moment. "I battled with Brother Jacob. I was lucky to get in the final strike."

"What do you think the Changelings will do next?" His tone turned deadly serious.

"There's no telling, but I doubt it will be good."

He and his dad discussed the possible outcomes—most of them bad. They were in the middle of the discussion when Lexi, who was standing at the food table, clutched her throat and dropped a spring roll she'd dipped in some yellow sauce.

Sam rushed to her side. "What's wrong?"

Her eyes widened. "Can't breathe."

His whole body tensed. "Did you eat any peanut butter?"

She shook her head as she grabbed his arm. "I don't... think so." She wheezed as she sucked in air. "Spring rolls. Maybe?" She rubbed her throat as if trying to massage more air into her body.

"Where's your EpiPen?" Sam demanded.

Her body shook. "Home," she whispered.

Devon was no doctor, but he understood that an allergic reaction like this could be fatal if she didn't get the proper treatment fast. Lexi and Sam lived at least three miles away. Driving would take too long.

Vinea!

She rushed out. *"Yes?"*

She might not be able to shift, but they could communicate telepathically. "Lexi needs her EpiPen from their house, stat!"

Close to ten people were crowded around her as Sam led his mate to the sofa. "Where is it?" she asked Devon.

Sam must have heard and interjected. "It's in the top left-hand drawer next to our bed, but it will take too long to go get it."

"Where do you live?" she asked. Sam shot back some quick directions. "I'll be right back," Vinea said.

"You don't have time to—" She disappeared before he could finish his sentence.

Sam rushed back to Lexi and held her hand, trying to keep her calm. "I'm calling 911. Just relax."

Lexi's eyes rolled back in her head, and Sam caught her. He placed her on the sofa and coaxed her to respond. The room went deadly silent as if they were all praying to the gods above to help.

Please, Vinea, hurry.

About a minute later, his mate reappeared with the EpiPen in hand. "Here," she said as she handed it to Sam.

His mouth opened, but he quickly shut it. Then without a word, he stabbed Lexi in the leg. "Back up, everyone, and give her some air."

Lexi roused rather quickly and looked around. Her eyes were unfocused but soon began to clear. She peered at the EpiPen in Sam's hand. "Where did that come from?" she asked as she gulped in air.

"Vinea got it for us. She teleported to our house," Sam explained.

Lexi reached out and took Vinea's hand. "Thank you."

"It was the least I could do."

"Vinea, we owe you," Sam said. "Right now, I need to get Lexi to the hospital."

Vinea smiled. "Just give me a moment. I can help."

Devon wanted to tell her not to heal Lexi since she was already so weak from the episode healing him, but he could tell it was something she needed to do. Vinea had many debts to repay, and doing something nice for Sam and Lexi was just one of them. She sat next to Lexi and placed her hands on Lexi's shoulders. Vinea closed her eyes and bowed her head, looking as if she were praying.

When her body began to shake, Devon had the strongest urge to pull her away and protect her from harm. When he moved toward her, she sent a not-so-polite telepathic message saying that if he interfered, he'd regret it.

Devon stopped. Vinea lowered her arms, looked up at him, and smiled. Lexi drew in a deep breath.

"That was amazing," Lexi said. "How did you do that?"

"It's just something I can do now."

Devon moved next to Vinea, and gently helped her up, surprised when she seemed to be at full strength. He didn't even detect any distress. "How are you feeling?"

"Never better."

"How is that possible?" The last two times she'd taken ill.

"I think being mated to you saved me."

Lexi reached up and placed a hand on Vinea's arm. "You two have mated?"

He guessed it was time to make the announcement.

VINEA COULDN'T HAVE been more pleased with how the evening

went, but now it was time to return to the guesthouse and enjoy Devon. To think she'd come to Silver Lake to repay him, Sam, and Zane for the bad things she'd attempted to do to them—and now she had. Her methods hadn't gone as planned, but she had accomplished her goal.

Devon held open the front door to the house and motioned her in. "So what did my mom and you talk about in the kitchen? You were in there quite a while."

She smiled. "I'm not telling."

He lowered his chin. "Vinea."

Vinea grinned. "She just asked if I loved you, and I said yes. Your mom then told me a few tips to remember about living with a wolf. It was all good. I think she likes me."

"What's not to like?"

"Funny man."

"How about I fix us a drink and we can plan our future?" he asked.

"What's there to discuss?" She was moving to Pittsburgh with him.

Vinea sat on the sofa while Devon poured two glasses of wine. When he returned, he handed her a glass. "For starters, we haven't really celebrated our mating."

What they did felt like a celebration to her. "Meaning what?"

He lifted his glass and tapped hers. "Normally, after a couple mates—assuming they both aren't shifters to begin with—they head on over to the lake and go for a run together since it would be the first time for the new shifter mate."

"But I can't shift."

"Exactly, which is why I thought we should do something different." He had a glint in his eye.

"Like what?"

"I've always wanted to go to Costa Rica. There is an area called La Fortuna where they have hot springs fed by a volcano. Cabana boys bring you drinks while you lounge in the secluded pools—or so

I've been told. It will be amazingly romantic."

Her pulse soared. "That sounds absolutely beautiful."

"After seeing a waterfall or two, we could head on over to the Pacific side and find a private beach. What do you say?"

Vinea had missed out on so much. While she'd had the ability to go anywhere on Earth when she lived in the dark realm, she hadn't, only returning to Earth to do her nefarious deeds. "I can't imagine anything more wonderful."

He grinned. "It'll be like having a honeymoon."

She set down her drink and hugged him. "When do we leave?"

"Do you have a passport?"

Her shoulders turned heavy. "No."

"Can you make one up?"

Her heart nearly broke at his disappointment. "It would take a while to alter all the records, and besides, it's not exactly legal. I am trying to live the straight and narrow life now. How about I just meet you there?"

He fingered her hair. "How about we just wait till you order one legally and go together?"

Vinea hugged him. "Did I ever tell you how happy you make me?"

Devon squeezed her tightly. "I hope just as happy as you make me."

Chapter Twenty-Five

VINEA AND DEVON exited the San Jose terminal in Costa Rica. He released his hold on his suitcase and embraced her. "We're finally here," he said. "Are you ready for some private one-on-one mating celebration?"

Vinea looked up at him and smiled, making his heart sing. "Absolutely. Ever since we mated, it's like we've become one. You're in my blood. I need you now more than ever."

"I couldn't have said it more eloquently." He kissed her lightly. Any more and he might shift. "Come on, we need to get this honeymoon started."

"I couldn't agree more."

Devon spotted the van to take them to the rental car agency. After a quick shuttle ride, they were on the road to La Fortuna in a large Mitsubishi. While it was a little hectic getting out of the city, once they headed north, all of Devon's anxieties fell away. Because the landscape was dotted with farms, small towns, and rolling hills, at times he was reminded of being back in Silver Lake.

Vinea leaned back and sighed. "Believe it or not, there's something to be said for moving from one place to another in a car."

He glanced over at her. "Oh, yeah? What's that?"

"For starters, I get to enjoy the countryside. And secondly, I don't have to worry about whether I'll land in the wrong place."

It did concern him every time she did her teleporting. The world would be forever changed if she messed up and appeared at the wrong spot at the wrong time. "I'd be worried too."

A short while later, they arrived at the hot springs where they would spend a few wonderful days relaxing before heading out for other areas of the country. While he'd never been to Costa Rica, he'd researched a few spots he thought Vinea might like to visit.

As soon as they pulled up to the reception area, Vinea jumped out and slowly spun around, a bright smile on her face. Yup. Coming here had been a good choice.

Once they checked into the room, Vinea changed into her swimsuit, causing Devon's cock to harden. "Ah, no way. Ain't gonna happen!"

She pressed her hands down her cute little body. "You don't like it?"

The skimpy suit showed off every delicious curve, and it had him rock hard. "I like it too much. Hell, so will the rest of the guests. No one gets to look at you in that outfit except me, ever."

Vinea laughed and changed. This time, she put on a very seductive green one-piece. A red-eyed frog graced the low cut front. "This better?"

No matter what suit she wore, she'd attract attention, so he might as well get used to it. "Perfect."

She grinned and held up a hand. "Now for you."

"Oh, no you don't. I brought a suit and am perfectly capable of putting it on myself."

He wouldn't be surprised if she tried to give him a pair of grape-smashers. No thank you.

"Fine."

Devon hurried to change, needing to hold her sooner rather than later. As much as his wolf was begging him to make love to her first, Vinea seemed too excited to want to stay in the hotel room. Besides, he had other plans to drive her wild.

Once he was ready, he led her outside. After passing the large swimming pool with the swim up bar, they entered a path that led to the totally lush gardens of the hot springs. Because there appeared to be so many hot spring pools, they continued walking until they came to an unoccupied one.

Vinea grabbed his hand. Without seeming to care whether the water was too hot, she walked right in and sunk down. "Ahh. Yes." Her groan caused his nails to sharpen and his bones to crack. "The light realm—what I remember of it—can't beat this," she said with an amazing glow on her face.

Devon stepped in and pulled her to his chest. When she wrapped her legs around his waist, his wolf starting celebrating.

Not here, he chided to his impatient animal.

No one's around, his wolf shot back.

Vinea grabbed his head and kissed him slowly, seductively, sensually. As he cupped her rounded ass, his world spun with desire and need, and all he could think about was sinking his cock deep inside of her. The fact someone might discover them added to the excitement.

Trying to suppress his wolf, Devon listened to the cooing of the doves and the squeals of the monkeys darting overhead. Voices sounded and another couple peeked into their little retreat before moving on. The fact they had a young child with them doused his desire to be amorous in this pool. From the brochure, there were more secluded places—ones designated for adults only. "How about we find a better hot spring where we have a little more privacy?"

"Why, Devon McKinnon, don't tell me I'll get to see your wild side."

He gave her a seductive wink. "You're going to see more than just my wild side."

"Show me the way." Vinea stood and stepped out of the pool. "Brrr. It's a bit chilly."

Devon's eyes were fixed on her protruding nipples. "You're wet, that's all."

He snagged his towel and rubbed her body to heat her up. "Better?" he asked.

"Yes."

"Then let's explore." When they came to a fork in the path where the sign read adults only, his pulse soared. "This way."

Grabbing her hand, he led Vinea to a secluded spot where two lounge chairs—or rather two beds with a canopied cover—sat next to a hot spring. If the drapes were drawn, they'd have total privacy.

"Ooh," Vinea squealed. "Let's sit in this one."

"Sit, yes." Not really. He intended to enjoy what she was offering.

Vinea stepped closer and looked deep into his soul. "Please don't tell me you're really a fuddy-duddy in disguise?"

Devon placed her hand on his erect cock. "Does this feel like I'm disinterested?"

She laughed. "No, so what are you going to do about it?"

Before he could answer, a young man wearing black pants and a white shirt with the hot springs logo on his shirt arrived. "Can I get the two of you something to drink?"

Vinea stepped in front of Devon. "Yes. I'd love a vodka Collins."

He didn't care what he ordered, just as long as it would take the kid a long time to retrieve it. "Make it two."

As soon as the attendant disappeared, Devon lifted her up and swung her around. "You are driving my wolf to drink."

"I like hearing that." She swiped a hand in front of her and instantly they were naked, his swim trunks nowhere to be seen.

"Vinea. Dress us right now." Devon's pulse rose. While no kids might find them, he didn't want to scare anyone who might happen upon them.

She sashayed over to the covered lounge, and then crooked her finger at him in a come hither way. "We only have a few minutes before our drinks arrive. Don't you want to take advantage of the time we have?"

"When we return to Silver Lake, I'll have to dunk you again in the lake to cleanse you. I can see your evil ways have returned."

She dropped back her head and laughed. "You know the old saying: You can take the goddess out of the dark realm, but you can't take the dark realm out of the goddess."

He hoped that wasn't true. "That's not quite how it goes."

Vinea landed on her back and spread her legs wide. Dear goddess in heaven. Did Naliana have any idea her sister was a devil in disguise? Devon was on her in a flash. She lifted her legs and managed to draw the curtains closed with her toes. "I can't wait any longer," she moaned.

He didn't need any more of an invitation than that. Devon pounced. His mouth crushed hers and then their tongues tangled. She scraped her nails down his back, ratcheting his desire to unbelievable heights. Once they mated, his need for her knew no bounds.

While there wasn't as much room inside their little cocoon as he would have liked, there was enough for him to feast on her tits. The first tug had her squealing in delight.

"Shh. We don't need anyone finding us like this," he said.

"Like you care."

Hell, maybe he didn't.

VINEA COULDN'T BELIEVE she was being so bold, but she'd finally found the perfect balance between being good and being a good girl—which meant she wasn't very good at all. It wasn't because she cared if that young man returned and found them in the throes of passion that she wanted to hurry, it was because she wanted—no needed—Devon now.

He moaned, and the next tug of her nipple had her soaring. She dug her nails into his skin, clamoring for more. Their tongues dueled for position, but because his teeth had sharpened, she had to be cautious.

"Please. I'm so fucking ready," she whispered in between breaths.

Ignoring her plea, he drew the nipple taut while he slipped a finger between her folds. Waves of lust shot straight through her, and her little world narrowed to just the two of them. She broke the kiss and nipped at his earlobe.

"Grr." Devon scraped his teeth against her neck, probably debating when to sink his teeth into her.

Vinea returned the favor by dragging her tongue down his neck, loving the slightly volcanic tang from the heated pool water. A second later, Devon placed his cock at her entrance, and a rush of hormones filled her. Not able to wait any longer, she lifted her hips, helping to drive his cock in, but only half of it fit despite her slickness.

Devon slid out and captured her lips once more. When he forged his way in again, her inner walls contracted around him, holding him tight. Vinea closed her eyes and floated into such an intense state of bliss that she almost forgot to breathe.

"Vinea, I can't get enough of you," Devon whispered after taking a deep inhale.

"Then don't stop."

Devon plunged in again just as she lifted her hips. She wasn't sure who was fucking who more, but with each foray, she soared higher and higher. Her body vibrated with delight, and the pleasure was so intense, it felt as if her inner goddess had returned to the light realm.

Devon nibbled on her lips and then her chin, before making his way back down to her neck. With each lick and kiss, her body came closer to exploding. When Devon finally sank his teeth into her, her climax swept her away, shattering her into a million pieces. She swallowed a scream as she buried her face against his shoulder. His hot seed pummeled her insides, and she held on tight.

The wind whipped the curtains around them, and the gurgling of the hot spring helped drown out the blood pounding in her ears.

"You're drinks are here," said a very unwelcomed voice.

Vinea groaned, and Devon withdrew. He glanced down at their naked bodies and grimaced. A second later, she'd dressed them both in their suits. She sat up, pulled open the curtain and smiled. "Thanks."

Devon told the waiter their room number and to put it on their tab.

"Yes, sir."

The young man didn't seem upset at all. Then again, she bet he'd seen more than his share of couples having sex.

Vinea held up her drink. "A toast to foiling the Changelings' evil plans, and to the start of a wonderful life together."

Devon tapped his glass against hers. "To us."

NO SOONER HAD they entered their room after another hour of soaking in the wonderful hot springs than Vinea's cell rang. It took a moment to locate her phone and glance at the screen. "I don't know who this is."

"You won't know until you answer it then," Devon said.

She swiped the button. "Hello?"

"Is this Vinea Summer?"

"Speaking."

"This is Claire from the Billard Georgia Hospital. I'm calling in regards to EmmaLee Donovan."

Vinea's legs weakened, and she grabbed onto the desk chair. "Oh, no. What happened?"

"Your name was on the contact list. I'm sorry to have to tell you that EmmaLee was assaulted a few hours ago. Her spleen ruptured, and we had to rush her into surgery. She's in recovery now and doing quite well."

Vinea's stomach lurched. "I can't believe it."

"We thought you should know."

"Of course. Thank you. Do the police know who did this?"

"I'm not the one to ask."

Devon rushed to Vinea's side and wrapped an arm around her shoulders, his comfort helping. "I appreciate you letting me know," she said to the nurse.

Vinea must have been standing in the room for a while saying nothing because Devon slipped the phone from her fingers. "Come sit down and tell me what happened."

Vinea let him lead her over to the bed. "EmmaLee was beaten, and the bastard ruptured her spleen. I'd bet anything it was Slater." She looked over at Devon who was white. "Are you okay?" she asked, quite ill herself.

"I'm feeling your pain. It's intense."

She'd completely forgotten that mates could sense each other's emotions. "I'm sorry."

"Don't be. Do you want to go to her?"

She hugged him tight, trying to absorb all of his goodness. "Yes and no. EmmaLee needs me, but we're on our honeymoon and having such a good time. I don't think I can be away from you for that long."

Devon leaned back and ran a knuckle down her cheek. "I'll catch a flight up there as soon as I can book one. I know you'd be fretting if you didn't see her."

"Are you sure?" Devon was such a good man.

"Yes."

Then it was settled. "The only good that might come of this incident is that EmmaLee might finally be convinced that Slater is no good for her."

Devon rubbed her shoulders. "Your friend will need protection. No telling if he'll try something else. I'll call Connor. He'll make sure she stays safe."

"That would be wonderful, but she can't pay."

"It's okay. We do pro bono work all the time. EmmaLee is important to you, which makes her important to me."

If she ever saw her sister again, she'd have to thank her for giving her the best man in the world to love.

Chapter Twenty-Six

CONNOR REALLY DIDN'T have time for a protection detail, but a woman was in trouble, and he'd be damned if something happened to her on his watch. Dev had assured him he would catch the next flight from Costa Rica to Atlanta, and then rent a car to drive to Billard. Once he arrived, he and Vinea would take over watching her friend.

The drive from Silver Lake to Billard took less than three hours, which was why Devon had asked him to go. Given the fact that EmmaLee had only recently been brought back from surgery, he doubted the hospital staff would let anyone visit her. That worked for him. His job was to make sure this Slater Coghill—assuming he was the one who did this to her—didn't cause any more problems.

Not knowing how long he'd have to stay, Connor packed a bag, checked into a hotel close by, and then headed to the hospital. As he approached the desk to ask about EmmaLee, Vinea rushed up to him.

"Thank you for coming," she said. "I really appreciate it."

"How did you get here so—" He waved a hand. "Never mind. And Dev?"

"He'll be here late tomorrow night. It was the first available flight he could get."

"How is your friend doing?" he asked.

"I haven't seen her yet. I was waiting for you."

"Let's check on her status to see if she's even allowed visitors."

Together, they walked up to the nurse's station. Because Vinea was on EmmaLee's contact list, he suggested she ask.

"Can you tell me what room EmmaLee Donovan is in?" she asked.

The nurse checked. "She's in room 307. They just brought her in from the ICU."

If it was that easy for them to find EmmaLee's location, Connor worried that Slater might be able to sneak in. As they approached her room, something strange began to vibrate in his chest. It wasn't another shifter signature, but rather something else—a feeling of urgency and need. Dismissing it, he followed Vinea to her friend's room.

Vinea knocked softly then pushed open the door. EmmaLee's eyes were closed, and her blonde hair was matted. The bruise on her cheek, along with her cut lip had his wolf growling. The tube attached to the bag of saline further incensed him.

Connor leaned close to Vinea. "Is Slater a shifter by any chance?"

"Yes, but don't tell that to EmmaLee. It will only make him more attractive."

"Perfect. I'd like nothing better than to rip out his throat."

EmmaLee moaned, and once more his wolf shot into protective mode. What the hell was wrong with him? Connor had protected many people. Why should this woman be different?

Mate, mate, his wolf said.

Well, hell. That was the last thing he needed.

VINEA WAS SICK to her stomach just thinking about the pain her friend had endured. Carefully, she walked up to the bed. "Emma-Lee?" she said softly.

Her friend's eyes fluttered open then quickly closed. Connor placed a hand on Vinea's arm. "We should let her rest."

He was right. "I'll just sit here in case she needs me."

"I'll stand guard in the hallway then."

Vinea was seeing a new side to Connor, and she liked it. She reached up and grasped his hand. "Thank you for helping."

He nodded and slipped out. For the next few hours, EmmaLee fought to wake up. Throughout, a sea of nurses came and went, checking in on her. Each time, Vinea would disappear until the nurse left. No doubt they'd tell her that EmmaLee would be better off without any visitors and Vinea didn't want to leave. She was certain if her friend could sense her presence, it would help her heal.

Finally, EmmaLee opened her eyes and kept them open. It seemed to take her a full minute before she recognized that Vinea was there. "What are you doing here?" she asked.

Vinea clasped her hand. "The hospital called and told me what happened. How are you feeling?"

EmmaLee lifted her hand and touched her cut lip. "Like someone beat me to a pulp."

Someone did. "Was it Slater?" Her friend looked away. "Emma-Lee you have to realize he'll never stop."

She turned her head back to Vinea. "I know."

When she tried to push herself up on her elbows, Vinea placed a hand on her shoulder. "What are you doing?" Vinea asked.

"I need to get out of here. Slater will sweet talk the nurses and come after me. I know he'll kill me this time."

"No, he won't. Connor is outside standing guard."

"Connor? I thought you were with Devon."

Even with the anesthesia still in her body, she remembered. "Connor is Devon's brother. Devon and I were in Costa Rica when the hospital called."

"Costa Rica? You shouldn't have come back from holiday for me."

Poor EmmaLee. Vinea's heart hurt for her. Slater hadn't just beaten her physically but he'd drained her emotionally as well. "It's all good. We can always go back."

EmmaLee shook her head. "You should have let the hospital deal with me."

"Nonsense. Someone has to protect you."

EmmaLee's smile came out weak. "You always did have this need to help me."

"You helped me when I needed someone."

Her friend nodded and then closed her eyes. "Tell me about Costa Rica," she said, her voice fading away.

As Vinea filled her in on what little she'd seen during their brief stay, her friend dozed off. About an hour later, voices sounded outside the door, and Vinea went to investigate, hoping it wasn't Slater. When she opened the door, Connor was speaking with Sam.

"Hey, what's going on?" she asked.

"Sam agreed to spot me. I'll need to sleep sometime," Connor said.

She faced the newcomer. "I can't thank you enough."

"It was Lexi who suggested I help out, though I would have come anyway. We're a team at McKinnon and Associates. We do what we can to help."

That made her feel good. "Thank you again."

"Why don't you get some rest?" Connor asked. "Sam and I will make sure nothing happens to your friend."

"I could use some shuteye." She wanted to talk to Devon anyway. "I'll be back early tomorrow morning. Don't be surprised if I just pop in."

They both shook their heads and smiled.

DEVON FINALLY ARRIVED two days later, unhappy with all the plane delays. Vinea met him outside the airport, and she was really excited to see him. As soon as he exited the security area, she ran up to him. The kiss that followed only served to add fuel to her desires.

"How's EmmaLee doing?" he asked.

"They're releasing her tomorrow. Fortunately, she's a fast healer."

Devon lowered his gaze. "Did you help?"

Vinea shrugged. "I might have placed a hand on her and drew out some of her pain. It wasn't enough to make anyone suspicious though."

Devon gave her another hug. "I can't wait to go the hotel."

She grinned. "Now you're talking."

"So what happens now with EmmaLee? You do know that Connor and Sam can't stay indefinitely," he said.

That had worried her. "I spoke to her about maybe moving to Silver Lake."

"But we'll be in Pittsburgh."

"I know, but Connor will be there."

He glanced over at her. "Connor?"

"From the way he kept avoiding eye contact, and how his eyes would turn that wonderful amber color when he looked at her, I'm thinking EmmaLee is his mate."

Devon laughed. "Really? If you're right, he won't be happy about that."

Vinea gave him a lustful look. "He'll have to deal. Are you ready to get out of here?"

"Damn straight, woman, let's go."

The End

Don't forget to sign up for my newsletter to receive three free books, as well as up-to-date information on my stories. If you prefer to only receive notices regarding my releases, follow me on BookBub.
http://smarturl.it/o4cz93?IQid=MLite
bookbub.com/authors/vella-day

I hoped you enjoyed Vinea and Devon's story. Up next is EmmaLee and Connor's story—HER WOLF'S GUARDED HEART. Here's the first chapter.

I 'M NOT LEAVING town." EmmaLee Donovan planted a hand on her hip as she spun to face her bodyguard, Connor McKinnon.

As much as she appreciated his help in keeping her safe, it was time to take back control of her life. It didn't matter that her ex-boyfriend had beaten her up in this very apartment; she had to remain in town in order to continue her important research. She hadn't worked all these years for a master's degree only to leave right before she finished her thesis.

Connor ground his teeth together. "Slater Coghill is still out there. Do you want him to come after you again? This time he might kill you, you know."

"You're exaggerating." Slater was too scared to attack her again—or so she wanted to believe. "With the cops looking for him, he won't come near me. He has this thing about being in jail."

Connor's brows quirked. "I'm glad to know he has one redeeming quality, but if he kills you, you won't be around to testify."

Now he was being ridiculous. "Slater's not a killer. He just has a bad temper."

"Bad temper, huh? He ruptured your spleen." He inhaled deeply then glanced to the side as if he was trying to come up with a good argument why she should move to another state. "Are you still in love with him? Is that it? Do you secretly want him to come back?" His voice escalated as his Adam's apple bobbed.

She had to blink to make sure she really had seen the hair sprout on his face. EmmaLee should be angry over his ridiculous comment, but he had some basis for his opinion. She had let Slater back into her life, time and time again since her ex was a master at apologizing. The last beating however had taught her a lesson; at all cost, avoid slick talking men who had a good heart but who were tortured by unseen demons.

Connor stepped even closer and her pulse sped up just like it always did whenever he was near. It was similar to the visceral reaction she had with Slater, except that with Connor, the sensation was more intense, deeper, and far more enjoyable. Perhaps she reacted the way she did to him because his eyes were more startling than Slater's. Right now, Connor's were hazel streaked with amber, but she doubted it meant this werewolf was interested in her— merely furious.

All he'd done in the last few weeks was grunt and growl when she came too close, or if she suggested leaving her tiny apartment. "No, I'm over Slater. He can burn in hell for all I care."

The muscles in his face softened. "Then what's the attraction of Billard?"

EmmaLee lifted her chin. "I've already told you. Not only do I make my living here, I need to finish my thesis."

"You can finish it in Silver Lake. We do have Internet there."

"You don't understand. There is a world-renowned professor coming for one semester to shed some light on dinosaurs and their possible link to dragons. I've already paid the tuition. I believe what he's recently learned while doing an archeological dig in Africa will be the final piece to my thesis." She held her breath, waiting for the ridicule that was sure to come.

"Are you saying you want to learn if dragons exist? Or rather existed? Is that where your stubbornness stems from?" Connor huffed then turned his back, but she refused to address the ache in her heart.

The only person beside her thesis advisor she'd confided in about her research had been Slater. The strange part was that her former boyfriend never mocked her belief in werewolves or werebears, but he did scoff when she spoke of dragons—just like Connor was doing now.

"I'm not saying dragons exist, but I believe dragon shifters do. A real dragon couldn't hide."

When he finally faced her again, one side of his mouth quirked upward. He was obviously fighting a smile—or heaven forbid that look was one of disgust. "What makes you think a dragon shifter exists?"

EmmaLee didn't know why she bothered explaining anything to this pigheaded man, but he was a shifter—the first one she'd spent any time with—and her curiosity about him and others of his kind was still off the charts.

"I've seen a picture of one. While I couldn't pinpoint the location, the background has the same type of hills and tall pines found around here. It's possible one might be lurking nearby." She'd only told the cops what she'd seen that fatal day, and their response convinced her to never mention it again.

"And you're willing to put your life in jeopardy because of a photograph you saw on the Internet?" He stabbed a hand through his hair.

Sarcasm didn't suit him. He acted as if she had no other proof. "As I said, it's for my thesis."

"What are you getting your degree in?"

"History with a specialty in Lore and Legends."

He chuckled. "Do you hear yourself? Lore and Legends? The words imply it's make believe."

"To you maybe, but I want to prove werewolves, wearbears, and weredragons exist. Don't worry, I won't reveal that I know a real life goddess or that my bodyguard is a shifter."

"Can you really be sure I am one?" Connor asked with a challenging tone.

"Yes. I've seen your eyes turn a color and your facial hair grow in seconds. But don't worry, I won't tell anyone that fact."

He held up a hand. "Thank you. We really don't need the world to know we exist. The panic alone could have dire consequences."

So she'd been told. "I will be discreet. As for whether dragon shifters exit, I'll show you why I believe they are here with us."

EmmaLee was taking a big chance in revealing what she'd found, but given he was a werewolf, Connor couldn't deny that paranormal beings existed. In her heart, she hoped he might provide her with some insight. Even if he could show her why the picture was a fake, she'd be closer to the truth. She wasn't ready to show him her tangible proof.

EmmaLee ducked into her bedroom, knelt by her bed, and pulled out the cardboard box from underneath. Her fingers hovered over the real evidence for a moment then lifted the photo she had printed off the Internet and returned to the living room. "Here it is."

Connor studied it. "I can only see part of a dragon, or rather what someone might say looks like one."

"I'm guessing the photographer had to hide, and as a result didn't have a good angle for the shot."

"Hmm. The head might have the right shape, and the scales are quite realistic, but the part of the wing we can see looks a tad oversized."

How would he know? Unless.... Her pulse sped up. "So you believe me? You told me you've never seen one before, or were you holding back?'"

He handed her the photo. "No. In all seriousness, it's too blurry to tell much. If I had to guess, I'd say it's someone in a costume."

EmmaLee tried not to let her shoulders slump. After all, it wasn't like she hadn't expected him to claim it was a fake. "I take it no one in your Clan has ever mentioned anything about dragon shifters?"

"No."

"What if I said I believed in giraffe shifters or even otter shifters? Would you still be so skeptical?"

She thought he'd say yes right away, but he did seem to think about it. "I suppose if the animal exists in the real world, it's possible a shifter could exist too."

"If you met a dragon shifter in human form, would you be able to tell he was one?"

"I can sense another shifter, but I can't detect if he's a wolf, a bear, or dragon—assuming one exists," Connor said, his confidence deflating.

Her mind raced. "So when you run into a person who is a shifter, you assume it is one of the more common varieties, right?" She rushed on. "Which means you might have met a dragon shifter and not even known it."

He held up his palms in surrender. "Okay, fine. A dragon shifter could exist."

From the flash of black shooting through those amber-brown eyes, he clearly thought she was just some kooky waitress and part time student who lived in the world of make believe. Oh, well. She had to ask to know for sure.

No matter what she said or did, he'd never change his mind. And if he didn't believe in her passion, she saw no reason to ask him to stay any longer.

After all, he wasn't here to date her, merely to protect her. EmmaLee needed to remember that.

While her body had healed from Slater's attack—in no small part to her goddess friend Vinea and her ability to speed up the process, EmmaLee wasn't stupid. She understood the dangers of Slater finding her, as he was still out there. After that last attack, Vinea had claimed she'd given EmmaLee the ability to ward off Slater, so she didn't really need Connor. She would have told him about this new power of hers a week ago, but Connor intrigued her. His eyes were pools of mystery, and while his nose was strong and straight, his full lips were slightly uneven, making him look like he had a permanent scowl—something she found sexy as hell.

Stop it. She'd fallen for Slater because he was charming and way too good-looking for his own good. Her friends were right when they said she was a sucker for a pretty face.

Because she understood her own weakness, Connor needed to leave, and she needed to get back to finishing her research and then polishing her thesis.

Once he understood she could defend herself, he'd be out the door faster than she could say his name. *Is that what I really want?*

EmmaLee was so conflicted. Even if she did mention her new talent, he probably wouldn't believe her mostly because she had no way of proving it to him—and Connor liked proof. This internal shield Vinea said she had given her would form around her if anyone attacked. So what if she'd never seen or felt it? She had to trust Vinea that it was there. Her goddess friend had no reason to lie.

"If you'll excuse me," she said. "I need to make a call."

"To whom?" Connor's body tensed.

"Not to Slater, if that's what you're thinking." She didn't want to keep secrets. "I need to discuss something with Vinea."

His shoulders relaxed. "About?"

The man would never stop. "Girl stuff."

"Oh. Well, tell her I said hello to Devon."

"Can do."

Once in her bedroom, she closed the door. Because shifters had good hearing, she walked to the far end of the room and pulled up a chair before dialing her friend.

The cell rang only once before she picked up. "EmmaLee? How are you?" Vinea sounded genuinely excited to hear from her.

"Good. Hey, I need your advice."

"Sure. Is Connor driving you crazy or something?"

She almost chuckled. "No, but I can't ask him to stay here any longer when I know he has a business to run. Physically, I'm good as new, and Slater hasn't been seen anywhere."

"That's good. How are you holding up emotionally though? Sitting on pins and needles waiting for him to show?"

How well her friend knew her. "Kind of, but I know Connor can take care of him if he does show up."

"I'm getting the sense that while you feel guilty keeping Connor there, you want him to stay."

EmmaLee did love Vinea. She always cut to the chase. "Yes. I know that once he leaves I'll miss his protective presence, but that isn't a good enough reason to ask him to put his life on hold."

She wouldn't mention that Connor starred in her nightly dreams. The man was this sleek animal, full of hot muscles, tightly wound, and ready for action. He moved with such grace it constantly made her fantasize about what he'd be like in bed. That unleashed power of emotion, if tapped, could be amazing, and she had no doubt he could wake up every cell in her body if he ever touched her intimately.

"What does Connor want to do?"

"Go back to Silver Lake and take me with him."

"Ooh, that sounds promising."

EmmaLee stood and then paced. "Remember I'm almost finished with my thesis. I don't want to leave."

"Let me ask you this. Do you like Connor?"

This wasn't about Connor. It was about what she'd worked so hard for. "Of course I do, but just because he is hotter than sin doesn't mean he's someone I should drop everything for. It's not like he's Mr. Perfect. Far from it." She glanced to the ceiling, hoping it would provide her with answers. "Fact of the matter is that he and Slater have a lot of traits in common besides their handsome faces and sophisticated ways."

"You're comparing them now? Trust me, Connor is absolutely nothing like Slater."

"You know what I mean. Both men are skeptics when it comes to dragon shifters, and they both keep too many secrets. I need to tell him to go."

EmmaLee admitted that she would fall for him if he stayed much longer. She also recognized that even if he wasn't the violent type toward women, he'd move on and she'd be hurt once more. No, it was time to break that cycle.

"Think of the bright side," Vinea said. "Silver Lake is full of shifters. You could get first hand knowledge about how they live and what their secret talents are. It could be a huge boon to your research."

She dropped down on the bed. The temptation to take Connor up on his offer tantalized her. "I've thought about that."

"Connor might be a skeptic, but one of the men who works for him, Jackson Murdoch, is not. You could learn a lot from him."

Vinea was only making this harder. "I'll think about it. Thanks. How are you feeling?"

"I'm still having morning sickness." She chuckled. "You'd think being a goddess, I'd have escaped those usual human issues."

That made EmmaLee laugh. "You'd think. Otherwise, are you're happy?"

"Happier than I thought I could ever be."

They talked a little bit longer and then Vinea had to go. Once they hung up, EmmaLee stayed in her bedroom, trying to decide what she should do. After much thought, she stepped back into the living room.

"Everything go okay?" Connor asked. "Is Vinea doing well?"

"Yes. She still has a bit of morning sickness but she's fine. Listen, we need to talk." Connor moved closer, disrupting her thoughts. *Focus.* "I appreciate all you've done for me, but since I'm healed, there's no reason for you to hang around," she said with as much compassion as she could muster. Unfortunately, her stupid lips wouldn't stop trembling. "I know you have a company to run back in Silver Lake."

He crossed his arms and widened his feet. All he needed were dark sunglasses and an earpiece, and he could pass for an FBI agent. "I'm not leaving you."

The force with which he delivered that statement surprised and delighted her, but EmmaLee didn't dare hope it was because he liked her.

He doesn't—not really. In the two weeks he'd been babysitting her, he hadn't as much as tried to steal a kiss or rub up against her accidentally on purpose. The opposite in fact had happened. He seemed to avoid her whenever possible, though he rarely succeeded. Her postage stamp apartment was just too damn small. She didn't want him to like her, as that would complicate things, because if he told her he cared, she'd be a goner faster than he could shift.

"EmmaLee? Are you okay?" His sympathetic tone snapped her out of her daydreaming.

What had he just said? Oh, yes—he wasn't leaving. "Why won't you just go?"

"The reason doesn't matter." Connor looked conflicted as he stabbed a hand over his short dark hair.

He had a hidden agenda and she wanted to know what it was. "This is my life and I think I have a right to know why you won't let me live it!"

Connor got right in her face and growled.

"I won't be responsible for another death!"

PACK WARS (Paranormal)
Training Their Mate (book 1)
Claiming Their Mate (book 2)
Rescuing Their Virgin Mate (book 3)
Box Set (books 1-3)
Loving Their Vixen Mate (book 4)
Fighting For Their Mate (book 5)
Enticing Their Mate (book 6)

MONTANA PROMISES (Full length contemporary)
Promises of Mercy (book 1)
Foundations For Three (book 2)
Montana Fire (book 3)
Hart To Hart (book 4)
Burning Seduction (book 5)
Montana Promises Box Set (books 1-3)

ROCK HARD, MONTANA (contemporary novellas)
Montana Desire (book 1)
Awakening Passions (book 2)

HIDDEN HILLS SHIFTERS (Paranormal)
An Unexpected Diversion (book 1) – FREE
Bare Instincts (book 2)
Shifting Destinies (book 3)
Embracing Fate (book 4)
Promises Unbroken (book 5)

SOUTHERN SHIFTERS KINDLE WORLDS
Bear 'N Dirty

WERES & WITCHES OF SILVER LAKE
A Magical Shift (book 1)
Catching Her Bear (book 2)
A Surge of Magic (book 3)
The Bear's Forbidden Wolf (book 4)
Her Reluctant Bear (book 5)
Freeing His Tiger (book 6)
Protecting His Wolf (book 7)
Waking His Bear (book 8)
Melting Her Wolf's Heart (book 9)

Author Bio

Want 3 FREE books? Sign up for my newsletter.

COPY AND PASTE INTO YOUR BROWSER:
http://smarturl.it/o4cz93?IQid=MLite

Check out my latest interview on You Tube:
youtube.com/watch?v=sQo5pyyVMDI

Not only do I love to read, write, and dream, I'm an extrovert. I enjoy being around people and am always trying to understand what makes them tick. Not only must my books have a happily ever after, I need characters I can relate to. My men are wonderful, dynamic, smart, strong, and the best lovers in the world (of course).

I believe I am the luckiest woman. I do what I love and I have a wonderful, supportive husband, who happens to be hot!

Fun facts about me

(1) I'm a math nerd who loves spreadsheets. Give me numbers and I'll find a pattern.
(2) I just moved to Costa Rica and live on the beach!
(3) I also like to exercise. Yes, I know I'm odd.

I love hearing from readers either on FB or via email (hint, hint).

Social Media Sites

Website:

www.velladay.com

FB:

www.facebook.com/vella.day.90

Twitter:

@velladay4

Gmail:

velladayauthor@gmail.com

www.ingramcontent.com/pod-product-compliance
Lightning Source LLC
Chambersburg PA
CBHW022005170626
46808CB00001B/291